"You're quick   e spun her in a quick circle

The flash-dance move left her smiling and reaching for his shoulder once again. "I don't appreciate my friends being treated like they aren't worthy," she replied.

Cash dipped his head and his mouth came within a whisper. "Are we friends, Red?"

His lips slid across hers in the lightest caress, like a feather tickling, teasing. Her fingertips curled into his suit jacket and she realized they'd stopped moving. The music continued, but she paid no attention to the tune or anything else going on around her.

"Cash," she murmured.

She didn't know what she was going to say. Maybe nothing at all. Perhaps she was pleading for more because no one had ever touched her so simply, so softly, and yet had her every single nerve ending standing at attention, anticipating more.

Then, in a move she saw coming but did nothing to stop, Cash completely covered her mouth, obliterating every last thought she had . . .

Books by Jules Bennett

WRAPPED IN YOU

CAUGHT UP IN YOU

LOST IN YOU

STAY WITH ME

BE WITH ME

HOLD ON TO ME

Published by Kensington Publishing Corporation

hold on to me

JULES BENNETT

ZEBRA BOOKS
KENSINGTON PUBLISHING CORP.
www.kensingtonbooks.com

ZEBRA BOOKS are published by

Kensington Publishing Corp.
119 West 40th Street
New York, NY 10018

All Kensington titles, imprints, and distributed lines are available at special quantity discounts for bulk purchases for sales promotion, premiums, fund-raising, educational, or institutional use.

Special book excerpts or customized printings can also be created to fit specific needs. For details, write or phone the office of the Kensington Sales Manager: Attn.: Sales Department. Kensington Publishing Corp., 119 West 40th Street, New York, NY 10018. Phone: 1-800-221-2647.

Zebra and the Z logo Reg. U.S. Pat. & TM Off.

First Printing: September 2019
ISBN-13: 978-1-4201-4500-7
ISBN-10: 1-4201-4500-2

ISBN-13: 978-1-4201-4501-4 (eBook)
ISBN-10: 1-4201-4501-0 (eBook)

10 9 8 7 6 5 4 3 2 1

Printed in the United States of America

Chapter One

Jade McKenzie would rather point her sporty car in any direction other than Haven, Georgia's small-town airport. Because heading to the airport meant she'd be flying on up to Nashville for her cousin's wedding, where she'd be forced to wear a hideous orange chiffon gown guaranteed to clash with her rich, red hair.

Orange? Who the hell chose that as a wedding color?

Oh, but it wasn't just the dress that had thrust Jade into a foul mood. Pretty much any family gathering drove her to the point of needing an entire bottle of cabernet to get through. Of course, if she had that, she ran the risk of getting a nice red wine all over her tacky dress. If she thought that would get her out of the whole ordeal, she'd gladly make the sacrifice.

Jade never fit in with her family; she never *wanted* to fit in. The high-class, pinky-dangling, pretentious group just weren't her people. Since birth, her parents had tried to mold her, to create her into someone she wasn't. Well, more her mother than her father. He'd passed away when Jade had been a toddler, so she didn't recall his role in her life. Her mom expected pleated pants, perfectly coiffed hair, and a smile at all times.

There was only one person in the entire McKenzie clan

Jules Bennett

Jade actually wanted to see, and that was her spunky, out-spoken, eighty-year-old nana.

Jade didn't know where she had ever truly fit in and felt like part of a unit, but she knew who her people were. The people who would have her back and share a glass of wine while discussing a bad blind date. They were her best friends and the sole reason she was still here in this tiny town with more specialty shops than streetlights.

As Jade turned on to the one-lane road leading to the small airport owned by her best friend, Livie Daniels, and her husband, Jax Morgan, Jade smiled. This place had been nearly falling apart when she, Livie, and their other friend, Melanie, had rolled into town over a year ago. Now, through the help of their small circle—not to mention several grants for funding—Livie and Jax were expanding and making this airport something grand for the town of Haven.

The movie industry had been all over Georgia for the past few years offering another option, one quainter and more personable, and to celebrities as their main goal once they were officially up and running.

Jade pulled her car up next to the hangar where Jax kept his Cessna Skycatcher. She'd learned quite a bit since coming to town and joining forces to revamp this place. Now she knew the difference between a taildragger and a nose wheel. Things she never thought she'd need to know at the age of thirty-two, but here she was, discovering aviation was not only fascinating, she found the sport rather sexy.

She parked her car out of the way of the construction crew's mess and shut off the engine. The main building was nearly complete, with the addition to allow for a restaurant and gift shop, and she positively couldn't wait to get that going. There wasn't a doubt in her mind that this place would become another tourist attraction for the growing town.

As Jade sat there, she imagined various landscape ideas for the bleak grounds. They would need magnolias for sure, plus some lush greenery and accent rocks. It couldn't get too feminine and had to look professional and classy.

And she was stalling. Jade would much rather think of the manual labor of planting shrubs than get on that plane for a wedding she'd rather give up her favorite running shoes than to attend.

On a deep sigh, Jade pushed her door open, grabbed her purse, and rounded the car to the trunk. Might as well get this over with. One rehearsal and dinner, one wedding and reception, then she'd be heading back home in two days. That was all she had to survive of her family and then she didn't have to see them again until . . . well, most likely another cousin got married and she was expected to pretend to be the doting bridesmaid.

The McKenzies had long ago given up asking her to join them for the holidays, for which she was eternally grateful. But there were still certain events she was obligated to attend because her mother never dropped the pretense that they were a loving, close-knit family. She'd only spoken to her mother on the phone a handful of times since "the incident"—her mother's words.

The incident would be the scandal Jade had the nerve to bring upon their family. Not that her mother cared, but Jade refused to put up with sexual harassment so, yeah, she'd come forward, and she wasn't the least bit sorry.

Jade jerked her suitcase from the trunk and extended the handle. As she wheeled it behind her, she clicked the key fob to lock her car and pushed "the incident" from her mind. She was over that whole nightmare and she'd come out on top . . . just like she always did.

She may be floundering her way through life, but at least she never failed. And honestly, she was having a good time not knowing what each day would bring. Who knew she'd start sowing those proverbial wild oats at this age?

The hot Georgia sun beat down on her back as Jade made her way across the grassy field toward the back door of the hangar. She gripped the suitcase with one hand and shielded her eyes with the other. The sun's reflection bounced off the new metal roof and nearly caused her to stumble, but she charged on and reached the door without so much as a scuff to her new gold sandals.

The wind whipped her hair across her eyes and a few strands clung to her lip gloss just as she pushed open the new metal door. The second she stepped inside and shook her hair away from her face, she stared across the hangar and nearly growled.

Could this weekend get any worse?

She shoved her sunglasses on top of her head. "What are you doing here?"

Vincent "just call me Cash" Miller stood beside his Cessna Skycatcher. Jax's plane sat in the opposite bay, but there was no sign of Jax.

Cash propped his hands on his narrow hips and flashed her that smile that curled her toes and made her wonder why she ever let this man affect her so. Her body betrayed her at every opportunity because while he annoyed the hell out of her, he also turned her on.

Damn him. Nobody infuriated her the way he did. He purposely pushed her buttons, and she could only blame herself. They'd started off on the wrong foot and stayed there for over a year. If she hadn't been in such a vulnerable place in her life at that time, she could've easily handled his charms and tossed them back in his face. As it was, she suffered each and every time she had to be near him.

Because he was sexy as hell and he knew it. Granted, he would never know that she thought so. Oh, no. There was no way she'd ever let him have that leverage. Cash Miller had that whole dark, brooding, tattoo thing going on. He wasn't the least bit polished, but damn it, he did have those good ol' boy, Southern manners.

In all honesty, it was simply absurd that she found him attractive at all. He had too much ink, too much beard, too many muscles . . .

Nope. None of that appealed to her—she wouldn't be so clichéd as to let that delicious packaging hinder her judgment.

Cash didn't answer; he merely smiled like he knew some secret she wasn't in on, and Jade tipped her chin and squared her shoulders. She gripped her suitcase handle and started across the hangar, the small heel on her sandals clicking against the concrete.

"Cash, what are you doing here?" she repeated as she came to stand within a few feet of him. "Where's Jax? And what the hell happened to your face?"

He had quite the shiner on his right eye, which for some asinine reason only added to his badass sex appeal. Probably got in some fight over a woman. That would be just like Cash. Throw punches and then throw a woman over his shoulder and cart her off to his lair.

"It's good to see you, too, Red."

He knew full well that predictable nickname grated on her very last nerve, which was why he always insisted on using it. It was like he got off on irritating her.

Well, he'd have to get in line, because her family took that spot for the next few days.

"What did you do to your eye?" she repeated.

He shrugged as he hooked his thumbs through his belt loops. O-kay. Clearly he wasn't going to enlighten her. Fine. She wasn't really in the mood for chitchat.

"Is Jax here?" she asked, glancing around, hoping to see her best friend's husband ready to save her. "I need to get to Nashville on time so I can relax before the show."

"I thought you were going to a wedding?" Cash replied, his brows drawn in.

"Show, wedding; same thing with my family. Everything is over-the-top." She pulled in a deep breath and prayed for patience. "Is he here or not?"

"Didn't he text you?" Cash asked. "Piper is sick, so he's home with her."

Jade looked toward the ceiling and attempted to count backward from one hundred. She made it to ninety-eight before turning her focus back to Cash and forcing herself not to scream. This did not bode well for her sanity today.

"No, he didn't text me." She shoved the tall handle on her suitcase down and crossed her arms. "I have to get to Nashville before five o'clock at the latest."

Cash spread his taut arms wide and assaulted her with that high-voltage smile once again. "I'll be your pilot for today. Welcome aboard."

Oh, he knew that announcement would go over about as well as a steak dinner at a vegan convention. When Jax had called because Livie was busy in a town meeting regarding the updated airport renovations and Piper had a fever, Cash had jumped at the chance to take Jade to her destination.

There was something about her that he simply couldn't resist. Perhaps it was how easy she was to goad, maybe it was the challenge she continually presented, or it could be the fact that nobody had intrigued him quite like her in a very long time.

She shook her head, waves of red hair shifted against her bare shoulders. "Hell no."

Cash couldn't suppress his smile. "You hurt me."

"Oh, please," she scoffed, rolling those striking green eyes. "Your ego needs to be knocked down a peg or three. Where's Tanner? He can take me."

"Working and keeping Haven safe." Okay, now he really was irritated. "Do you want to get to this wedding or not? Because I'm it and you're wasting time."

Jade shoved her hands through the mass of red hair and closed her eyes. He wasn't sure if she was praying or thinking of ways to drive him out of his mind even further. Regardless, he didn't care. They may constantly rub each other the wrong way, but Jade McKenzie was drop-dead gorgeous and it was definitely no hardship spending time with her.

Besides, considering his two cousins were in committed relationships with her two best friends, Jade and Cash couldn't exactly dodge each other.

Livie had married Jax and they were fixing up this airport once owned by Livie's father, all while raising Jax's daughter. Melanie and Tanner were planning a Christmas wedding and expecting a baby shortly thereafter.

They were all just one big, happy family—present company excluded, because she looked ready to shoot steam out of her ears and throttle him. So five out of the six were happy family members, so to speak.

"I'll take your bag."

He stepped forward but stopped cold when those emerald eyes snapped to him. Wow. Did she rehearse that look in the mirror?

"You fly me there and keep your snarky comments to yourself," she demanded. "Got it?"

Cash reached for the handle and stepped just close enough to see the faint sprinkle of freckles across the bridge of her nose. Since when did he find freckles sexy?

"No snarky comments? Then what should we talk about?" he asked, pleased when her eyes widened and her lips thinned.

With the most unladylike growl, she marched around him and headed for the Skycatcher. He and Tanner shared this beauty, but they were both saving for something just a little larger. With the airport expansion coming right along, they were going to need something that carried more than three other passengers.

Cash spun around and followed those swaying hips and that mass of red hair. She'd questioned his eye, but there was no way in hell he'd be getting into that conversation. Because as much as he loved to get under her skin, he knew she'd be humiliated if he told her what really happened. He had no intention of ever purposely hurting her, so he let her draw her own conclusions.

Cash didn't even attempt to help her climb inside because he fully enjoyed keeping all of his limbs intact. He quickly stowed her suitcase and went to retrieve the winch. He'd just completed the preflight check when she'd burst through the door with her hair all about her face.

Which conjured up yet another mental image to add to his ever-growing fantasy list where Jade was concerned.

Cash made quick work of hooking up the winch and easing the plane from the hangar. This wouldn't be a long trip, but long enough that they'd have to talk, and likely the incident from two nights ago would settle between them until they brought it to light.

Because two nights ago Cash had seen firsthand what

happened when Jade became upset and disgraced. It was in that moment that Cash had wanted to slay every single one of her dragons.

Instead, Cash had allowed some asshat to punch him just so Cash had a valid excuse to flatten the guy to the ground. Cash wasn't typically a fighter, at least not now that he was a grown man. But when he witnessed this jerk making a spectacle of Jade, Cash had lost it—and he wasn't the least bit sorry either.

It had been an interesting night, and one he didn't necessarily want Jade to discover. There was no reason to add more salt to her already exposed wound.

Once the plane was in position, Cash took the winch back into the hangar and put it away. Now he was ready to settle in for a four-hour ride. He'd drop her off, refuel, and head back. They could get through this like adults. He vowed to be on his best behavior and not irritate her . . . at least not too much.

Cash had rescheduled his clients for the day and his assistant manager was more than capable of running the gym without him.

As much as Cash loved being a gym owner and personal trainer, he didn't miss an opportunity to get back into the sky. Flying had been his outlet and stress reliever during his stressful times—like his wife leaving him and his father turning to the bottle to cope with reality.

The extra income didn't hurt, but he'd fly for free because there was something so peaceful about being up in the clouds. Problems didn't exist, there was nobody to interrupt you, time passed without a worry, and he was actually looking forward to the long trip.

Cash climbed into the cockpit and settled in. He fastened his belt and grabbed a set of headphones from the center and handed them to Jade. She put her sunglasses on, shoved her hair back, and settled the earpieces in place before adjusting her mic well below her chin—a clear sign she wasn't in a talking mood.

"So who's getting married?" he asked, simply because he couldn't help himself.

There went that vow to not agitate her, and they hadn't even made it to the runway yet.

Cash concentrated on checking the windows, the belts, his flight log. When she didn't answer, Cash glanced sideways. He wasn't disappointed to see those vibrant eyes glaring back at him.

"Are you trying to make small talk?"

He smiled. "I wasn't trying. I was succeeding."

"Yeah, well, I'll have to do enough small talk and smiles this weekend," she explained as she focused her gaze straight ahead. "I don't have the mind-set right now."

Going through the familiar routine, Cash checked the wings and gauges. Even though he knew every single motion by heart, he still double-checked with the list that stayed in the pocket of the door. Most aviation accidents stemmed from lack of awareness or rushing or even omitting preflight checks. Flying may be a fun, relaxing sport, but there was still the need to be safe and smart.

"I take it you're not chummy with the bride?" he asked as he eased the plane forward.

Jade let out an unladylike snort. "If you knew my cousin Ruthie, you wouldn't ask that question. I just can't believe she found someone who'd want to declare 'til death do they part."

Cash couldn't help but smile. He reached across and tipped up her mic closer to her mouth, which earned him a swat of her hand.

"Since we're going to be chatting," he explained.

Cash lined the plane up at the end of the runway and

did one last check of gauges and wings. He announced his departure into the headset and started down the runway. As he picked up speed, he caught from the corner of his eye Jade's clenched fists and white knuckles.

A gentleman wouldn't call her on it, but . . .

"I didn't know you were afraid of flying."

"I'm not afraid of anything."

Cash wasn't going to point out that her teeth were clenched and there had to be nail marks on her palms.

He lifted the plane and started their ascent. Through the headset came her swift intake of breath. If anyone else sat in that seat so close to him, Cash would've reached across and offered a comfort squeeze. But Jade was tough and she was proud. She didn't want to appear weak—just another reason why the other night shouldn't be brought up.

Jade had always been that way. In school she'd been the tough girl. Rich, but tough. Some mistook her for being snotty or too uppity, but Cash never saw her that way.

Oh, sure, she dressed nice and probably used all the proper forks in the right order, but that was her upbringing. Her parents were wealthy and had high expectations. Which was probably why Jade felt she had to attend this wedding. The woman was loyal; nobody could ever deny that.

She'd come to Haven with Livie when her father passed, and Jade had ended up staying. She now lived in Livie's childhood home, but he honestly had no clue what her future plans were. He knew she'd started teaching hot yoga classes in the next county, and try as he might, he couldn't get her to come to his gym to teach. He couldn't even get her to discuss it. Anytime he broached the subject, she instantly came back with the argument that they should never work together.

Once the plane leveled out, Cash risked a glance at her. "All right?"

She blew out a slow breath and nodded. "I'm not a fan of takeoffs."

"Duly noted."

"Or landings," she quickly added.

Cash surveyed the gears and controls. "I'll be sure to give you a smooth landing."

"Why don't we discuss something else?" she suggested. "Or better yet, not talk."

"For four hours?" he asked, glancing to his controls and then to the bright-blue horizon. "You think you can ignore me that long in this tight space?"

"I could if you'd be quiet."

Cash shook his head. "Not likely. You can pick the topic if that makes you more comfortable."

She toyed with the hem of her little black dress, which stopped right at her knees. He really shouldn't be admiring her tanned knees, but he couldn't help himself.

"Fine. Let's talk about that shiner. Did you spar with the wrong guy?"

"Oh, he was the wrong guy all right," Cash muttered. "Let's just say I had my reasons for letting him take a swing."

Jade grunted or laughed, he couldn't really tell.

"I never would've taken you for a guy who let anyone get the best of him."

Cash ground his molars to keep from defending himself . . . because at the time, it had been more important to defend her. A black eye was nothing in comparison to the way that bastard had treated Jade. Even thinking about it now set Cash off, made him angry all over again. No man should ever treat a woman like she's not worth everything in the world. Breaking up is one thing, but being a complete bastard is unacceptable.

"So where's the wedding?"

Jade shifted in her seat and smoothed down her dress. "You really don't want to talk about that fight, do you?"

"No."

"Male ego, I get it," she said with an extra bit of confidence, though she had no idea his reason for the fight. "Fine. We can move on. The wedding is at some country club that no doubt Ruthie's parents were founding members and are on the board of, or some such nonsense. I'm sure it's the most prestigious in the state and there will be a flurry of wedding planners and photographers racing around to make sure her day is nothing short of perfection."

Cash watched the horizon and listened to her sultry voice come through the headset. He'd known Jade since junior high, but it wasn't until she moved back a year ago that he'd gotten to know her better. Not that they were chummy by any means, but they'd tolerated each other for the sake of their friends.

In school, Jade had been three years older than him and definitely not hanging in the same circles. Cash's circle had been so minuscule, with only Jax and Tanner. Cash had been too embarrassed to get closer to anyone else. With his mother gone and his dad hitting the bottle every waking minute, it wasn't as if Cash felt like inviting friends over.

Girls were easy, though. They never expected to come to his house. He dated quite a bit, then ended up in the Air Force and came home and married the first woman he thought he might love. Turned out, there was no love from either of them and he'd been desperately seeking someone to fill a void.

His father's bottle habit had turned to pills; then he just decided to combine them both and currently was slowly killing himself. Cash had urged his dad to seek help and this time really stick to the program. Each day that passed without a call that his father had checked himself out was a success.

"Don't even get me started on the dress," Jade went on, cutting through his thoughts. "I'll shut up. You don't need me grouchy for the rest of the trip."

Cash shrugged. "At least your anger is pointed at someone else, not me."

Silence settled between them, only the hum of the engines filling the space. Cash enjoyed the view; it wasn't often he took longer flights. He typically did short jaunts, so this was even more enjoyable, even if Jade would've rather had any other pilot.

"You haven't brought up Taps yet," she said after several minutes.

Taps, the local bar in Haven where Jade had been with her boyfriend the other night. Well, Jade had walked in and caught her boyfriend of a few months on a date . . . with another woman.

A few weeks ago, Cash had tried to tell Jade that there had been less-than-complimentary locker-room talk at the gym regarding Brad. Jade had simply rolled her eyes and told him to mind his own business.

She may have used more colorful lingo, but that was the gist. And he had been minding his own business, he just happened to see the disturbing scene two nights ago.

"Didn't figure you wanted to discuss it," he replied.

"I don't, but we should just get it out of the way."

Cash glanced her way. "Get what out of the way?"

Her vibrant eyes landed on him. "You saying 'I told you so.'"

She stared at him, had the nerve to raise one perfectly arched brow, as if challenging him to say just that. Her low opinion of him really grated on his nerves. Of course, from what he'd heard about her life in Atlanta, Jade hadn't had the best run of luck with men in her life, then add in Brad, and, well . . . her bitterness was justified.

Cash shifted his focus back to the horizon and replayed the night at Taps. The shock on Jade's face, the hurt that quickly followed, the way she had confronted him like her nerves were made of steel, and the way she proudly walked out with her shoulders back and head high.

But he'd caught the flash of humiliation, the slight vulnerability that maybe nobody else saw, but he didn't miss anything. Not when it came to Jade McKenzie. He'd been intrigued by her for far too long.

"I didn't say I told you so," he replied.

"No," she agreed. "But you want to."

"Actually, it didn't cross my mind." Which was the complete truth, not that he expected her to believe him.

Jade laughed. "Oh, please. Of course it did. You tried to warn me about Brad, and then you were there to see the whole thing unravel."

The annoyance in her voice confused him. Was she upset that he'd been there, or was she upset that he had indeed tried to protect her?

Regardless, she had already formed her opinion of him and there wasn't much he could do about it. He'd spent most of his adult life wanting people to see who he really was, but they rarely did. The persona he put out led people to believe he was shallow, a ladies' man, just some buff guy who didn't get feelings.

He got them . . . all too well.

"You're better off without him," Cash stated. More truth.

"Yes, I am."

Jade shifted again and stared out the side window. She was nothing if not resilient. She may be hurting and wounded, but she would put up that concrete wall of protection if she had to. The woman never wanted to be seen as weak or vulnerable—a trait he not only appreciated but found downright sexy as hell.

Finding Jade sexy and acting on it were two different things, though. He'd gone that route before, of letting his hormones guide him. They'd guided him right down the aisle and a few years later right into divorce court.

Perhaps he was shallow. He did simple relationships, he did one-night stands and short-term flings. There was no way he'd ever permanently get tangled up in a woman ever again. Why take the risk of brutally damaging his heart even further?

And getting involved with someone like Jade? That was ridiculous to even begin to comprehend.

Sure, she may be stunning and successful, but she had her own issues, same as everyone else. Not to mention they were too opposite. They barely got along on a good day, and she didn't have the highest opinion of him. Just another person who didn't know the truth and didn't want to take the time to find out.

Cash was quite happy with his life, though. He ran the most successful gym in the entire area, he had clients from all over the state, and online, he hosted a boot camp once a month that reached across the country. He didn't have time to feed a relationship.

"So why all the animosity with the family?" he asked, more to pass the time and to take the topic away from Taps. "I mean, I understand you making an appearance at the wedding, but a bridesmaid?"

"You don't know my family," she stated, shaking her head. "Appearances are everything. Even the black sheep has to remain loyal."

Black sheep? He couldn't imagine Jade being the black sheep of anything, ever. What were the other family members like if this polished, controlled, successful woman beside him was considered the outcast?

"You're an adult." Way to state the obvious. "You're not obligated to anyone."

"I owe them," she replied simply.

Her voice slid through the headset, her tone so soft he wondered if he'd heard correctly.

Before Cash could ask her what she meant, a loud boom replaced the hum of the engine . . . and then a clicking, sputtering sound. The plane started to shake, and Cash gripped the controls as his eyes snapped to the gauges.

"Cash?"

Jade's panic came through loud and clear, matching his own anxious worry. But there was no time to panic. He needed every ounce of his focus on finding a spot to land, because that engine wasn't going to hold up when it sounded like a toy whose batteries were dying.

No, don't think of dying.

"What's happening?" Jade asked, gripping the dash.

"Engine's out." He surveyed the land, looking for a road, an open field, anything that didn't involve homes or population. "We're about to make a hard landing. Hold on."

Chapter Two

Jade was certain her fingers were permanently embedded in the dash of the Skycatcher. Cash, on the other hand, seemed calm and in control as he radioed their dire situation.

She closed her eyes and focused on his soothing voice. How the hell could anyone be so calm at a time like this? The unusual sounds coming from the engine were terrifying—and even more terrifying when they just went silent.

"We're making an emergency landing," he warned in a stern tone. "Make sure your belt is tight."

With a quick jerk, Jade tugged the excess belt and prayed like she'd never prayed before. Because isn't that what people were supposed to do in a dire situation?

Jade seriously didn't want to die like this, and certainly not with Cash. Oh, mercy, she was sorry she said she didn't want to go to the wedding. She'd much rather go and wear the hideous dress and blow fake air kisses than not to make it out of this aircraft alive.

The plane dipped, and she let out a cry when her stomach sank. There was no way to describe her fear because she'd never actually been this petrified before. Nausea consumed her and she had to focus on her breathing, focus on the feel of the dash beneath her hands, focus on Cash's arm brushing against hers . . . anything to keep from zeroing in on what could be her final moments.

"It's okay," Cash stated in that still, calm tone that should settle her but only infuriated her. "I'm dropping altitude to try to get us to that field up ahead. Don't panic on me now, Red."

"Really? Don't panic?"

She wasn't even addressing the whole "Red" reference because they were well past that. She hated it, he knew it, but they had much bigger issues to deal with.

The plane dipped again, and Cash's knuckles turned white as he gripped the controls. Maybe he wasn't as calm as she thought, and perhaps she should keep her eyes closed.

Cash radioed their situation again, but there was no reply. The radios in small aircrafts were mainly for other planes in the vicinity, so there was no magical air-traffic controller who could respond and help save the day out here in the middle of nowhere. They were on their own, and she had to put her trust in Cash to save them.

Jade watched as the ground kept getting closer and all she could think was that they were going way too fast to live through this. Her heart thumped heavily against her chest, her sweaty palms slid against the dash, and she was fighting back a serious case of queasiness.

"I can do this."

Cash's voice came through the headset, and she wasn't sure if he was reassuring her or trying to convince himself. Either way, she prayed he was right.

As the ground got closer, she squeezed her eyes shut.

"If you kill us, I'm going to be really pissed."

Cash grunted. "Duly noted. Now brace yourself."

She gritted her teeth as her entire body tightened, preparing for the worst while desperately hoping for the best.

The plane hit the ground with a hard bounce, then lifted up again. Back down, then up. Jade's body jarred with each hit, and she just knew the plane would fall apart if this kept up. Cash's mutterings and string of curses filled the headset, so she tried to hone in on that instead of all the fear that consumed her. She didn't dare open her eyes because she didn't want to see where they were.

When they bounced again, they stayed on the ground, sliding, but she could tell they were slowing down. Jade risked opening one eye and then the other. A tree line in the far distance had her worried they may not stop in time, but for the most part there was nothing but an open field. Not a telephone pole, not livestock, nothing.

With a shuddering jerk, the plane finally came to a stop. She didn't know how long the whole ordeal had lasted, but she did know it took at least five years off her life. Her heart might never beat a regular rhythm again.

She glanced to Cash, who still gripped the control as he stared straight ahead. The corded muscles in his forearms remained tight, his jaw clenched, his breathing harsh. Cash wasn't nearly as unaffected as she'd thought.

Without thinking, Jade flicked off the seat belt as she shifted in her seat. "You did it," she exclaimed, throwing her arms around Cash's neck.

"Damn," he whispered. "That was . . . way too close."

One strong arm banded around her waist and he buried his face against the side of her neck. Cash held her tight and Jade inhaled, pulling a heavy dose of raw masculinity and a hint of woodsy cologne. An unexpected curl of lust hit her hard.

Cash eased back and smoothed her hair from her face.

That dark gaze seemed to roam over her as if making sure she was indeed all right. Silence enveloped them, and for several moments, Cash continued to cling to her . . . or maybe she was clinging to him.

"Are you hurt?" he finally asked.

For the first time since she'd gotten to know him, Jade didn't hear a hint of sarcasm, ego boosting, or flirting. Cash expressed genuine concern, and the way he was looking at her, like he was devastated to have put her in this situation, had a brand-new emotion rolling through her. Everything about this side of Cash appealed to her.

Jade dropped her gaze and landed on his lips. What would it be like? Just one taste. Nobody would have to know, right? If she just leaned in a little more . . .

Cash gripped her face in his rough hands. "Not a good idea, Red," he growled.

She blinked and mentally pulled herself back. What had she been thinking? She couldn't be attracted to Cash, and right now she had much bigger issues than worrying about these unwanted feelings.

"Jade, are you okay?" he repeated.

Disconnecting herself from whatever trance she'd been in—had she seriously gotten caught up in the way his mouth moved and that short beard along his jaw?—Jade nodded, but then noticed the side of his head.

"You're bleeding."

She reached up and touched beneath the wound, causing him to wince. Jade jerked her hand away and cursed herself for hurting him even more.

"It's fine," he assured her, taking the bottom of his shirt and pulling it up to swipe the wound. "Just hit my head on that landing. Are you hurt anywhere?"

Cash released his shirt, covering up his taut abs. That

dark gaze landed back on her and he continued to visually assess her.

"I'm fine, I think." She eased away from him before the adrenaline rush had her making decisions she may regret. "I can't believe we made it."

Cash blew out a deep sigh and sank back against his seat. "I'm not sure we made it, considering I have no idea where the hell we are."

"You don't know where we are? Aren't you supposed to track those things?"

"Oh, I know we're in Tennessee," he corrected, raking a hand over that stubble on his cheek, generating a scratchy sound. "We were only about eighty miles from Nashville just before the engine went. I need to check the plane to see what the hell happened and assess any damage."

He jerked on the handle of the door and climbed out. Jade watched as he walked to the front of the Skycatcher, then around the sides. Cash circled once again before bending down out of sight. She may not know very much about aviation yet, but she was pretty sure this plane wasn't going anywhere.

On a groan, she reached down to grab her phone from her purse. But her purse had dumped somewhere between bumps one and eight and scattered her belongings all around her feet. She shuffled around through lip gloss, her planner—yes, she still carried one—her wallet, ah . . . finally. She gripped her cell like a lifeline and tapped the screen. She would get help and be on her way—

No service.

Fan-flippin'-tastic.

Jade tugged on her door handle and climbed out of the Cessna. She quickly adjusted the short skirt of her dress and held her phone up in the air, desperately searching for a signal. Just one bar . . . was that too much to ask? Could this weekend get any worse?

No. She didn't even want to answer that rhetorical question.

"Your cell is pointless." Cash moved alongside her and propped his hands on his hips. "The plane isn't going anywhere either."

Jade dropped her hand to her side and spun in a slow circle, hoping she'd merely overlooked some semblance of civilization. But, no. That would be too easy.

"So, now what?" she asked as she circled back around to face him.

"We start walking," he said, as if the fix could be that simple.

"What direction? There's literally nothing in sight."

He pointed behind her. "We came in from the southeast and passed a highway just before landing. There will be a town or someone to help us."

Jade raked a hand through her hair and let out a laugh. "This is just great. I didn't exactly dress for trekking through . . . wherever we are."

He went to the back side of the plane and pulled on the storage compartment. "Well, Red, unless you packed your hiking boots in this suitcase, you're going to have to make do with what you have."

She barely resisted the urge to strangle him, but he *had* saved her life, so she cut him a break. Her suitcase consisted of a pair of tacky orange shoes to match her equally tacky bridesmaid's dress, toiletries, underwear, running shoes with shorts and a sports bra, and another sundress to ride home in. Some may not believe it, but she truly was a minimalist.

Cash tugged out her suitcase and sat it in the grass. "We need to start walking. I can take this."

"Let me at least change my shoes."

She squatted down and unzipped her suitcase. When she flipped the top back, she found her tennis shoes in the top compartment.

"That's the dress?"

Glancing over her shoulder, she caught Cash standing behind her. Her bridesmaid's dress wasn't in some fancy garment bag. She'd been spiteful and rolled it up and put it right on top. Her mother would have heart palpitations if she saw this packing method.

"I'm tempted to leave it here in this field." She slid off her sandals and threw them into the case before zipping it back up. "It's hideous."

"It's quite . . . orange."

Jade came to her feet and shot him a glare. "Either my cousin truly hates me or she's fully grasping this autumn-themed wedding. I choose to believe both."

She reached out to grip his shoulder as she shoved her feet into her tennis shoes. Not the cutest fashion statement with her favorite black cotton dress, but whatever. She wasn't too concerned at this point, considering she was still thankful to be alive.

"I'm never going to make it to the rehearsal," she muttered.

Cash grabbed the handle on her suitcase and started walking. "Probably not, but we can't stay here. We need to find transportation and I need to call Jax."

Right. The plane. A much more important issue than the wedding she'd never wanted to be in to begin with.

"How the hell will you get that thing out of here?"

"Hopefully, we can figure out what went wrong with the engine and use that field to take back off. If not, we'll have to call in a team to extract it and get it back to Haven—which won't be cheap."

Jade followed at his side and wished she would've thought to take a rubber band from her toiletry bag to pull her hair up. She slid her purse down to her wrist and opened it up as she kept up the pace. Surely she had something in there, because at this rate, the heat from the sun would have her hair all frizzled and plastered to her back by the time they found civilization.

She could already hear her mother throwing a fit about "Jade missing the rehearsal and dinner and how that would look." No doubt she'd twist her pearls in a frenzy and then paste a smile on her face and make some lame yet convincing excuse as to where her rebellious daughter was.

Jade let out a laugh as she thought of what her mother might say to all of her stuffy country-club friends.

"What's so funny?" Cash asked.

She smoothed her hair over one shoulder to give some relief to her back. "Everything, actually. Not the broken plane, but the fact that I'll miss this evening, my mother's reaction when she realizes it, and how she'll fumble around trying to come up with a plausible excuse as to why."

Cash glanced her way and grunted. "It's just a rehearsal. You'll make it to the wedding."

Jade pursed her lips. "Doesn't really matter. She'd be upset even if I did make it to the rehearsal because I didn't bring my plus-one."

"Plus-one?" Cash asked.

Jade stepped over a small dip in the ground. She'd have to be careful or she'd twist an ankle. Wouldn't that just top off this disastrous day?

"You know, my date," she explained. "I'll show up alone, which will just add to her ever-growing list of my disappointments."

"Your mother can't be that disappointed in you," Cash

defended. "You're a successful woman and making it on your own."

Jade shrugged. "Yeah, well, I'm not married and supplying the next generation of McKenzies. I also have yet to do any type of showy parties where she can invite her friends and talk about my greatest accomplishments. I haven't logged in charity time for the sake of bragging about helping others less fortunate. I like to run marathons and teach yoga and I left my seven-figure job in Atlanta over a sexual assault claim—forget the fact I was the victim. Trust me, I'm quite the failure in her eyes."

Wow, saying it out loud made her growing list seem even more of an issue than Jade originally thought. Her mother had numerous things to bitch about next time she saw her.

"I really don't see where any of that is a reason to be let down. Clearly the sexual assault wasn't your fault. From what I heard, your coworker was a bastard. I hope he's out of a job and his dick fell off."

Jade stopped and stared at him. After a few steps, Cash stopped, too, and glanced over his shoulder. "What?" he asked.

Her heart did some weird flip thing she didn't want to analyze or allow when Cash was the topic. Still, she couldn't deny that having him immediately come to her defense was not only a surprise but also quite sexy.

"I never thought you'd take my side," she muttered.

Cash let go of the suitcase and took two steps to close the gap between them. Jade took a step back but stumbled. Cash snaked an arm around her waist and hauled her against his chest.

The way he towered over her had her pressing her palms against him. "Cash."

He stared at her for what seemed like several minutes,

and Jade wished she knew what he was thinking . . . but maybe it was better if she didn't. They annoyed each other on a daily basis, so what was all this about? The tingling and the long looks and that damn heart flip earlier?

Cash muttered a curse before shaking his head. He righted her, then raked a hand through his hair.

"You think I wouldn't defend you?" he asked, something akin to shock and hurt lacing his tone. "I'm not that much of a jerk, Red."

"No, I just . . ." Jade shook her head and attempted to get control of herself. "I didn't know if you were aware of why I left Atlanta. But the issues with my previous employer made it impossible to stay in a thankless, stressful job."

"Which is why your mother should be supportive." Cash propped his hands on his hips and leveled that dark gaze her way. "I'm not sure why you think you have to keep pleasing her, but I can solve one of your problems."

"And what's that?" Jade asked.

He flashed that smile that some women might find toe-curling. Okay, fine. Her toes might have curled, but why did she feel that he was about to throw down his secret plan? And why did she suddenly let his naughty grin fill her with anticipation?

"I'm your plus-one."

Cash turned away from Jade's dropped jaw and speechless expression. He gripped the suitcase handle and started pulling and dragging it behind him once again.

What the hell had he been thinking, saying he'd be her plus-one? He didn't do weddings. Hell, his own had started at a courthouse and ended in disaster a short time later, so why would he want to attend another? They were ridiculous, over-the-top shows in a vain attempt to impress people. Cash lived in the real world, where infidelity thrived and loyalty could only be found in dogs.

"You aren't going to be my date," Jade announced as she came stomping up beside him.

He didn't dare look over at her. Even with those tennis shoes on and her hair starting to cling to her sweat-dampened skin, she was so damn sexy, he'd do best to remember all the reasons she drove him crazy.

Perhaps the way she'd flung her arms around him when they'd landed, coupled with the way he was seeing a clearer picture of her background, made him see her in a different light.

But still, they were clearly from different worlds. Despite the fact that they went to school together years ago, she was older than him, she was loaded, she had never had a good opinion of him . . . the list was seriously endless.

If her best friends and his cousins hadn't gotten involved, Jade never would've said a word to him. Which really made this all the more hilarious.

Well, not the plane issue. His heart still hadn't started a proper steady rhythm since they'd landed. He had rolled over and over in his mind what could've gone wrong, and all he could think was, there must be some computer glitch, because everything else looked perfectly fine. But Jax was the airplane mechanic and would no doubt find the problem.

"Are you ignoring me?" she demanded.

"No. I'm just not arguing," he clarified. "I'll go as your date so your mom has one less thing to hassle you about."

"Why on earth would you do that?"

Because he was a masochist? Because he wanted to see how the other half lived? Because there may be an open bar?

Cash stopped again and shifted to face her. "Listen, I'm trying to be nice here. Do you want help or not?"

Jade stared back, and for a minute, he thought she'd tell him to forget it. He'd be fine with that, but he really was just trying to help. Call him a fool, but that underlying vulnerability she so desperately tried to hide had gotten to him.

Maybe they were more alike than he thought. Cash understood the need to keep weaknesses a secret.

"You don't even have anything to wear," she added.

Cash smiled, letting the victory settle in. "I'll take that as a yes."

"I'm serious."

"Let's worry about finding civilization." He started walking again, and dragging that damn suitcase behind him. "What time is the wedding tomorrow?"

"Five, but I have to be there for pictures at three."

Two hours of smiling for a camera. He'd rather be hit up the side of the head with a kettlebell. Another reason he found weddings to be a waste of time and money.

"Plenty of time for me to find something," he stated. "It's Nashville. How hard could it be?"

They walked along in silence, and Cash couldn't help but wonder what she was thinking. What would it be like to come from such a shallow, loveless home? Cash's father may be a deadbeat now, but he was once a robust, strong man. The untimely death of his wife had sent him spiraling out of control into a world of darkness and empty bottles—booze and pills.

Cash still loved the man, though. He took nearly every dollar he made to keep his father on the road to recovery. One day his father would get over this addiction. Cash wouldn't settle for anything less. He had enough energy to fight for the both of them.

The silence grated on his nerves. He wasn't used to the quiet. In the gym the music blared, weights clanged together. In the plane he usually talked to his passengers, and there was always the roar of the engine. But right now, the silence hovering between Jade and him was making him twitchy and he didn't like being alone with his thoughts.

"Would you rather read the book or watch the movie?" she asked.

Cash glanced at her. "What?"

"Just trying to pass the time," she mumbled. "I keep checking my phone for service, but until there is, I figure we could at least talk. So, would you rather read the book or watch the movie?"

Answering random questions was fine by him. He had nothing else to do. "Always the movie."

"I figured you'd say that," she replied. "Okay, would you rather eat sushi or pasta?"

That was easy. "Both."

"You can't answer both," she informed him.

"I'll try to do better."

Jade let out an unladylike snort. "How about would you rather vacation in a cabin in the mountains or an ocean-front house?"

"I love the mountains, but I'd vacation at the beach."

"That was just you skirting around saying both again, but I'll let it slide." She took a few steps and hummed as if she was thinking. "I think I'd take a cabin in the woods. In the winter, though. Being snowed in and surrounded by beauty like that sounds relaxing."

His body stirred. He wouldn't mind being snowed in with her . . . if she was asking, which she wasn't.

"I've got another one," she said with a smile. "Would you rather be rich or smart?"

"Why can't I be both?"

"Because that's not how the game works," she scolded. "Pick one."

"I'd rather be smart, because then I can make good business decisions and get rich."

Jade laughed again. "Still dodging and not answering directly."

"Would you rather go forward ten years or back ten years so you could change things?" he asked.

"Oh, definitely forward."

Cash glanced her direction. "Really? I wouldn't think you'd want to be older."

Her hand flung out and smacked his abs. He had to admit, he didn't mind how she put her hands on him. Now how pathetic was that admission?

"I don't care about age," she stated. "But I wouldn't want to change anything. All my experiences have led me to where I am today."

"Stranded in a field?"

Her shoulder brushed against his as a warm chuckle escaped her again. He hadn't seen this playful side of Jade and, circumstances aside, he was rather enjoying himself.

"Not exactly here, but in Haven," she amended. "It's giving me the time I need to think about the next step."

The next step. Did that mean she had no intention of staying in Haven? She'd hightailed it out of there years ago, and someone like Jade was too big for a small town. She had ambitions and she may have joked about teaching yoga, but that wasn't where she'd stay. He didn't see her happy with that decision at all, considering how she was raised and what all she'd left behind in Atlanta. Even if her job had left her jaded, she was still accustomed to seven figures and city life.

Over the past several months Jade had been a huge help

in getting the ball rolling on the new airport renovations. She'd written up the draft to help them get grants and she'd worked on the budget side of things as well.

She was an extremely smart businesswoman and he hoped like hell the firm she'd left in Atlanta felt the sting of her departure. From what he'd heard, she'd been put in a position no woman should ever be put in and her boss hadn't believed her. But in the end, the truth came out, and Jade had not only come out on top, they'd begged her to come back. She basically had told them to go to hell.

Jade was a strong, independent woman and it would take a special town, a special man, to keep her.

The idea of someone treating Jade like less than she deserved made him furious, and that had nothing to do with his attraction. Women deserved respect.

Cash may throw snark her way as a hobby, but that didn't mean he didn't respect her. Besides, she usually dished it right back at him, which was what made her so damn fun.

"You really don't have to do this, you know."

Jade's matter-of-fact tone pulled him back to the moment.

"What's that?" he asked.

"The wedding. It's kind of silly for you to go with me."

"Too embarrassed to have me on your arm?" he asked, not the slightest bit joking.

"I'm not a snob," she defended as she held up her phone in another vain attempt to check for service. "I know what people thought of me when I lived here growing up. Obviously you still think I believe I'm better than others. I'm not embarrassed to have you there, Cash. I just don't want to put you in an awkward position and my mother . . . no, most of my family, is rather difficult."

Ah, well. Maybe she wasn't embarrassed because of

him; perhaps she was embarrassed because of her own family. How bad could they be? Everybody had family members they'd rather keep hidden.

"I think I can handle it," he assured her. "If you want to go alone, that's up to you, but I'm offering you an out."

She kept walking, her eyes focused straight ahead as she continued on without answering. He honestly couldn't understand why she was even going to this damn wedding. She was an adult and could make her own decisions. Couldn't she have just told them no?

Cash had a feeling something, or someone, kept a hold over Jade, made her loyal to this crazy clan.

"I'll be fine on my own," she told him. "But thanks for the offer."

Fine. He wasn't going to beg. He'd never begged a woman for anything, ever. He sure as hell wasn't going to start now.

A hum in the distance had him halting and straining to hear.

"What—"

Cash held up his hand to silence her. Yes, that hum was steady and slow and absolutely music to his ears.

"Do you hear that?" he asked, smiling at her.

Jade whipped her head toward the sound. "Tell me that's cars."

"On a highway," he added.

"Then let's get moving, Flex."

He let the annoying nickname pass. There were more important matters to deal with now.

Jade took off ahead of him and his gaze landed on her ass. He was human. Besides, she'd checked him out a time or two over the past year she'd been back. Jade had a certain sexiness about her that was hard to find. A great body was one thing, but the confidence that went along with it wasn't something he often found in a woman.

So he followed those swaying hips and cursed himself for even offering to be her date. What had he been thinking? Jade and him even faking being a couple never would've worked. It was better this way.

So why was his ego bruised?

Chapter Three

By the time they reached a small town, finally had cell service, and found a rental car, Jade was about ready to call the whole weekend off. And she would have if it weren't for her grandmother.

"I've never been so happy to see a hotel." Cash pulled the rental car into the lot. "I'll walk you in."

"You don't need to walk me in," she told him. "Just pull beneath the canopy and drop me off."

"Now what kind of gentleman would I be if I didn't walk you in? I've taken great effort in seeing to your safety today; I'm not going to stop now."

It was true. From the emergency landing to keeping her sane up until this point, he hadn't been a bad companion. Maybe the near-death experience had been some strange turning point. Leave it to them not to do things the conventional way.

Cash parked the rental and Jade opened her door as he shut off the engine. Before she could do anything, he was out and had the trunk up, pulling out her suitcase.

"I can get it," she told him. "You've lugged it enough today."

"You're dead on your feet." He gripped the handle and gestured for her to go ahead. "Lead the way."

Jade wanted to argue, but she was honestly out of steam.

Ah, steam. What she wouldn't give for a nice, hot shower and fresh clothes. She didn't need a mirror to know she was an absolute disaster, and she didn't even want to think how gross she smelled.

"Jade McKenzie, where have you been?"

She cringed and stilled as she reached the front door. It slid open; all she had to do was keep walking on in to the lobby and pretend she didn't hear the screeching of her cousin behind her.

"Jade." Footsteps pounded on the pavement. "Good heavens, what happened to you?"

Jade turned around to the perfectly polished, overly exaggerated bride-to-be. Let the miserable weekend family reunion begin.

"Ruthie." Jade pasted on a smile that she knew full well looked fake. "You look beautiful."

And that part was true. Her cousin had her raven hair all straight and silky sleek. Her body-hugging, hot-pink dress and nude shoes was a signature Ruthie look. Her diamond rock glittered in the lights of the entrance.

Ruthie's eyes raked over Jade, and it took everything in her not to come to her own defense. Honestly, though, Ruthie's thoughts were the least of Jade's concerns. She was hungry, tired, grouchy, and not in the mood.

Then her cousin turned her attention to Cash, who remained slightly off to the side, still clutching Jade's suitcase.

"Oh, my." Ruthie's perfectly manicured hand went to her chest. "And you are?"

"Cash."

Ruthie blinked, clearly waiting on a better introduction. Jade chewed the inside of her cheek to keep from smiling, but that was Cash. He was a man of few words.

"What happened to your face?" she asked, then looked to Jade. "And why are you wearing a dress with tennis shoes? Your hair . . . Jade, really. Your mother said you couldn't be here tonight because there was a last-minute issue with a charity you were working on."

Cash grunted, but Jade didn't spare him a glance. Of course when Jade hadn't shown up, her mother had quickly come up with something to save face.

"Actually, we had a problem with our plane and had to make an emergency landing when the engine started to go," Jade explained. "I'd love to stay and chat about your perfect day, but I'd really like a shower and a bed."

Ruthie's eyes widened. "Oh, well. Um . . . of course. I'm glad you're all right. I was just leaving when I saw you pull in, so I wanted to say hi."

More like check on them and find out gossip to spread to the rest of the family, but whatever.

"I thought your plus-one's name was Brad," Ruthie stated, her brows drawn in . . . well, as much as they could be, considering the amount of Botox she'd had injected. "What did you say your name was again?"

"Cash. I'm sure you're familiar with that term."

Jade didn't even try to hide her laughter this time. "Good night, Ruthie. I'll see you tomorrow."

"I hope you don't miss the ceremony," Ruthie added. "I'll be sure to text your mother to tell her you and your date have arrived. Nighty-night."

Ruthie clicked away on her kitten heels and Jade resisted the urge to groan and roll her eyes.

"I'd hate to see the poor man who's going to be saddled with that the rest of his life," Cash muttered for only her to hear.

Jade faced him and shook her head. "I'm sure he's loaded and they'll put up pretenses like the rest of the family. Nothing will ever be wrong in their worlds, and if it is, they'll throw money at the problem and make it all go away."

She smoothed her hair away from her face and turned back toward the double doors. "Let me get checked in and we'll see if there's a room for you. I'll put it on the wedding party's tab."

Cash headed into the lobby right at her side. "I'm sure that sounds appealing to you, but I'll pay my own way."

Jade shrugged and headed to the counter. She checked in to her suite, complete with Jacuzzi tub and a king-size bed. Both sounded so fabulous, she might weep with joy.

"Do you happen to have another room available?" she asked. "My friend is in town last minute."

The guy working the desk tapped a few keys and stared at his screen. "No, I'm sorry. We're all booked up for the McKenzie/Walsh wedding and a skydiving convention."

She nearly laughed. The irony of a skydiving convention was certainly not lost on her.

"Jade! Is that you?"

Again, she cringed at the sound of her name. She thanked the worker for their help, grabbed her key card, and turned to see who was beckoning for her now.

The sight of the bride's sister coming at her with wide arms had Jade pasting on that fake smile once again. She might as well practice up for tomorrow.

"Hey, Margot."

"Of course that's her name," Cash muttered from behind her.

Jade stifled a laugh as Margot came in for a half-assed hug and air kisses. "We missed you at the rehearsal. Your mother said you were busy with a charity."

Margot's eyes darted over Jade's shoulder. "Is he the charity?" She giggled.

Ugh. A giggling woman. Was there anything less attractive?

"This is Cash," Jade stated. "Cash, this is my cousin, Margot. She's Ruthie's sister."

"Pleased to meet you," Cash replied, but didn't step forward to shake hands.

Margot frowned. "What happened to your face?"

"Rough flight," Cash explained.

Jade couldn't help but laugh, and Margot seemed even more confused as she stared between Cash and Jade.

"Well, um, I won't keep you two. I'm sure you're eager to get to your room to relax. Your mom mentioned you were bringing someone, but I had no idea he'd be so . . . blue collar and rugged."

Jade stilled, not at the verbal smack to Cash, but at her cousin's assumption. Jade's room had been reserved for her and Brad to share, so of course everyone thought her plus-one would be staying here. Well, damn. If Cash wasn't seen coming and going with her, they'd know he wasn't actually her date and there would be another host of questions and lies to dodge.

"Actually, I'm not—"

Jade reached back for Cash's hand and squeezed it to silence him. "See you tomorrow, Margot."

She all but pulled Cash toward the elevators and smacked the button for her floor. When she turned, Cash leaned against the opposite wall, still holding her luggage, but giving her a sample of that side smile . . . which only looked more menacing with his black eye and the cut on his forehead.

"Not one word," she growled through gritted teeth. "Not. One."

He started whistling some annoying tune—was that "Achy Breaky Heart"? Jade refused to comment, so she shifted her focus to the numbers above the panel. Finally, the elevator stopped on the fourth floor, and Jade stepped out the second the doors slid open.

She clutched her room card in her hand and led the way to her suite . . . which she might have to share with her plus-one because she'd run in to both Margot and Ruthie and no doubt word would get back to her mother. Though it was highly likely that word had already gotten back to Lana McKenzie.

Jade pulled in a deep breath and pushed thoughts of her mother aside and slid her key card into her door. She shoved it open and plastered herself back to allow room for Cash to enter with the suitcase.

And he was still whistling that damn song.

As soon as he was in, Jade moved out of the way and let the door slam at her back. Cash shoved his hands in his pockets and did a slow perusal of the main room.

"Did everyone get a room this fancy?" he asked, his gaze finally landing on hers.

Jade glanced around, taking in the double doors leading to the bedroom, the kitchenette, the patio doors for the private balcony, and the large sectional sofa plopped right in front of a large television.

"I have no clue." Thoughts whirled around in her mind, all of them leading her to one conclusion that made sense, even though she didn't like it. "But the couch is all yours."

Cash cocked his head, then stalked toward her. "Aw, Red. I figured you for more of a missionary type in a bed. You know, more vanilla-type sex. But the couch is a step up, so . . ."

Jade narrowed her eyes. "You'll sleep on the patio if you don't cool it."

He came to stand within a breath of her. Jade flattened her palms against his chest.

"You know, most men would take into account that I was a victim of sexual misconduct by a coworker and not crowd my space."

Cash smiled, flashing those perfectly white teeth. "I'm not most men, and you know I'd never make a lady uncomfortable or force her into anything."

Yeah, she did know that, which only made her stomach flutter all the more. Cash may be egotistical and snarky and, yes, maybe a ladies' man, but he would never take advantage of a woman—of that Jade was certain.

"Fine, but give me some space." She took a step back, only to come in contact with the wall. "Seriously. I'll throw you out on to the patio and lock the doors if you don't cool it."

He didn't bother backing up, but at least there was some semblance of space between them.

"You were ready to give me a thank-you kiss when we landed."

As if she needed the reminder. That moment had rolled over and over in her mind because had she leaned forward those last few inches, their relationship would've crossed a line they couldn't return from.

"That was adrenaline," she defended, crossing her arms over her chest. "I was just thankful to be alive."

A corner of his mouth kicked up, which drew her attention back to those lips. Damn him. He did that on purpose.

"So you would've been ready to thank anyone with a kiss who had landed safely?"

Jade narrowed her eyes. "Don't you need to go call Jax?"

In an instant, Cash was all business. The smile vanished and he stepped away, pulling his cell from his pocket.

"I do," he agreed. "This could be a while."

Once he stepped out onto the patio for privacy, Jade thunked her head back against the wall and closed her eyes. She could do this. Spending the night with Cash was no big deal. He'd be on the couch, she'd be in the bedroom with the doors closed. How difficult could this be?

That was one question she wasn't even going to entertain answering.

Jade pushed off the wall and went to her purse. She pulled out her phone and saw she'd missed three calls from her mother and six texts. Yup. She'd discovered Jade was in town and not the polished charity volunteer she'd tried to paint her out to be.

Whatever. Jade wasn't in the mood to defend herself or explain where she'd been. Right now, that Jacuzzi tub was calling her name. Hopefully, she wouldn't fall asleep and drown, but it was a chance she was willing to take.

She grabbed her suitcase handle and started toward the bedroom. A quick glance out the patio doors and she stopped. Cash had the phone to his ear, his head down, his free hand raking back and forth over the back of his neck.

Guilt stirred within her. If she hadn't needed a ride, he wouldn't be stuck here with her and the plane wouldn't be abandoned in some field outside the city. She couldn't imagine how terrified he'd been, knowing their safety had literally been in his hands, and now worrying about the plane he and Tanner had invested so much in.

Jade could've turned down the request to be in the wedding party, but her grandmother had asked her to be in it, and there was no way Jade could say no to the woman who had kept her sane all those years growing up with Lana as a mother. Jade's father had passed too soon. He'd been all Irish, and they actually resembled each other, even though the biology didn't match up. She often wondered how her life would've been different had he lived. Because living with Lana had been quite the struggle as Jade attempted to find her place . . . which hadn't been at society functions with her mother.

But her dad's mom, the one woman Jade had felt a connection to, had been there when Jade needed an escape from pearls and teacups and gossip over who had the latest-model Jag.

Cash turned and raised his head, his dark eyes instantly locking on hers. Nightfall had settled in, but the glow of the patio light seemed to shine down directly onto him, making him appear like some sort of dark angel.

Jade blinked and pulled herself from the trance.

A bath. That was what she was working toward. Not these crazy stirrings toward Cash. She was tired, she was confused, she was ready to get this weekend over with.

Jade turned toward the bedroom and pushed open the double doors. Shedding this rank dress and her running shoes were top priority right now. Long glances toward her new roommate were not.

How long should he wait before checking to see if she'd passed out in there?

Cash stood outside the bedroom doors and listened. When he'd hung up with Jax, he'd heard the water running, but for the past hour, there had been nothing at all.

Jax had been upset about the plane, even though the aircraft didn't belong to him, he didn't like knowing his friends had been in danger. A crew would be called in the morning to come and check the plane and work on getting it back to Haven. The entire ordeal would be a mess and a hell of a hit to their renovation budget, but Cash would figure something out.

He'd called Tanner, too, considering they shared the Cessna, but he didn't answer. Cash ended up shooting him a brief text.

And now he was waiting for Jade. He didn't know why he was waiting on her. She'd likely get out of the tub and crawl into bed and ignore him. But he wanted to see if she was okay. Jade had a tendency to use sarcasm or the cold shoulder to deal with things . . . or maybe that was just the special treatment he got.

Regardless, as much of a tough front as she'd tried to put up earlier when running into her cousins, Cash had seen beyond the forced smiles. She truly didn't want to be here.

He wanted to know why or who kept her loyalty. He'd always thought Jade was upper class, and she was, but after seeing a brief sampling of her family, Cash realized she was nothing like them.

There was no need for him to barge into the bathroom to see if she was breathing or submerged underwater. Surely to goodness she was just relaxing, like she'd been wanting to do.

Cash turned from the closed doors and stared at the couch. This day sure as hell hadn't gone as planned, but he could think of worse ways to spend the night. He still needed to text his clients to reschedule them because he wasn't going to be back in Haven for a couple of days.

Tomorrow he'd have to find somewhere to get something to wear for the wedding. No doubt it was a black-tie affair, but because he technically wasn't invited, he didn't feel he needed to follow those rules.

He crossed to the sectional, which would prove to be his bedroom, office, and living room. Pulling his cell from his pocket, he sank into the corner seat and stretched his legs out before him on the cushions.

After several minutes of scrolling through his schedule and contacting clients, he set his phone aside and glanced over his shoulder toward the closed bedroom doors. Still nothing.

Was she done talking for the night?

Considering he was only here by default, Cash wasn't going to bother her. She'd booked this room thinking she'd have some romantic getaway with her jerk of an ex. A stirring of jealousy slithered through him, which was absolutely absurd because he never got jealous. He wasn't even jealous when his wife cheated on him . . . twice. He was mad as hell, but not jealous. That had been a glaring sign that he wasn't in love with her.

Cash came to his feet and went to the closet in the entryway. He found spare blankets and pillows and took them back to the couch to make his bed. He had no spare clothes, so he'd just have to sleep in his boxer briefs. No way in hell was he going to be modest and try to sleep in jeans. He wasn't that much of a gentleman.

Stripping down to his underwear, he already felt more comfortable. He grabbed the folded blanket and gave it a hard shake before sending it fluttering down onto the sofa cushions.

"Hey, Flex   "

Cash shifted his attention across the suite to the open door of the bedroom, where Jade stood wearing a fluffy white hotel robe, her hair up in a towel and those eyes wide with wonder. Even at this distance, he didn't miss the way her mouth dropped open as her gaze darted down, then struggled to make the return trip back up.

"Need something?" he asked, not bothering to shield his body or hide his smile.

Jade blinked and clutched the vee in her robe. "Um . . . yeah. I was going to see if you wanted to order room service and—damn it. Would you put clothes on?"

"I'm wearing clothes."

She stepped from the room and glared at him. "Your underwear is hugging parts I shouldn't be looking at."

Cash couldn't help himself; he stepped around the couch to give her a better look. "Can't control yourself, Red?"

She crossed her arms over her chest and cocked her head to the side. "You wish. I think you adore yourself enough for both of us."

"There's nothing wrong with being proud of your body," he told her. "I work damn hard to stay in shape and I know you do, too, with as much as you run."

Her eyes traveled over him once again. "I love running. It's therapeutic. So is yoga. I'd say you're one of those guys who is constantly taking gym pics in the mirror and splashing them all over social media."

Cash couldn't help but laugh as he raked a hand over his abs. "I don't take pictures of myself. I do take pictures of the gym, of people working out, of partners spotting each other. It's all part of my marketing. I mean, there are photos of me because I'm the business, but I'm not that shallow, Red."

He took another step closer, and she darted her eyes up to the ceiling. "All right. Put clothes on or I'm giving you this robe."

"What are you wearing under it?"

Jade groaned and rolled her eyes. "You're ridiculous."

"I'm not the one staring at the ceiling because the sight of a man wearing the equivalent of swim trunks is making her uncomfortable."

Her eyes darted back to his and held them. "Fine. Put

some damn pants on and let's order food. We're not paying
for it anyway."

Cash laughed. "You really don't like your family,
do you?"

Her lips thinned and one corner of her mouth quirked.
"Well, they saved me, but they have regrets, so . . ."

Saved her? What the hell did that mean?

Cash was about to ask just that when she turned back
to her room and called out, "I'm ordering room service.
When I'm done, I expect your junk to be covered by more
than spandex."

Damn, that woman could make him laugh and drive
him crazy at the same time. Who knew this little im-
promptu trip would turn into him wanting to learn more?

She had so many layers, more than he'd ever given her
credit for. Jade might be wealthy, she might have high
standards, and she was most certainly out of his league,
but maybe they could actually get along.

Of course, there was this sexual tension they had to
contend with. There was no way she could deny her attraction, not when her mouth practically had fallen to the floor
when she'd come out of her room. The attraction and
physical admiration definitely went both ways. Jade was
sexy as hell. Just because he was a gym owner and personal trainer didn't mean he expected a woman to be
perfect by society's standards. He appreciated a woman
who took pride in her health, but size had never mattered
to him.

He didn't want this pull toward Jade McKenzie. Sex
was one thing, but sex with Jade would seriously make
things messy for their tight group. They were all working
on this airport renovation. While the other two couples
were in committed relationships, Cash had no aspirations
of committing himself to anyone, let alone Jade.

But that wouldn't stop him from agitating her or getting in all the visual licks he wanted.

Her low, sultry voice filtered out into the living area. He chuckled as he thought of all she must be ordering on her family's dime. While he could pay his own way, he'd let her have this.

As he went to retrieve his jeans, because he had no other pants, Cash kept rolling her comment through his head. What had her family done to save her? Was that why she felt obligated to attend this wedding? Had her life been in danger before?

Sometimes he thought he had her pegged, then other times he realized he didn't know her at all. Despite the fact they'd grown up in the same town, despite the fact he'd been around her for the past year, Jade McKenzie was one hell of a complex puzzle. And he always did enjoy a challenge.

Cash had just tugged his pants over his hips when Jade stepped from her bedroom wearing a pair of black, snug shorts that showcased her long, toned legs and a gray tank top.

Was she doing this as payback? If she wanted to fight dirty, she'd found the right guy to play with. He invented the damn game.

"How is that any better than what I was wearing?" he asked.

Jade shrugged and came over to the sofa. "I didn't plan on having a guest, so this is what I packed," she explained as she took a seat in the corner of the sectional.

"Don't mess up my bed," he growled.

Jade kept her eyes on his as she reached out and grabbed the blanket he'd just gotten out. She gave it a tug and had it on her lap, covering the legs he'd been imagining around his waist.

No. Absolutely not. No sex fantasies concerning Jade. He had to set some boundaries, damn it.

"I'll remake the bed," she said sweetly, with that smile that used to drive him crazy, but now it drove him crazy in a whole new way.

"Why don't you find a movie?" she suggested.

Cash stared down at her, his eyes darting to the sliver of hot pink bra strap poking out from her gray tank. Mercy, he could not be thinking of her lingerie . . . and he'd bet his last dollar she had some amazing pieces.

"Cash?"

Right, the movie.

"So, are we going to do each other's nails at this slumber party?" he asked, reaching for the remote on the coffee table.

Jade stuck her hands out in front of her, then flipped them around for him to see. "I actually already did them for the ceremony, but thanks."

He took a seat on the couch, just below where she had her feet curled up.

"There's a whole other section to this couch," she stated.

Cash pointed the remote toward the television and started flipping through their options. "You have the blanket and I may want to snuggle."

"Oh, please. I doubt you've ever snuggled with a woman in your life. You're not the type."

"And what type am I?" he asked, dropping the remote to his lap as he shifted to face her. He stretched his arm along the back of the sofa and waited for her answer.

She lifted one delicate shoulder. "I don't know."

"Well, you've given it some thought."

She shifted, and her bare feet brushed against his thigh, definitely not helping the situation. The situation, being his attraction for her, was exploding by the minute.

Why this woman? Maybe there would be another woman at the wedding tomorrow that would take his mind off his current roommate.

Well, hell. That wouldn't work, because Cash was pretending to be her plus-one. Damn it. He was stuck with her until they returned to Haven. Which meant the only person he'd be flirting and dancing with was Jade.

"I just never took you for being compassionate, that's all," she finally stated.

She didn't make an attempt to shift back her feet.

"Is this because I didn't let you kiss me when we landed?" he joked, mostly because he couldn't get wrapped up in this woman or this moment, which was teetering way too close to the line of intimacy.

"I wasn't going to kiss you," she insisted.

"Is that right?" Cash leaned toward her just a bit more. "Then why were your eyes on my mouth, just like they are now?"

Those vibrant green eyes snapped back up. "You are delusional. Now put on a movie."

She was the delusional one for denying what she wanted, because her heavy-lidded stare told him more than her lips ever would.

Cash picked the remote back up. "Would you rather action or comedy?"

"Are you taking my game and using it for your own purposes?" she teased.

"Maybe I am." He flashed her a smile and patted her feet, where they still rested against his side, poking out from the blanket. "Or would you rather nix the movie and play strip poker?"

Her mouth hinted at a grin, but she replied, "You're a jerk."

She kicked her foot at him, but he caught it. The second

his hand clamped around her arch, her eyes flared wide, her chest expanding as she sucked in a deep breath.

"That's not how you felt when I saved your life," he murmured, inching just a bit closer.

"I got caught in the moment," she defended herself. "So what if I wanted to kiss you? Believe me, the feeling has passed."

Cash barely contained his smile. "Is that right?"

He slid his hand from the bottom of her foot up to her ankle, her calf . . . all the while keeping his eyes locked on hers. She made no attempt to move or to stop him.

Why was that? More importantly, what the hell was he thinking? This was a standard case of playing with fire. Sure, he'd been burned before, but hadn't he learned his lesson?

Apparently not.

"Stop playing games, Cash."

Yes, Cash. Stop playing games.

"I'm just making sure you're relaxed," he explained. "You had a pretty rough day."

He massaged her calf and took great pleasure in watching her lids flutter. But then she recovered and shot him that glare once again.

"You think this is making my day better?" she scolded.

"I think if you'd lay back, you might enjoy this."

"Maybe I would, but I'm not sure where you'd stop."

With the haze his mind was in right now, he wasn't sure either. But she wasn't putting up any resistance other than feeble words. He figured she was about two strokes away from moaning.

"You know this isn't smart, right?" she asked, her voice huskier than it had been moments ago.

"I'm just trying to relax you and figure out a movie to

watch. You said I wasn't compassionate, so I'm proving you wrong."

She let out a slight laugh before stretching out her legs until they landed in his lap. Well, maybe they were making progress. He slid his hand to her other foot and started the slow process all over. He'd never rubbed a woman's feet before, but he didn't mind one bit getting his hands on Jade.

"Stay below the knee," she ordered as her head dropped against the back of the sofa and she flung an arm over her eyes. "And stop staring at me. You're supposed to be picking a movie."

Ah, there she was. The mouthy, snarky friend he'd come to know. Wait. Friend? He wasn't sure what their label was exactly. Was there even a term for people who drove each other insane, had mutual friends, and somewhat worked together?

The shrill bell echoed through the room. Cash patted her legs and eased out from under her.

"That's the food," he told her. "Sit still, Red. Let me get that for you."

For a man who'd always thought of her as pampered and spoiled, he sure was treating her like a princess . . . and damn if he didn't like it.

Chapter Four

"Maybe I shouldn't have ordered so much food."

Jade surveyed the spread on the coffee table, then glanced up to the food cart, where even more silver-domed lids sat untouched.

"I can't eat anymore," Cash stated as he leaned back against the couch.

They'd both sat on the floor and used the table as one giant tray. The fruit, the pasta, the steak, the brownies, and so much wine . . . she may have gone just a tad overboard.

In her defense, her mind hadn't been in the right place when she'd placed the order. She'd spent all day with Cash, she'd seen him in those marvelous boxer briefs, which showcased every ounce of muscle tone and perfection. So her call to the room-service operator may be a bit hazy—and that was before he'd put his hands on her.

If she'd had to communicate after that, she probably wouldn't have been able to make a complete sentence. Had she ever had a foot massage from a man before? Cash's hands had been damn near magical and so, so strong. She'd put in that below-the-knee stipulation mainly for herself because the way he kept working his fingers all over her skin, she was afraid if he traveled up too high, she'd offer up the rest of her body.

Since the food arrived and they'd started a movie, he'd reverted back to the regular Cash she knew. No touching, but a wealth of sarcasm and ego. At least that side of Cash she could handle and had actually grown accustomed to. The touchy-feely side . . . she wasn't sure she'd ever be ready for that.

The man was too potent for words, and if she ever mentioned as much, she'd never hear the end of it. Cash would use her jumbled feelings as fodder to stoke that inflated ego.

At least they'd finally agreed on something to watch. That may be the only thing they had in common. They'd stumbled upon a documentary about some drug lord and the federal agents who went undercover to take him down. True crime and biographies were her go-tos when she wanted something to watch. She'd been quite pleased when that nugget of information surprised him. Jade hated being predictable.

"It's getting late," she told him as she came to her feet. "I should put this food in the fridge and get to bed. I'll need my energy for tomorrow."

"Actually today," he corrected, pointing to the screen of his phone. "It's one in the morning."

Jade raked her hands through her hair and realized she'd forgotten to brush the knotted mess before it dried. That would be a bitch to get through tomorrow.

"Let me get this food out of your way so you can get some sleep, too."

She started to grab the bowl of Alfredo when his hand clamped around her. That strong hand circled her wrist with ease and made her feel petite and feminine. She'd never had a man make her feel like that before, so why Cash? Why did those large, rough hands make her wonder just how they'd feel on other places of her body?

"Go to bed," he told her. "I've got this."

"Don't be silly."

Her heart kicked up and she really hoped he couldn't feel her pulse. Why did she have to have such a strong reaction to his touch? Just because he continued to hold her in that firm, arousing grip and those forearms flexed so gloriously . . .

"Red, listen to me for once." He released her as he came to his feet and closed the narrow distance between them. "Go to bed. Your mother won't like it if you don't look rested."

Jade laughed. "It's like you already know her."

He didn't even attempt to crack a smile, he just continued to stare in that intense, maddening manner. He'd never acted like he found her attractive before; perhaps this was all still leftover adrenaline, or the fact that they were alone in this hotel room in the middle of the night.

Regardless, Jade couldn't do this. Not the touches, the glances, the flirting, and sure as hell not him parading around in that, that . . . ball-hugging underwear.

"You're not heading to your room," he murmured.

Did his voice just get lower? Why was he standing so close?

Jade backed up and nearly tripped over the edge of the sofa. "I'm going, I'm going."

She made quick work crossing the suite to the entrance of her room. She stopped and glanced over her shoulder, her heart stuck in her throat when she caught Cash staring at her. His eyes locked right onto hers and she had that warm sensation flooding through her again.

"Thanks." Jade pulled in a deep breath and attempted to regain control over these absurd emotions. She offered him a smile. "For the safe landing, the plus-one, the foot rub."

"My pleasure."

Oh, mercy. Those two words coming from that sexy, shirtless man . . .

Jade quickly went into her room and closed the double doors. There would be no sleep for her tonight, not when she was so revved up and justifiably confused. She needed some distance from Cash before she crossed some invisible line neither of them could come back from.

Tomorrow, she vowed, she'd have her thoughts in order and she wouldn't let Cash affect her in such ways again.

Cash had been gone all morning. He'd gotten up early, ordered room service for Jade to have breakfast, waited for the delivery, then left her a note before he headed out to find wedding attire.

And what a bitch that excursion had turned out to be. He just needed something between a tux and his worn jeans and tee, which he'd been wearing since yesterday. The whole black-tie thing didn't work for him. He hadn't even worn one to his own wedding . . . not that he could base much on that mistake.

After nearly five hours, Cash had been felt up and groped and, for a while, he had regretted walking into that store as a last resort. But turned out with the measuring and never-ending dressing room changes, Cash ended up with the most expensive suit he'd ever owned.

The black suit, black shirt, black patent leather shoes were all in a garment bag and ready to go. Cash pulled out his key card and slid it into the suite. He had enough time to shower and hopefully get Jade to the venue on time. He didn't know what he'd do for those two hours while she did photos, but he'd figure something out.

Cash stepped into the suite and the assault of something floral hit him. Not just floral, but money. He couldn't describe the aroma exactly other than expensive. Some perfume he didn't recognize, perhaps.

"Red," he called out. "I found a suit but opted not to pay extra for the tie."

After getting measured, standing on a minicircular stage in front of a wall of mirrors, and having no less than three workers waiting on him at a time, he was ready to relax before the real show began. He wasn't sure what to expect, but from the picture Jade had painted, he didn't know that he could actually prepare for something so over the top.

Cash laid the black garment bag over the back of a dining chair and headed toward the open double doors of her room. One quick peek inside and he wasn't sure if they'd been robbed or if she'd made this mess in an attempt to get ready.

Clothes were strewn all over the messy bed, and her empty suitcase lay on a chaise in the corner. There was no sign of her, which meant she'd probably come to her senses and decided to go to this hell fest alone.

Whatever. He wasn't going to cry over missing some snotty gathering. He couldn't return the suit because they'd pretty much tucked in some spots and let out others, after his chest and biceps had been measured. But he'd at least hit up another store for a pair of jeans, a fresh T-shirt, and some underwear.

As he crossed the suite back toward the living room, he noticed his blanket folded with the pillow on top and a folded note atop that with his name in all caps across the front.

Cash reached for the note and flipped it open.

Had to leave early. Apparently we're all getting our hair and makeup done together. I'm sure you won't recognize me once they're done. Meet me at the country club at five.

J

Cash smiled. Her sarcasm came through, and he'd read each word in her sweet, Southern tone. Though he was positive he'd recognize her. Someone as striking as Jade would always stand out in a crowd.

Now why the hell was he still standing here smiling at her note? Hadn't he just mentally rejoiced that he didn't have to go?

Yet he couldn't deny that part of him actually wanted to be on her arm. Maybe because he wanted to see firsthand just how ridiculous this shit show could be, maybe he didn't fully believe her family was that pretentious, but Cash knew the truth. He wanted to be with Jade to offer support. She clearly didn't want to be there, and damn it, he may be the complete opposite of what Jade preferred, but that didn't mean he wasn't good enough.

He'd be there as her friend and to offer support, nothing else. He sure as hell didn't want to go because he thought he'd seen something in her eyes last night. After Jade had gone to bed, Cash had convinced himself all he'd seen was exhaustion. They'd had a difficult day, to say the least.

But he wanted to see her again today, just to make sure that crackling tension between them was a figment of his imagination.

Cash decided to go ahead and get ready. She may have

told him five, but that was probably because she was trying to save him. He could head over early and have her back. From the little he saw yesterday of her cousins, Jade would need it. Any real boyfriend would offer the same, right?

He plugged the country club address into his cell and saw it was only ten minutes away. Plenty of time to shower and change.

Grabbing the garment bag and the toiletries he'd purchased, Cash headed toward the master bath. He laid his bags on her bed, ignoring the stir of emotion at the sight of his masculine things intermingling with hers.

Get a grip. This was just a last-minute, temporary arrangement. There was certainly no reason for him to be reading into each and every little thing.

His cell vibrated in his pocket, pulling him from his self-induced pep talk. He pulled out his phone and saw Tanner's name.

"Hey, man," he answered. "The Cessna—"

"Obviously you didn't do anything on purpose," Tanner interrupted. "I'm just glad you and Jade are okay. Listen, I just hung up with Jax and he's on-site with a crew."

"What's the verdict?" Cash sank down on the edge of Jade's bed, only to jump back up again.

The bright-red blow-dryer didn't make a comfortable seat. When he went to move it, he uncovered an emerald green bra beneath. His gut tightened. That bra matched her eyes perfectly, and he bet if he glanced around, he'd see matching panties.

Jade may not be the most predictable person, but he would've laid any amount of money on her being a lingerie lover—ironically, something else they had in common.

Raking a hand through his hair, Cash started toward the bathroom. Hopefully, all he'd encounter in there would be lotions and hair products.

". . . and the electrical is all a mess," Tanner went on.

Damn it. He'd been sidetracked by a damn bra and the visual of Jade and missed the first part of Tanner explaining the issue. But from the little bit Cash caught, the plane would be an expensive fix. As much as that would sting, Cash was still thankful he and Jade had made it out with barely a scratch. The thought of her getting hurt, especially by his hands, made his gut tighten with a fear he'd never felt before.

"Jax is working on getting it back to Haven," Tanner added. "But the local paper got wind of the issue and already called, wanting to know if this was an extension of the expansion and what new clients should expect. The guy was a total ass, but Livie handled him with that sweet charm of hers, and now he's waiting on an exclusive statement."

Well, hell. An idiotic thought like that never crossed his mind. Why did everyone glom onto the negative aspect of aviation? It was one of the safest sports and means of transportation there was. Yet one malfunction and the media was all over things.

"How the hell did they know?" Cash asked.

He caught sight of himself in the mirror over the vanity that stretched along the far wall. Damn, he needed to shave or get a haircut. He hadn't thought to pick up an extra set of beard trimmers. Oh, well, the black eye would distract from the unruly facial hair.

Part of him wanted to laugh, knowing he'd be showing up at a country club looking like a savage. The other part of him felt sorry for Jade because she'd have to deal with her mother.

"I have no clue how they found out," Tanner replied. "Livie is already working on the press release, but if you could ask Jade to jump on that as well? We're going to have to do some major damage control before we lose business we don't have yet."

Cash sighed as he glanced toward the ceiling. "Yeah. I'll talk to Jade today. She's at the wedding, but we'll start brainstorming. Listen, man, I know we share this plane, but I'll pay for anything that needs fixing."

"Like hell," his cousin all but shouted. "We have insurance that will cover most of the cost, and it could've happened with me behind the controls. I know it wasn't pilot error."

"Still . . ."

"Forget it. Just worry about dealing with Jade when she gets back from the wedding," Tanner warned. "From what Melanie told me, Jade's family can suck the life right out of you. Good thing you're not attending."

Apparently, Jade hadn't told Melanie or Livie he was joining her at the wedding. Nothing to tell really. It wasn't like they were dating or even pretending. As far as Cash knew, he was just here as a friend, to keep somewhat of the peace.

"I'll keep an eye on her," Cash promised.

"What? Wait a minute, Cash." Tanner muffled something in the background. "Melanie said to be nice to Jade and not irritate her too much."

"What about her irritating me?"

Like with her booty shorts and lingerie?

Tanner chuckled. "Just passing along the message, buddy. We'll see you back here tomorrow."

Cash disconnected the call and rubbed his eyes. Tomorrow Jax was coming back up to give Jade and him a ride home so they didn't have to take the rental car back to Georgia. Likely Jax thought Jade and Cash would kill each other before they made it back if they were left alone too long.

Focusing on things he could control today, Cash took a quick shower and attempted to smooth his hair back so he didn't look completely unruly. Of course, now with the sleek hair and the black eye he was giving off the image of a mob boss, but better than homeless . . . right?

He knotted the towel tighter around his waist and flattened his palms against the vanity as he leaned in to examine the beard. Might as well, he thought. It was only hair.

A laugh escaped him as he grabbed Jade's razor from the shower and got to work. He hadn't fully shaved his beard in several years, but something made him want to attempt to look his best for Jade. He didn't want to be a complete embarrassment to her. He drew the line at trying to fix his facial injuries. He wouldn't be borrowing any of her magical makeup potions to cover the eye or the cut on his forehead.

Once he was done, Cash ran a hand over his smooth jaw. His face felt colder, almost naked now. He made sure to rinse the razor extra before he put it back on the small ledge in the shower. She'd probably throw it away if she knew he'd used it.

All that was left to do was get dressed. He checked the time and figured they'd be starting pictures now. Likely she was bored out of her ever-loving mind. He still wondered if there was one family member she actually looked forward to seeing, or if she got along with any. Surely she had something in common with her own family.

Cash finished getting ready and headed out. It only took him eight minutes to get to the country club, where he was greeted by a valet when he pulled up. As soon as the valet took the car, a golf cart waited to take him on up to the outdoor venue.

Fall in Tennessee was rather amazing. Not that he'd

ever get married again, but this was a perfect day for any outdoor activity. There was a slight breeze, the temps were hovering at a perfect seventy degrees, and the foliage had hit peak season. No money in the world could buy this type of setting.

Cash was dropped off right at the entrance to the ceremony. There were tall floral arrangements on gold stands on either side of the brick pathway that led toward the grove of trees. As he headed down, he heard laughter and chatting. All at once, nerves assaulted him.

What was he really doing here? He didn't belong in a place like this. He'd obviously stand out, considering he wasn't wearing a tie, and he looked like he'd been on the losing end of a boxing match. Hell, he'd never been on a golf course in his life, let alone a country club. His father was a pill-popping alcoholic and Cash was a bitter divorcé.

Growing up, though, he'd been in a regular, middle-class American home. His mom and dad had been in love, had worked hard for everything they'd had. Then his mother died suddenly in a car accident, and his father had closed in on himself. One moment in their timeline had changed the future forever.

Cash pushed those memories aside. He'd need his full mind-set to handle his current situation.

In the distance, standing inside a large, white gazebo, was a whole host of ladies in hideous orange dresses. He recognized that shade and still couldn't believe anyone would purposely choose it—not that he knew much about fashion. His wardrobe consisted of workout gear and jeans.

Cash kept walking, his eyes searching for the one person he knew. He scanned back and forth but couldn't spot her.

"Excuse me, sir. This is a private ceremony."

Cash stopped on the path and turned at the female voice. A lady in her midfifties, if he were guessing, came toward him. The dark green suit and pearls looked a little more first lady and less like bridal party.

"I'm with one of the bridesmaids," he explained.

The lady gasped and reached up to touch her pearls. "Is that so? I know every single bridesmaid and I've never seen you before."

"Mother."

Cash turned as Jade came striding toward them. No wonder he didn't recognize her. Damn, she'd been right on guessing that.

Whoever did her hair had slicked it down and back so tight into a bun that it was amazing her face wasn't stretched into a permanent look of surprise. And the makeup plastered all over her face looked more like it was for a stage production. What the hell had they done to her?

"This is Cash," Jade stated as she came to stand beside him. "He's with me. Cash, this is my mother, Lana McKenzie."

Lana's eyes widened. Cash's first thought was that this woman looked nothing like Jade. She had blond hair almost to the point of being bleached white and the most vibrant blue eyes—blue eyes that seemed cold as ice. He'd never understood that statement until this moment.

"Jade Erin McKenzie." Lana clutched her gold purse and squared her shoulders. "Tell me this is not your date."

Cash started to speak, but Jade slid her arm through his and used her other hand to place over his chest.

"Mother, Cash isn't just my date." Jade paused and looked up at him, smiling wide. "He's my boyfriend."

"What?" Lana exclaimed.

What?

Jade sent him a wink and squeezed his arm. What the

hell game was she playing? Obviously something he'd ask her later, but for now, apparently he was playing the doting boyfriend. When that thought went through his head earlier, he'd only been joking.

"This is Vincent Miller, Mother."

"Everyone calls me Cash," he stated with a side grin he knew would never melt the ice.

"And where are you from, Vincent?" Lana asked in the most uninterested tone he'd ever heard.

Next she'd probably ask for his family's lineage.

"Haven, Georgia, ma'am."

"And your family?"

Cash refused to let his smile falter. "My mother was a nurse, but she passed away when I was a teenager. My father is currently retired and lives about an hour from me. I'm an only child."

Lana muttered something under her breath before her angry gaze landed on her daughter. "And you two went to school together?"

"I was a few years ahead of Cash," Jade stated. "We've recently reconnected."

"Is that right?" her mother stated. Her sharp eyes darted back to him. "I assume you work?"

"Yes, ma'am. I'm a personal trainer at the gym I own."

"Is that how you injured your face?" she asked, clearly disapproving.

Cash reached up and slid his hand over Jade's, which was still wrapped around his arm. "The cut is from the emergency landing we had to make yesterday. That's why your daughter missed the rehearsal, so stop making excuses and lying for her."

Jade gasped. Cash ignored her, tightening his hold on her hand as he forged onward. Because this woman was a grade-A bitch and Jade didn't deserve the condescending treatment. Lana could throw out whatever she wanted to him, he didn't give a shit, but he wouldn't just stand here and not defend Jade.

"The black eye came from a fight at Taps. I'm sure you remember the local bar from when you lived in Haven," he stated.

"A bar fight?" Lana repeated, her hand to her heart. "Really, Jade. This is what you bring to meet your family? And on the day of Ruthie's wedding no less."

"Maybe you missed the part about the emergency plane landing," Jade defended. "Cash controlled the plane that could've crashed and saved my life."

"Yes, and I'm grateful. I'm focusing on the bar fight right now."

"Mother—"

Cash moved his arm and wrapped it around Jade's waist, tucking her into his side and settling his hand perfectly over the curve of her hip. She fit his palm too damn good—something he couldn't concentrate on right now.

"The bar fight came from when some asshole publicly humiliated your daughter. I approached him, gave him an opportunity to apologize to her, but he mouthed off and I provoked him. I let him get in one good punch so I'd have a reason to beat the hell out of him."

"What?" Jade whispered.

He glanced to her, taking in her wide eyes, rimmed with too much dark liner. Even with all the spackle on her face, Jade was a beautiful woman, and right now he couldn't tell if she was just shocked or if she was pissed at his admission. He'd never wanted her to find out about his altercation with Brad, but Lana needed to know her daughter was worth more than a verbal punching bag.

"I love him already."

Jade pulled from Cash's side and turned at an elderly

female voice. When she gathered her skirt and moved away, Cash shifted to see a petite lady embracing Jade.

"Millie, this is not your concern," Lana said. "I'm having a conversation with my daughter and her supposed boyfriend."

Jade eased away from the women, but for the first time since arriving, he saw a genuine smile on her face.

"Cash, this is my Nana Millie. She's my dad's mom."

Jade introduced them with pride, and Cash had a feeling he'd just met the reason Jade had come to the wedding.

"Nana, this is Cash."

The petite woman, in a navy dress, sans pearls, and bright red lipstick, stepped forward. Cash thought she'd shake his hand, but she pulled him into a fierce hug with more strength than any nana should possess. This little sprite of a lady was strong and damn impressive.

"I heard enough to know this young man is a real hero." She stepped back and patted his arms. "And quite beefy, too. Well done, Jade."

For the first time ever, Cash noted Jade's flushed cheeks. He couldn't help but laugh.

"I'm a personal trainer, ma'am," he explained. "I try to stay in shape."

"I'd say you do more than try." She sized him up with her blue eyes. "Former military?"

"Yes, ma'am."

She nodded her approval. "I can tell. Your self-control around my outspoken daughter-in-law and the way you came to Jade's defense are all telltale signs."

"Shouldn't you be getting back to the pictures?" Lana scolded Jade like a child.

Jade's eyes landed on him, and he couldn't stop the dramatic thump to his heart. Where the hell had that come from? He hadn't allowed his heart to be a factor with any woman since his wife left. There was no way he could let this happen with Jade.

"Go on," he told her. "I'm sure Nana and I can get along just fine."

Millie laughed and hooked her arm through his. "Come on, young man. Let's go get a drink before this shindig starts."

"Millie, you're due for pictures, too," Lana stated, crossing her arms over her chest. "You're already late as it is."

Jade's grandmother waved her free arm in the air. "I have time for one drink. This wedding party is so large, nobody will notice I'm missing for the next ten minutes."

Jade continued to stare at him as her mother started to lead her away. The only way he could describe her look was that she had big plans for an epic talk later. He definitely had some explaining to do regarding the fight at Taps. There was no way he could deny what happened, not now that he'd let the secret out.

Millie patted his arm. "Shall we?"

Cash nodded and let her lead the way to the bar. He was going to need that drink to make it through the rest of the day.

Chapter Five

Jade made it through the ceremony, she'd made it through another round of photos, and she'd even made it through the cheesy introductions of the wedding party as they entered the glamorous outdoor seating area for the reception.

But she was done with her duties and on the hunt for Cash.

What the hell had he meant, he got in a fight with Brad over her? She hadn't asked him to do that, and she didn't appreciate him telling her mother about that humiliation.

What on earth had happened when she'd left that bar? Why did Cash get involved in the first place?

Though, if she were being completely honest with herself, the fact that he'd stood up for her against Brad had her feeling all sorts of warm and tingly and, damn it, completely turned on. She could take care of herself—she had for years—but knowing he'd done so really clicked something inside her. He'd not only come to her defense, he'd done so without boasting or bragging about it.

Maybe there were more layers to Cash's ego than she'd thought. Clearly, there was a humble side to him.

She had so many questions that only he could answer,

and she found she wanted to get away and just see him. My, how things had changed just since yesterday morning when she'd walked into that hangar and seen he was her pilot.

Jade's eyes scanned the reception area. Whoever Ruthie had hired for a wedding coordinator and decorator really had pulled off something magnificent. Not that Jade wanted to get married and not that she needed all the frills and glam, but there was no denying this place was something from a fairy tale—hideous dresses aside.

Rich, brown velvet couches sat beneath cream canopies. Circular, gold ottomans served as spare seats or mock tables for drinks. Clusters of fall flowers in a variety of colors were used to secure the openings on all four sides of the canopies, leaving an open and airy ambience. The sun had just started to descend behind the hills and trees, the twinkling lights draped all around, and the lanterns suspended from trees were giving off a gorgeous glow.

Jade gathered the skirt of her dress and grabbed a flute of champagne as a waiter came by with a tray. She needed something to keep her hands occupied and she wasn't going to turn down a drink right now. Her nerves were on edge between her mother's embarrassing reaction to Cash and Jade's sudden attraction to the man.

She planned on ignoring the attraction because she assumed it was just a temporary bout of insanity. But they seriously needed to talk, and she owed him an apology. She'd warned him how upper crust her family was, but she never would've guessed her mother would be so blatantly rude.

"If you're looking for your man, he's been standing in the back with his eyes on you."

Jade hadn't even realized her nana had come to stand right beside her. She'd also not corrected the whole boyfriend comment . . . another reason she owed Cash an apology. She'd completely blindsided him with that little bombshell, and he'd gone right along with it and hadn't taken Lana McKenzie's mouthy greeting.

Jade sipped her champagne, not wanting to turn around and see Cash eyeing her. Was he really staring at her? Or was Nana only seeing what she wanted to see? Perhaps he *was* staring. The combo of hair, dress, and makeup was certainly something he'd never seen her in before . . . and never would again.

"You're wasting a perfectly good opportunity to dance," Nana continued. "I already got mine in. He's got some moves."

Shocked, Jade jerked her attention to the woman who'd always been Jade's rock and biggest fan. "Nana. You danced with Cash?"

Millie McKenzie smiled and held her champagne flute up to her mouth. "He asked me, for the record. And like any Southern lady with manners, I accepted."

Jade leaned in and kissed her on the cheek. "I love you. I'm going to go check out those moves myself."

"You'd better, before someone else does. That whole dark, broody thing he has is rather sexy."

"Nana, if you were younger, I'd think you were making a play for my guy."

The second the words slid through her lips, she wondered why the lie came so easily. Cash wasn't her guy, and she had only been pretending such for a few hours.

"Darling," Nana stated with a hand on Jade's arm, "you know I'll never love anyone like I loved my Walter. Now, you go. Your young man is waiting."

Jade tossed back the last of her drink and turned until she spotted him. He stood off in the distance, but there was no denying that dark gaze was directly on her. There was also no denying that tingly feeling that started in her toes and crept all the way up, hitting all of her like an assault she'd never known.

A waiter came by and plucked the glass from her hand, but Jade's gaze never wavered. What was this trance he'd put her in? Perhaps it was that whole clean-cut look he was going with. But the clean jaw, the groomed hair, still made him seem mysterious, sexy, alluring.

"You and I need to have a talk." Her mother stepped in front of Jade, completely blocking the fascinating view.

Jade released her skirt and pulled in a deep breath, shifting her focus to her mother. "What is it?"

"That young man you brought is not a good match for you, Jade. If you're trying to rebel or get back at me, you're only hurting yourself." Lana clasped her hands and tipped her head. "I only care about your future; I always have."

Jade didn't even bother to suppress the eye roll. The only thing her mother cared about was putting on the perfect front. Jade refused to apologize for Cash or for bringing him.

"Not everyone has to look or act a certain way to be a good person," Jade stated. "Would you rather I date some stuffy, uptight CEO in a three-piece suit who treated me like shit or someone who actually cares for me?"

"Watch your mouth around me, young lady."

A large, firm hand slid across the small of her back an instant before a strong, familiar body came to her side. "I believe I owe my girl a dance."

Jade turned toward Cash. "Yes, you do. I've heard all about your moves from my nana. I'm jealous."

He flashed that grin and stared down at her like he didn't want to be anywhere else . . . which was utterly absurd for her to even think. Of course he wanted to be somewhere else. Hell, *she* wanted to be somewhere else.

"This discussion is not over," her mother declared.

Jade tossed a glance over her shoulder. "Then you'll be speaking alone because I'm done."

She let Cash lead her away toward the live band and the other couples caught up in the romantic evening. She'd dated over the years, though nothing serious, and she never really had a romance. For now, there was nothing wrong with pretending. Why stop now?

Though she had to keep in mind, they were simply playing a part. A part that was entirely her fault because she hadn't had to say he was her boyfriend; the words had just slipped out last night and now Cash was here, going above and beyond. As annoying as they were to each other, Cash was a good guy.

"I'm sorry."

Cash wrapped his arm around her waist and took her hand in his, pulling her flush against his broad chest. "How did I know you would try to apologize for her?"

She rested her arm on his shoulder and stared up at him. "Because she's never going to."

A corner of Cash's mouth kicked up in a sexy grin. "Red, I've dealt with worse people, and you don't get to say sorry for something out of your control."

His hips shifted against hers, and even through the layers of chiffon, she couldn't ignore the way her body heated at brushing against his with each step.

"Okay, then. I'm sorry for pulling the boyfriend card."

Now he did laugh as his firm hand dipped just a bit lower on her back. "You're not the only woman to use me for her dirty little secret."

"You're not a dirty little secret."

The defense came instantly, and she wondered who else had used him and why he seemed okay with it. Because nothing about this was okay. Not the lies, not the way her feelings were all jumbled, nothing.

Well, this friction between their bodies didn't seem wrong. It was delicious, actually. Too bad nothing would come of this sudden physical attraction. Acting on temporary hormones was definitely not the way she should wrap up this nightmare of a weekend.

"You're quick to defend people," he stated as he spun her in a quick circle and pulled her back in.

The flash-dance move left her smiling and reaching for his shoulder once again. "I don't appreciate my friends being treated like they aren't worthy," she replied.

Cash dipped his head and his mouth came within a whisper. "Are we friends, Red?"

His warm breath washed over her. His fingertips grazed the top of her backside through her dress and her entire body clenched, trying to hold in all the glorious euphoria spiraling through. There was nothing wrong with capturing all that arousal inside. She wasn't going to admit it, not to him.

"Red?"

What? What was the question?

His lips slid across hers in the lightest caress, like a feather tickling, teasing. Her fingertips curled into his suit jacket, and she realized they'd stopped moving. The music continued, but she paid no attention to the tune or anything else going on around her.

"Cash," she murmured.

She didn't know what she was going to say. Maybe nothing at all. Perhaps she was pleading for more because no one had ever touched her so simply, so softly, and yet had her every single nerve ending standing at attention, anticipating more.

Then, in a move she saw coming but did nothing to

stop, Cash completely covered her mouth, obliterating every last thought she had. The hand on her back pressed tighter, pulling her hips against his. He parted her lips with his tongue, proving that Cash was a man who took what he wanted . . . and she suddenly found herself more than ready to give.

Jade's hand tightened in his as he brought them to his chest. He let out a low growl, then nipped at her lips before easing back.

"That should do it," he murmured.

Jade blinked. "Wh-what?"

He started leading her in a dance again as one slow song flowed into the next one. Dancing, right. That's what they'd been doing before he completely knocked her for a loop and had her more than ready to strip off this sad excuse for a bridesmaid's dress.

"Your mother was watching," he stated as he continued to lead. "Just keeping up the charade you started, Red."

A slight burst of humiliation slid through her. He'd kissed her as part of the act. She wanted to be furious, but that wouldn't exactly be fair. Hadn't she started this farce? And how could she be angry when that one kiss elicited more from her than any sexual experience in her thirty-two years?

Jade attempted to smile, but her lips still tingled. "Well, thanks."

Those dark eyes landed on her and held. "My pleasure, Red."

Oh, the pleasure had been all hers.

The ride back to their hotel had been made in complete and utter silence . . . accompanied by a heavy side of sexual tension. Surely he wasn't the only one replaying that brief kiss over and over. Did that kiss have any hold over her? Because he was positive he'd fall asleep tonight with her taste on his lips and a new fantasy in his mind.

Never in his life had he thought he'd be fantasizing about Jade McKenzie in such a vivid way, but what had happened on that dance floor left him little option.

Yet he'd lied to her earlier. There hadn't been a soul looking in their direction, let alone her mother. Not that he saw, anyway. He'd only been able to see Jade. When she'd plastered her body against his and started moving, he knew he was trying to hold on to a slippery slope and failing miserably.

Why was it this woman he lost his control around? Jade had used him to get a jab in to her mother and he hadn't minded one bit; the woman really deserved to be knocked down a peg or five.

But why shouldn't he kiss Jade? He'd wanted to, she'd wanted to. Might as well test it out, right?

Only now that she was sliding her key card into the door of their suite, all he could think of was how he could still taste her and how they would be alone again all night.

As soon as she stepped inside, he followed and closed the door at his back. The second he flicked the lock in place, she set her purse on the dining table right inside the door and whirled around on him.

"Do you want to tell me why you started a fight with Brad? Or, more importantly, why you didn't share this information with me?"

O-kay. Not what he thought she'd lead with, though he was surprised it had taken her this long to circle back to that bombshell he'd dropped earlier.

Jade stood in front of him with one hand braced on a high-backed leather chair and the other propped on her hip. Was now a bad time to think how much he wanted to mess up that hair and makeup and take her into that bedroom and do . . . hell, everything. He wanted to do everything to that woman.

Over the past year she'd been back, he'd had stirrings. Random licks of lust here and there, but he'd brushed them aside. Unfortunately, over the past two days, that lust had curled all through him and threatened to strangle him if he didn't get a grip on his hormones.

Cash cleared his throat and slid out of his suit jacket. He'd been confined long enough. She continued to stare, waiting for an answer, as he crossed and laid his jacket over the back of one of the dining chairs.

"He deserved it," Cash stated simply. There really was no other reason. The guy was an ass.

Emerald-green eyes narrowed. "I don't want you fighting my battles."

Oh, she was pissed, and he had a feeling it had nothing to do with Brad and everything to do with the fact that he'd kissed her and she'd liked it. At least that's what he was telling himself. Maybe part of that idea was to feed his ego, but the majority was because he wanted it to be true. He wanted her to like his mouth on hers . . . and he wanted her to crave more.

"No?" he asked, shoving his hand in his pocket to resist reaching for her and finishing what he'd started on the dance floor. "You needed me to pretend to be your lover, so I think you do need me."

"My boyfriend, not lover," she corrected, crossing her arms over her chest.

He purposely let his eyes drop to her lips and smiled. "Same thing in this case."

"Well, the game is up," she told him, back to that stuffy tone he'd always associated with her. But now he realized that was just a defense tactic.

Without a word, he stepped forward and reached out.

"What . . . what are you doing?" she asked, her eyes wide.

He reached around with both hands and started pulling pins from her hair. So damn many pins.

"What did they do to you?" he asked softly.

Her natural waves tumbled around her shoulders, gliding through his fingers. So silky and soft . . . so the opposite of him.

"Nothing good," she muttered. "I can take my own hair down."

"You can do quite a bit on your own." He dropped a handful of pins onto the table before reaching back up for more. "But I'm still helping."

Her eyes searched his. "Why?"

"Because I'm trying to get you back to yourself."

She bit down on her bottom lip and closed her eyes. "Sometimes I don't know who that is."

Cash's fingers stilled in her hair and he clenched his teeth. He hated her family for making her so confused and ashamed of who she truly was.

He also hated her family for putting him in this position. He couldn't feel, not for Jade or anyone else; he didn't have it in him anymore.

But he could help her. He saw now that she wasn't some prima donna with a padded bank account expecting life to hand her everything she wanted. Jade was much more, and he had a feeling he'd barely scratched the surface.

"Sometimes I get tired of being someone else." She opened her eyes and looked up at him. "I'm tired of being the girl who does everything right, who cares what people think, who spent years trying to be the devoted daughter only to fall short every single time."

Once the last of the pins were in a pile on the table, he

couldn't resist putting his hands back in her hair and tossing those curls all around her shoulders.

Even when they'd had her hair all slicked back, once it was released, the strands had gone right back to their natural state. Just like the woman. Once she'd been turned loose from the grip of her family, she turned back into the woman he wanted.

"I just don't want to be me right now," she whispered.

His gut tightened. "Then don't."

Her eyes held his for about a half second before she stepped into him. "Maybe I do need your help."

Cash's hands tightened in her hair as he pulled her head back. "I'll help you get the hell out of this dress."

"Yes."

The simple word came out on a sigh, and it took every bit of his willpower not to rip this ugly thing to shreds. As he was contemplating where a zipper would be hidden in a dress like this, Jade gripped his shoulders and pushed him back until his back hit the wall next to the door. Her mouth covered his, and Cash had never been so shocked or turned on in all his life.

A woman who took control was so damn sexy. He'd never imagined Jade in this manner, but he wasn't about to complain.

His hands went to her ass and he groaned when he fisted layers of silk or whatever the hell this dress was made of.

Jade's delicate, soft hands framed his face as she plastered herself against him. She wasn't just kissing him, she was full-on making love to his mouth and driving him out of his ever-loving mind. Just when he thought she couldn't get any sexier.

Cash slid his hands up over the waist of her dress. He

fumbled around, looking for a zipper like some horny teen who had no experience. Why was there so much material?

While he was busy getting nowhere at all, Jade continued to kiss him. Her hands slid between their bodies and she had his shirt untucked and unbuttoned in about two-point-five seconds.

She stepped back and stared at his chest before peeling the material apart. He started to shrug out of the shirt, but his cuffs were still buttoned. She gave a yank at the material and the buttons popped to the floor, followed by the unwanted shirt.

Cash laughed. "What's the hurry, Red?"

"Shut up, Flex."

She reached to the side of the dress just beneath her arm and jerked the zipper down. In the next instant, a puddle of orange had slid down her luscious body and pooled at her feet. She stepped out of it and kicked it aside, standing before him in a white strapless bra and high-cut matching silk panties. And heels. Mercy, those heels in combination with those long, lean, runner's legs nearly brought him to his knees.

"Well, that shut you up," she stated.

When she reached for the button of his pants, Cash laid his hand over hers. "I'm in charge now," he warned with a growl.

Her eyes widened and she looked like a woman who had already been thoroughly messed up by her lover. Ringlets of red hair hung down her back, over her shoulders, in front of one eye. Her lipstick was all but gone now, and he didn't mind one bit that he was likely standing there half-dressed wearing the most hideous shade.

Cash spanned his hands around her waist and picked her up, earning him a squeal as he took three steps and sat her on the edge of the dining table. He flattened his hands on her thighs, his thumbs raking the inside of her legs as he spread them wider.

He never took his eyes off hers. He wanted to see every bit of her pleasure, to know what turned her on and what didn't.

Jade rested her hands behind her on the table, the motion thrusting her chest up toward him. The woman was going to be the death of him and they hadn't even gotten all of their clothes off yet.

Cash kicked off his shoes, unfastened his pants, and shed every ounce of his clothes—grabbing a condom from his pocket—before coming to stand between her legs again.

"Cash."

His name coming out on a groan had his body tightening even more. "Right here," he promised.

He slid his fingertip from the top of her panties up to the front closure of her bra. Her skin prickled beneath his touch and he used his thumb and forefinger to expertly flick the bra open, sending it falling to the table.

In about one second he was going to climb up onto this table and take everything he wanted, but he had to get her out of those panties.

With one quick jerk, Cash had them torn and no longer a problem. He thought the act would shock Jade, but when he let his gaze travel up her bare body and finally land on her face, he found her smiling back.

As if he needed another tug of arousal. The fact that he'd ruined her panties and it had turned her on was a common thread he never would've figured tied them together. So many things over the past two days had come to light about their similarities.

But those were things he couldn't think about now. Having Jade naked on a table was all he wanted to focus on.

Cash tore open the condom package, then covered himself. Jade relaxed back on her elbows as she lifted her knees on either side of his hips.

A man could get lost in those vibrant green eyes staring back at him. Another man, but not Cash. He was going into this with his eyes wide open, knowing this wasn't the start of anything permanent. She wanted to use him to forget and he was all too happy to offer up his assistance.

Cash braced his palms on either side of her face as he joined their bodies. The second he did, Jade arched up and met him. Seizing the opportunity, he dipped his head down to taste the creamy skin along her neck, that sexy spot where the curve met her shoulder.

Jade's fingertips dug into his biceps as she let out a groan. He didn't only want to taste her, he wanted to consume her. Cash's lips slid up over her neck, her jawbone, and captured her mouth.

When she locked her ankles behind his back and jerked her hips harder, Cash wondered just who was in control here. Somewhere along the way, they'd silently volleyed back and forth.

Her damp body clung to his as she tightened all around him. Cash broke the kiss, easing back slightly to see her face. He wasn't disappointed when she squeezed her eyes closed and tossed her head to the side. A flush crept up over her pale skin and he wanted to freeze this moment in his memory bank forever.

Cash couldn't hold out any longer. Jade did something to him he couldn't explain. Witnessing her undoing had been his breaking point. While she tightened all around him, Cash found his own release.

He gripped the back of one of her thighs and lifted her leg just a bit higher. He simply couldn't get enough.

Jade continued clutching his shoulders, and he caught her eyes locked on to him. As he came back to reality, he attempted to take in his surroundings. They had slid down the table and were on the verge of going off the other end.

Cash's entire body eased down on to hers, his forehead resting against hers as his trembling ceased.

Jade's fingers threaded through his hair and she gave him a gentle tug. "Flex, you're crushing me."

Cash thought he was out of energy, but her playfulness pulled him out of his postcoital haze. He slid off the side of the table and, before she could push her messed hair out of her face, Cash picked her up and plastered her against his body. He gripped her legs, giving her no choice but to wrap them around his waist.

She smacked his shoulder. "What are you doing?"

"We're going to the bedroom."

"I never said there would be a repeat."

Cash laughed. Had there been any resistance in her voice, he would've stopped, but she didn't put up much of a defense.

"And I never took you for a bed type of guy," she added. "You seem more adventurous."

Cash kicked the door open to her room, filled his hands with her backside, and smiled as he met her gaze. "There you go, thinking of my sex life again."

He dropped her onto the bed and climbed up after her, chasing her until she had her back against the upholstered headboard.

"And Red, I'm damn adventurous. You're about to see just how much."

Chapter Six

"Tell me about the wedding."

Jade felt the blush creeping up and heating her face. Thankfully, she was only on the phone talking with Livie, not in person.

She'd barely stepped in the door of her house—well, Livie's old house—before Livie called. Jade felt like she'd been through a war and away for a month, when in reality she'd been gone for only three days.

In three days she'd been in a near plane crash, humiliated by her mother, and had the most satisfying sexual experiences of her life with a man she technically couldn't stand.

But he'd come to her defense with Brad and her mother. He'd saved her life in the plane and calmed her when she nearly had an anxiety attack.

"Jade."

Blinking away her memories of the weekend, Jade finished unpacking her suitcase. "Sorry," she stated. "The wedding was just as elaborate and ridiculous as I figured it would be. The decorations and the outdoor setting was beautiful, but the dresses, the hair, and the makeup were something of a nightmare."

"That selfie you sent wasn't your best look," Livie

agreed. "How are you after the plane incident, though? I know we texted, but it's not the same as hearing your voice. I was worried, but then Jax assured me that Cash would take care of you. I was more concerned about you two killing each other on the way there. I never thought about the plane."

Jade swallowed and pulled her torn panties from the suitcase. Images of what they'd done on that dining table flooded her mind. Mercy, that man had some mad skills, and she wasn't so sure she'd ever recover from Cash's touch . . . or his mouth.

"He handled the landing like a pro." Jade went into her adjoining bath and tossed the panties in the trash. "How did the meeting go with the city council?"

"Pretty good. They appreciate the monthly updates on the renovations and are eager to bring in more business to the city. They'd heard about the plane incident, so I briefly touched on it, but they're going to want more information."

Working on damage control was easy. What wasn't easy was dealing with all these emotions surrounding Cash and everything they'd crammed into that weekend getaway.

Jade was relieved when her friend didn't mention the fact that Cash had stayed the weekend. Maybe he hadn't said anything to Jax. Because if Livie or Melanie knew Cash and Jade had shared a room, the questions would be endless and her friends would've been waiting for her on her doorstep.

Focusing on the airport renovations and teaching her yoga classes would hopefully keep her occupied and her mind off the way her body still tingled.

"The council even voted to extend some more funding because the airport is a historical building," Livie went on.

"With the grants, plus that boost from the city, we may not all go into debt."

Jade smiled. "I don't mind going into debt when I know it's for a good cause and I'm pretty sure I'll get a return on my investment."

"We're all in now," Livie said with a nervous laugh. "But seriously, I'm so glad you're fine. What do you say about girls' night in? I'll get with Melanie and I can bring Piper. She'd love some girl time."

Piper was absolutely the sweetest little girl and so lucky to have Livie as a stepmother. "Yes, bring her. I'd love some girl time. After the hideous hair and makeup I had this weekend, I'm ready to do something normal and just relax."

"Oh, I'm not sure about normal," Livie corrected. "Piper did my hair the other day and I ended up with some teased nest on top of my head, three ponytails in the back, and random bows to complete the style."

"Pretty sure that's still better than the slicked-back onion look I had."

"Ouch. Well, I'll bring wine and sparkling juice for Melanie and Piper."

"Plenty of wine," Jade added. "Even if it's just you and me drinking it. I need a good night in where I don't have to worry about driving."

"You can count on us," Livie promised.

"I know I can. See you in about an hour, if that sounds good."

"We'll be there," Livie assured her.

Jade disconnected the call and stared down at her opened suitcase. The glaring orange dress was such an eyesore. Pretty much the only thing it was good for would be rags for dusting or tossed in a fire for roasting marshmallows.

She clutched layers of the thin material in her hands, remembering how Cash had nearly torn it off, along with her panties. How often would she replay that night over and over in her mind? Because they may have started at the dining table, but then they'd progressed into the bedroom, the shower, the couch in the living room.

No wonder she was worn out and tired. She'd barely slept with Cash last night.

Had that only been last night?

Throwing the dress onto her bed, Jade went to her suitcase and zipped it up before putting it back in her closet. She'd be better off if she went to the kitchen and put together some snacks for ladies' night in. She should stick with her shake and veggies, but chocolate and wine were on the agenda for tonight. She could get back to her regular routine tomorrow.

As she headed down to the kitchen, she couldn't help but worry. What if Cash talked? What if he ended up telling Tanner and Jax that he'd shared a room with her?

Dread curled in her belly. What if he told them even more? Guys were different from girls, and she didn't know Cash well enough to know if he was a bragger.

Oh, please don't let that be the case. They hadn't discussed what happened. When they'd gotten up this morning, Jax had flown them back to Haven. She'd sat silently in the back while the two men in front dissected the reasons the Skycatcher had engine trouble. Their verbiage was foreign to her, but she could make out a little. The bottom line was, they were going to have quite a mess on their hands in repairing it.

Jade stopped at the kitchen island and pulled out her phone. She stared at the open message to Cash but wasn't quite sure what to say. She started about three different texts, deleting each one, before she decided.

We need to talk. Alone.

She hit Send, then realized she should've added "with our clothes on."

With a groan, Jade set her phone on the island and shoved the image of a naked Cash from her mind.

Okay, fine. She didn't shove that image from her mind at all. She actually let it roll through her head over and over because she'd never in her life seen someone as magnificent as Vincent "just call me Cash" Miller.

Why? Seriously. Of all the men in the world, why did her body have to respond so intensely to this one?

But sexual attraction was just physical. There was no reason to dissect this any further. Just because her heart had done a flip at the idea of him sticking up for her with Brad or the way he'd defended her to her mother, that didn't mean anything at all. She was thankful for his protectiveness, but she didn't need him fighting her battles.

They were home now. Their night was in the past and would remain in Nashville. There was no way she could let their encounter enter their lives here in Haven, because she planned on staying. She had no reason to go anywhere else. Her best friends were here, and she enjoyed coming back to her hometown more than she thought she would.

Maybe living in the big city had left her jaded; maybe she was over the snobs and the fake smiles. Something about Haven just felt right at this moment in her life. She'd been in such a hurry to leave when she'd been eighteen, but now she couldn't imagine herself anywhere else.

As she pulled out the ingredients to make snacks, she

caught herself glancing to her phone. She wasn't waiting on Cash to text her back. She *wasn't*.

Nearly an hour later, when she'd finished putting cute little plates together for her friends, she refused to admit the disappointment at her still-silent phone.

"I think you've had enough cookies."

Livie Morgan eyed her stepdaughter, but Piper just smiled and slid her hand up over the edge of the island in the kitchen and swiped another snickerdoodle.

"Your dad isn't going to be happy when you're too wired to sleep," Livie said, shaking her head.

"Come on. It's girls' night." Melanie rested her hand on her belly. "Besides, we never know when we'll have another one. I feel like I'm about to pop."

"You'll bring the baby when we do our next one," Jade insisted. "We have to break in the next generation."

Melanie laughed. "What if I have a boy?"

Jade shrugged. "He can hang with us for a while, or Tanner can take him for guys' night. Though I can't guarantee his first word won't be 'hell' or 'damn.'"

Piper's eyes widened. "You can't say bad words around me."

"Sorry." Jade reached for her wineglass. "Don't repeat them."

Livie rolled her eyes. "Believe me, she's heard worse when she's helping the guys at the airport."

"Yeah, and Daddy has a bad-word jar now and Livie makes him put money in it when he says bad words," Piper said with a wide smile. "Daddy says I get the money."

"I think my plan has backfired," Livie muttered. "Now she wants him to get in trouble."

Jade laughed as she finished off her Pinot and headed

to the fridge for a bottle of Moscato. They'd polished fingers and toes and the ladies had let Piper choose their shades. Jade cringed as she reached for the chilled bottle and spotted her bright purple nails. But she could live with it for a few days . . . she hoped. It was still better than a hideous orange dress or that showgirl-style makeup.

Melanie sported a bright, shiny red that was the complete opposite of her personality. Livie may have gotten the worst of the bunch with her school-bus yellow, but Livie didn't seem to mind too much. Livie had seriously mellowed out since coming back to Haven and stepping into the role of stepmom. Piper was impossible not to love, and if yellow nails made her happy, so be it. Though Jade was glad she didn't get the yellow.

Jade poured herself another glass and couldn't help but smile at the scene in her kitchen. Granted, although this house was still technically in Livie's name, Jade called it home.

The old, two-story white cottage was a far cry from what she'd been used to in Atlanta. Her condo had all the amenities and she took advantage of the gym, the sauna, the laundry service, the coffee bar. While she missed that part of her life, she didn't miss the rest.

Haven was where she was supposed to be. The résumés she'd sent out a few months ago had been a vain attempt at trying to reclaim the professional businesswoman she'd created. But being in this town, with these people: that was more important than anything else. She'd never thought she'd ever get to this point, but the temporary trip back just rolled from one day to the next. Now it was a year later, and Jade was in no hurry to be anywhere else.

She couldn't imagine not being here with her friends as they raised their children. Who knows? Maybe one day

Jade would have a family of her own with a man who loved her.

When Cash's face popped into her mind, Jade jerked at the unexpected image. Her hand tapped her wineglass at just the wrong angle and her Moscato went all over the island.

"Oh. Sorry, guys."

Melanie grabbed a towel from the counter and sopped up the wine before it could hit the food dishes. The wine surrounded Piper's bottle of water and Livie's stemless wineglass.

Jade grabbed a roll of paper towels and ripped off several. "I don't know what came over me," she mumbled as she picked up snack plates and utensils and swiped the soaked counter. "I wasn't paying attention."

Livie put her hand over Jade's wrist. "Is everything all right?"

Jade impressed herself by keeping her maniacal laughter inside. "I'm fine." If she didn't count the man who lit her up and forgot to extinguish the flame. "Just daydreaming."

"Anyone we know?" Melanie asked with a knowing smile and an irritating gleam in her eye.

"Believe me, you guys would know if I was seeing someone."

And she wasn't. She and Cash were nothing more than a one-night stand. The faux wedding date didn't count either.

"My friend Josh needs a mom," Piper chimed in. "His dad doesn't have a girlfriend. You want him to call you?"

Jade wasn't sure if this was a new low, having a five-year-old play matchmaker for her, or if the gesture was so utterly innocent and sweet. Either way . . . no.

"I'm not really looking for a boyfriend right now."

Piper's face fell, so Jade hurried on. "But when I am, I'll let you know, and we'll see if you can help me out."

Piper nodded. "Deal. I just want Josh to get a good mom like I got, and I know you'd be awesome."

Tears threatened to prick Jade's eyes, but she blinked that nonsense away. Damn it. Stupid wine was getting to her, that's all. The idea of her becoming a mom wasn't something she'd entirely dismissed. Oh, sure, her own mother was ridiculous, but that didn't mean Jade would be.

Lana McKenzie probably had great intentions somewhere deep down inside. Even though she'd adopted for the sake of the exposure and the accolades from her high-society friends, Jade wanted to believe there was a decent human being inside her mother.

Jade's mommy issues aside, Piper was right. She had gotten a wonderful mom when Jax and Livie had gotten together. They made quite an adorable little family.

Jade tossed her soaked paper towels into the trash and came back to where Piper sat perched on a wooden barstool.

"Thank you, sweetie." She wrapped her arms around Piper and kissed the top of her head. "I hope one day I'm an awesome mommy and have a sweet little girl just like you."

She met Livie's gaze above Piper's head and her friend smiled. Jade couldn't imagine their lives not here in Haven. They'd all loved Atlanta, but they had all agreed they needed a change. They just hadn't known exactly what that change would be.

Over a year later, here they were. Livie with her family, Melanie well on her way to her own family, and Jade . . . well, she was slowly finding her way, and she wasn't a bit sorry for the good time she was having along the way.

She'd been prim, proper, and confined for too long. Most of it was her own doing, in an attempt to make her mother proud, but that would probably never happen, so she was finally starting to live for herself. And it felt damn good.

"It's getting late." Livie grabbed the wet towel from Melanie and took it into the adjoining laundry room. When she stepped back out, she looked to Piper. "We'd better get going; it's a school night."

Jade glanced to the clock and realized three hours had already passed. Her phone, which sat charging in the corner on the kitchen counter, had remained frustratingly silent.

Fine. Whatever. It wasn't like she was begging him to give her attention or that this was some new relationship and she needed him to confirm his affection. But damn it. Couldn't he at least reply? The more time that passed, the more she worried he'd say something.

Perhaps he'd already written off their encounter and he'd moved on. Jade did tend to overanalyze things, and Cash didn't strike her as that type. He was likely either at the gym, training a client, or at the airport with the guys, trying to find a solution to the broken plane.

"I guess that's my cue to leave as well because I drove them," Melanie stated. "Are you sure you're all right, Jade? I know you had a difficult weekend with the plane incident and then spending time with your mother."

She'd gone over every detail of the over-the-top wedding, the horrendous hair and makeup, the condescending mother. She did leave out the fact that Cash had been her date, that he'd stood up for her with her mother and with Brad at the bar, and she'd definitely omitted the whole naked, dining-room-table sex.

Keeping secrets from her friends wasn't something she ever did; granted, neither were one-night stands, but she did feel a bit of guilt keeping something from them. They'd been through so much together and had shared everything over the years.

"I promise, I'm fine." Jade offered a smile as her friends gathered their things. "I'm still decompressing, but nothing the wine, some laughs, and a good night's sleep won't fix."

Livie stopped as she pulled her purse up on her shoulder. "When you get a chance, could you write a press release about the aircraft? The engine trouble was clearly unexpected, we always do preflight checks, give the stats of how rare that was, throw in some schmoozing about our stellar record and our eagerness to be the obvious choice for clients who want personal experience and—"

"I get it," Jade said, holding up her hands. "I'm well aware of how to do damage control. I already started making notes on my phone, so I can have this ready to go in the morning. It won't be difficult because this was the first incident with any aircraft from this airport and nobody was injured."

Well, minus the cut on Cash's forehead, but all things considered, they were both damn lucky.

Livie smiled as she sighed with relief. "Thank you."

"I'll be sure to layer in more details about the renovations and the grand reopening in the spring. I'll make it all upbeat and impossible for any potential client to worry. Who better to do this than the one who survived the incident?"

Livie wrapped one arm around Jade's shoulders and hugged her. "Thanks for staying. I don't know what we'd do without you."

Jade eased back and looked at her friends. "I can't leave you guys. So, because you're staying, I guess I am, too."

She'd probably have to find her own place at some

point, but for now, she just paid rent to Livie. They'd all done some minor renovations to the house when Livie had planned on selling, but as events unfolded, Livie couldn't sell and Jade had landed a fabulous place to live.

Was this all too easy? Could starting over and coming home really be this simple? If she let it be, yes. There was no pressure right now, and she was in charge of her own destiny.

Once everyone left, Jade figured she'd work more on that press release. She ignored the glasses on the counter and just grabbed the bottle of wine as she headed into the living room. She settled down on the oversize chair in the corner by the window and booted up her laptop.

If her mother could see her now, with her purple nails and chugging straight from a cheap, convenience-store wine bottle . . . well, she'd probably officially disinherit her.

Jade worked from her notes and managed a few solid paragraphs but needed to look up some statistics to throw in for good measure and to drive the point home of how safe flying really was.

If she thought too much about the incident, fear and nerves curled all through her. She would definitely leave any personal feelings from the piece. Facts were needed and they were all that mattered. This airport needed all the positive press it could get as a foundation for building a successful business.

Yet they'd come so close to crashing if Cash hadn't expertly handled the plane . . .

When Jade tipped back the wine bottle, she realized she'd already emptied it. Weird. She didn't remember drinking that much.

A knock sounded on the front door. Jade jerked her attention to the foyer and wondered who would be stopping by this late. She slid the laptop onto the seat, set her empty wine bottle on the floor, and came to her feet . . . which didn't seem as steady as they had earlier. How long had she been in that chair working and drinking? She really should've had more snacks earlier with the girls.

The warm, tingly sensation spiraled through her, and she wondered just how high the alcohol percentage was in that bottle of . . . she honestly couldn't remember if she'd grabbed the Pinot Grigio or the Riesling.

Jade glanced through the sidelight, and suddenly her warm, tingly feeling had nothing at all to do with the wine and everything to do with the man peering back at her.

Why was he here? Couldn't he just text?

With a flick of the dead bolt, Jade pulled the door open and rested her arm on it, trying to look casual, but really, she needed the support.

"Hey, Red."

Why did that voice sound so sexy, and why did she instantly think of sex when he spoke?

Stupid alcohol. She should've known better than to drink that much. She had only been drunk twice in her life. She wasn't drunk now, but she would be well on her way if she had any more. She was actually at the dangerous state where she spoke her mind, her truth, without filter.

"What do you want?"

"Nice to see you, too."

Without asking permission, Cash waltzed right in, brushing by her as he went. She didn't just shiver at his touch. She *didn't*.

"Won't you come in?" she muttered as she shut the door.

She didn't miss the way Cash instantly zeroed in on the empty bottle next to the chair, then back to her. "Partying without me, Red? And here I thought we'd gotten close."

Jade propped her hand on the newel post and glared across the room. "Why are you here? To judge my crazy Monday night?"

"I'm here because you said we needed to talk."

Oh, he was so infuriating, considering she'd texted him hours ago. Infuriating and too damn sexy. She hadn't been alone with him since he'd ripped her clothes off—which she would absolutely not think about right now.

"I texted you quite a while ago," she reminded him.

Cash lifted one shoulder in that frustrating way that set her nerves on edge. Everything about him set her on edge lately . . . even more so than usual.

"Been busy with training earlier, then helping Jax work on the plane."

She took in his full appearance. His hands were filthy, a small streak of grease over his left brow right beneath the cut, and his hair was a complete mess. The black eye was healing into a purple bruise and his jaw had already started that thick stubble of regrowth. His light gray T-shirt with his gym logo over his pec was all stained as well. Even covered in grime, Cash exuded sex and confidence.

Apparently, their brief time apart had done nothing to squelch her desire.

"You could've just texted me back," she retorted, still holding on to the banister.

If she inched any closer, she wasn't sure she'd be able to prevent herself from reaching up and swiping that streak off his face; then that would lead to trailing her hand down his cheek to feel that day-old stubble beneath her palm, toward his chest to appreciate those taut muscles, then his abs . . .

Also because she needed to cling to something right now. Clearly, she couldn't hold her liquor like she used to, because she'd been doing juice cleanses for far too long and now her body thought she was betraying their healthy pact. Wine was grapes, though, so she was totally counting this as her fruits for the day.

"Maybe I wanted to come by instead of text."

Oh, that low, almost menacing tone of his did things to her that she couldn't even describe. Her body should only respond in such a way when being touched, yet Cash was still across the room.

She had to get to the point and get him out of here. All she needed was a nice, hot bubble bath and a good book. In the morning, she'd get up and go for her run to clear her mind and decompress.

"Did you tell anyone about Nashville?"

"Nashville?" he repeated, then shook his head and laughed. "Is that our code word for sex?"

"It's not a code word for anything," she countered. "Did you tell anyone?"

That sexy smile vanished, replaced by a sneer. "Why? Don't want anyone to know you might have been attracted to me?"

"That's not it at all," she defended, but she could see how he'd perceive things that way. "I just don't do flings, and there's no reason for anyone to know our private business, especially because it won't happen again. We shouldn't let our friends think we're the next happy couple."

He seemed to be weighing her words for several moments, but then he started closing the distance between them. Why did she feel like the prey right now? Why wasn't she opening that front door and ushering him out? She'd said she didn't want their secret out and that's all she'd needed to tell him. They had nothing else to discuss.

"So I'm your dirty little secret?" he asked as he stepped into her. With each inhale, her chest brushed against his.

Warning bells went off in her head. Red flags waved in vain. Common sense didn't exist because she found herself reaching for him, stroking her fingertip over that streak above his dark brow just like she'd been imagining doing since he stepped through her door.

"Careful there, Red," he murmured. "You're playing with fire."

"Fire? No. You'd never burn me."

She swayed slightly, and Cash's hands circled her waist as he steadied her. "I think you had too much wine."

"Fruit cocktail?" she asked with a smile. "No such thing."

Cash reached up and grasped her hand, pulling it between their bodies. Someone moaned, and when Cash chuckled, she realized she'd let that sigh of desire slip. Oops.

Wine and Cash? The most potent combination she'd ever experienced.

Jade slid her other hand up over his broad shoulder, enjoying the excellent muscle tone beneath her palm. When she threaded her fingers through his hair, Cash hissed in a breath.

"Were you saying something just a moment ago about this not happening again?" he muttered.

Jade recalled some such verbiage, but her body clearly hadn't grasped that concept. She was ready to climb all over him if he'd just take this ache away. Why did engine oil or whatever he had all over him smell so damn good? He was just so . . . so masculine, and quite the opposite of any man she'd ever been attracted to.

Maybe that just added to the allure and desire.

Leaning forward just a bit, Jade skimmed her lips along that stubbled jawline. She missed his beard, but she'd never say so. Considering he'd shaved to appear more clean-cut for her family, she couldn't be upset. Though she did love the feel of his coarse hair beneath her touch. She stroked back and forth. His fingertips dug into her sides.

"Do you even know what you're doing?" he ground out.

"I'm pretty aware," she muttered as she nipped at his chin.

In a swift move that left her head spinning, and not just because of the wine, Cash had taken her face in both hands and silently demanded she look at him. That controlling attitude used to piss her off, but now she found his bold behavior impossible to resist. So why try?

"Maybe you want this, but how can I be sure it's not the alcohol?" he asked.

Jade blinked but never glanced away. "I'm well aware of what I'm doing and who I want to do it with. Are you with me or not, Flex? This stays right here and it's just tonight."

He covered her lips with his in an angry, frantic kiss before jerking away. "You want to keep this just between us? Fine. But we're far from over."

When he swept her up into his arms and mounted the steps, Jade rested her head against his chest as anticipation curled through her.

Cash wasn't done with her? Jade would have to analyze that statement later . . . much later.

Chapter Seven

Cash called himself all kinds of a fool with each step that took him closer to her bedroom. He only knew which one was hers because he'd been the one to paint it when Livie had wanted to sell the place.

Jade practically purred in his arms as her fingertips stroked along his jaw, his neck, up over his lips. The woman had had too much to drink and he was fully aware of that . . . but she still wanted him.

Had he not seen how passionate she was in Nashville, he would've denied her tonight. But the way they'd been once they came together . . . there was no way in hell they were finished with each other.

So what if she did want him to be her dirty little secret? He could handle that . . . for now.

Honestly, Cash wasn't looking for more anyway, and if their friends knew what they were doing, he and Jade would have too many questions to answer. There was nothing wrong with sneaking and taking what they wanted, so long as they were both on the same page. And from the way Jade's fingers kept raking along his jaw and feathering over his neck, he'd say that wasn't an issue.

The second Cash stepped into her room, he kicked the door shut. A light from the bathroom filtered in and slashed a glow across the bottom corner of her king-size canopy bed. This room screamed woman and romance. He didn't do romance, and that certainly wasn't what tonight was all about.

He knew sex, and he knew this woman in his arms wanted him just as much as he wanted her. Thankfully, she wasn't asking for more.

When he'd stopped by, he'd wanted her, but he'd also been realistic enough to know she might not feel the same. He followed her lead, he relinquished control for her to do as she pleased. Alcohol or not, Jade wanted him, and he wasn't about to turn her down.

Cash eased her to her feet, making sure her body brushed against his along the way. He kept his hands on her hips, pulling her to align their bodies just right, and waited for her lids to flutter open.

"Look at me," he demanded when her response was slower than his sanity could take.

Those bright green eyes landed on him and he tamped down every emotion except need, because it would be all too easy to fall into those eyes and get wrapped up in her world. Sex had to be simple and physical. Nothing else.

This was the only way he knew how to fully guard his heart.

"Tell me you're sober enough for this."

A smile spread wide across her face, and he hated how easily this woman affected him. Of course, now that he'd had her, she was under his skin, and he'd been pretty damn proud he'd restrained himself for a whole day. Now that he was here, he wasn't leaving anytime soon.

"I've got a great buzz going on," she purred, sliding her body all over him. "But I already told you, I'm good. I'm very aware of who is going to strip me out of this dress and have his wicked way with me."

Mercy. This woman would be the death of him. It was like she read his mind. Who knew for as much hell as they verbally gave each other, the bedroom was the one place they'd mesh perfectly?

"Did you honestly think I'd just text you back and not come over?" He gathered the hem of her dress and bunched it in his hands until it hit her hips. "Did you really think once we left Nashville I was done with you?"

She held her arms above her head, a silent, sexy-as-hell gesture for him to rid her of the dress. In a swift move, he whipped the material over her head and tossed it over his shoulder.

His eyes landed on her nearly naked body. The pale-gray bra and matching lacy panties were nothing less than he expected. He'd already come to realize that Jade was a lover of finer undergarments . . . and he was more than happy to help her enjoy them.

"I didn't expect Nashville," she stated, her hands going for the hem of his shirt. "I never expected to enjoy your company and get along with you outside the bedroom, let alone inside."

He helped her discard the shirt but swatted her hands away when she reached for the snap on his jeans. "Well, the first time was actually on the dining table, so . . ."

Jade trailed her fingertip from just above the snap, over his abs, and up to his chest. Then she went agonizingly slow back down. "Your sarcasm used to drive me insane."

"Is that so?" he asked, trying his hardest not to suck in his breath as she continued to torture him. How was this tipsy woman holding so much control here? "And now?"

Her eyes followed the path of her finger. "Now you drive me insane in other ways. Like when you're not touching me when I need you to."

Jade had to be drunk. She'd never say these things

otherwise. There was some truth to her words, at least the truth of her feelings, or she wouldn't be so aggressive. He wasn't about to let her regret this or forget everything. Come tomorrow, he'd be all too eager to remind her.

Cash circled her waist, lifted her, and tossed her onto the bed, which earned him a little squeal. Once she was sprawled out in the middle of her mound of pillows and thick comforter, Cash made quick work of removing the rest of his clothes. He grabbed a condom from his wallet and laid it next to her hip.

When he focused back on her face, he caught her staring. In all honesty, he didn't know if he'd ever get tired of being studied by those emerald eyes. He wanted to know what she was thinking, but from the flush on her cheeks and the heavy breaths coming out, he had a pretty good idea.

Seeing her looking like a damn princess in the middle of this frou-frou bedroom had him wondering what the hell he was doing. Perhaps he *was* the dirty little secret. Maybe he *was* pretending he would one day be good enough for someone like Jade McKenzie.

Damn it. He was a filthy mess from working on that stupid engine. He didn't know what turned Jade on, but he would bet it wasn't engine oil and sweat.

"I should probably shower before climbing in that bed with you."

Jade came up onto her elbows and quirked an arched brow. "Maybe we should get into that shower together and then come back here. You know I'm good for more than one location."

Yeah, he knew. He'd replayed their entire night over and over in his mind. It had been damn difficult to concentrate on the conversations with Jax and Tanner while working on an engine and digging into the computer programming. Jade's playfulness and passion had taken over every part of his thought process, and he had been of no use to his cousins.

Showering with Jade had images flooding his mind. "I don't think you can stand on your own, let alone when you're all wet."

As if to prove him wrong, she slowly rose to her feet, took the condom between her fingers, and held her arms out to the sides. "I'm perfectly fine, Flex. Besides, I think you can find ways to hold me up."

Cash didn't need any more invitation than that. He lifted her up in a fireman's carry and stalked to the bathroom.

"I can walk, you know."

"I'm working on those ways to hold you up."

She smacked his ass, and he laughed as he reached into her glassed-in shower and turned on the water. Then he stepped in and eased her back to her feet.

"I'm still wearing clothes," she squealed as the water pelted them.

And she looked every bit the fantasy he'd envisioned with her bra and panty set soaked to her creamy skin. Cash grabbed the condom from Jade's hand and tore it open, then covered himself.

"Better get you out of those wet things," he growled as he backed her into the corner. "Then I can hold you up properly."

He grabbed the material at her waist and tore the panties away. Then he reached for that closure nestled between her breasts and flicked it open. Jade shrugged out of her bra and it fell to the wet tile of the shower floor.

Cash gripped her hips and lifted her against the wall, stepping into her as she wrapped her legs around his waist.

"Getting right to the action?" she asked, her tone mocking.

"Red, we've danced around each other long enough and we both know what this is and what it isn't."

She gripped his shoulders and rocked her hips. That naughty smile and the gleam in her eye was more than he could take and he was done waiting. Nearly two days without her was long enough. There was an ache, a need in him that only Jade could fill.

Cash joined their bodies, eliciting a low moan from her. She tipped back her head and arched her body against his as he braced his hands on either side of her head. The hot spray peppering his back felt good, but nothing like being with Jade once again.

He raked his tongue up the column of her throat and nipped at her chin until she brought her lips to meet his. Cash gripped the back of her thigh with one hand while keeping the other by her head. He simply couldn't get enough, and if he thought Nashville had been amazing, it was nothing compared to now.

The whimpers that escaped Jade had his body tightening and nearly ready for release. No woman had ever been so potent and so addictive. Jade knew what she was doing, knew the power she held over him, and damn it, he was letting this happen.

Cash tore his mouth away and pressed his forehead to hers as her body quickened. Those whimpers became louder, longer, and a moment later, her body tightened and arched.

This was why he couldn't quit Jade. This right here, the passion, the abandonment of anything but her pleasure. She became a completely different person, and one he wanted to spend more time with.

Before he could get too carried away with such ridiculous notions, Cash felt that coil of anticipation a moment before he joined Jade in falling over the edge. He gritted his teeth and started to close his eyes but caught her watching him as he let the climax slam through him. Perhaps she enjoyed the show as much as he did.

Cash forced himself to keep his gaze on hers as his body started to calm. He blew out a breath he hadn't realized he'd been holding. Jade smiled and reached up to swipe above his brow.

"We didn't get very clean."

As tired as he was, as amazing as that had just been, he wasn't too far from needing another round with her.

"Then maybe we should try again," he stated, then covered her mouth with his.

Jade responded by tightening her ankles behind his back, her knees digging into his sides.

When he eased from the kiss, her lids fluttered open and those eyes locked him in place. Water droplets formed on the tips of her lashes, her red hair seemed so much darker now that it was wet and plastered down. Even with her makeup smeared, her hair a mess, and a little drunk haze to her eyes, Cash couldn't recall a time she'd looked more beautiful . . . or more his type.

Damn it, though. She wasn't his type. Just because their bodies were compatible didn't mean anything beyond that. He didn't need or want a relationship and, clearly, neither did she. Sex was great, their sex was off the charts, so why screw it up thinking of anything beyond what they had right here?

"Someone is thinking too hard," she murmured. "Maybe I should wash all this grease off you to take your mind off your troubles."

Yeah, maybe she should. Then he could focus on having a wet, naked woman at his command instead of wondering why he still hated that kernel of disappointment at the idea that she didn't want anyone to know they'd been together.

The second Jade dropped her legs and reached for the soap, Cash's thoughts vanished. Nothing and no one existed outside this shower, this moment.

Jade watched him sleep. Silly really, to be this infatuated with any man, especially Cash. They were completely different, yet there were so many ways in which they were the same.

She wasn't looking for boyfriend material, but she couldn't ignore her body. The man lit her up, did things she'd only read about in books.

The moonlight filtered in through the opening in the sheer curtains. She had just enough light to see his face, his body. Only a thin sheet draped over his waist, covering the magnificent form.

Jade propped herself up on her elbow and resisted the urge to reach for him, to trace each and every tattoo and wonder what the story was behind each one.

Her eyes traveled back up to his face, to the black eye, which now was only a pale purple and not swollen. He still had the small cut from the plane, but that was healing as well.

The tattoos held their own stories, just as those injuries did—and her name was all over them. Whose names were attached to all of that ink?

Jade glanced to the small gold antique clock on her nightstand. Nearly six in the morning and she had a hot yoga class to teach at eight, which meant she needed to leave by seven. She had no clue what the protocol was here. Having Cash spend the night in her bed hadn't exactly been on her planner, but then again, neither had drinking so much wine and having the hottest shower sex of her life.

Sitting up straighter in bed, Jade blew out a sigh and glanced over her shoulder to the man who slept as he lived . . . without a care. That dark skin with scars and tattoos was quite the contrast to her white sheets and thick white duvet. Her world had always been so pristine, so perfect and polished—the exact opposite of Cash.

Was that why she was so drawn to him? In some warped way, did she see him as a metaphorical middle finger to her mother?

Guilt and anxiety churned deep, and Jade shifted back around. She sure as hell hoped she wasn't that shallow. In all honesty, she never, ever would've guessed she'd end up naked with Cash. They never spoke in school, and when she came back to Haven, they got on each other's very last nerve.

Yet here they were, completely naked and completely spent. There was no explanation other than . . .

No, she couldn't even think of a lame excuse as to why they'd tumbled into bed together not once but twice. Was this it? Were they really done now? Could she go back to only seeing him at the airport or hanging out with their friends?

Considering they were still naked and he was within arm's reach, she couldn't answer that right now.

Jade was going to have to wake him up because he needed to start getting ready and he had to get out early. Neighbors were nosy in this town, and the last thing she needed was someone spotting Cash doing the walk of shame when they went out to get their morning paper.

Jade resisted the urge to groan. How the hell did she go about this? Just wake him up and hand him his clothes? Did she make him coffee before she kicked him out? This was precisely why she never did flings. Too messy—much more than a relationship, in her opinion.

A cell chimed from the floor. Jade glanced around, realizing that wasn't her cell and that the noise came from his jeans, still in the heap where he'd left them . . . on her side of the bed.

Jade hopped off the bed and reached for his pants. Digging out the phone, she turned back to the bed, where Cash sat straight up. The stark white sheet pooled at his waist and his hair stuck up everywhere. He rubbed his chest in that good-morning,-I-know-I'm-sexy kind of way. Could he not turn that off? The whole appeal thing that made her only want more?

Without a word, Jade thrust the phone at him and turned to get some clothes. She needed that barrier because she didn't have time to crawl back into bed with him, and they really, really needed to end this. Having him here was too risky, especially once they hit daylight hours.

He answered the call, and Jade tried to block out his throaty, morning voice. Who would be calling at this time of the day anyway? His gym opened at six, so perhaps there was a problem. None of her business really, because they weren't actually involved on a personal level.

"He did what?"

Jade threw on a T-shirt and turned at Cash's frantic tone. He was on his feet now and heading for his clothes. He paid her no mind, but there was no way she could look away. She'd seen Cash naked, of course, but not just to stand back and admire. Perhaps that made her a bit of a creeper, but damn, that man's body demanded that someone look. He was absolutely magnificent.

With the phone tucked between his shoulder and ear, he hopped into his jeans. "I'll be right there . . . No, I'll be there. Tell him I'm on my way."

Muttering a string of curses that would've shocked her mother right to her bleached roots, Cash ended the call and shoved the cell into his pocket. Jade wasn't sure what to do, but this at least answered her question of how to get him out of here.

"I have to go." He searched for his shirt and found it laying over the trunk at the end of her bed.

"What's wrong?" She cringed as soon as the question came out. It really was none of her business.

He hesitated, then shot her a quick glance before turning to search for his shoes. "Nothing."

Okay, then.

"Listen, last night I had some wine and—"

Cash let out a bark of laughter as he tied his running shoes. "Seriously? You're trying to make excuses for what happened? What are you going to do the next time we hook up?"

"Next time?" Jade crossed her arms, wishing she'd at least put on underwear to have this conversation. "What do you mean, next time? We 'hooked up,' as you so eloquently put this, and now we're done."

Cash shrugged into his shirt and stalked across the room in two long strides. "Done? Because you don't want anyone to know, or because you're already tired of me? Because I'm pretty sure that was you moaning into my ear only a few hours ago."

Jade's body heated all over again. They hadn't actually slept much, but that didn't mean continuing was a good idea. How could she keep lying to her friends? She'd never been sneaky or devious a day in her life.

"I just don't think that—"

Cash snaked an arm around her waist and pulled her against his chest as he covered her mouth. Before she could catch her balance or grab his shoulders, he released her.

"As much as I'd love to stay and chat, I have to go."
He turned toward the door, but before he hit the hall, he
glanced over his shoulder. "And Jade . . . We are going to
keep this up. If you want to be secretive about it, fine, but
I'm still not done with you."

He left her standing there confused, frustrated, and
completely aroused at his parting promise . . . or threat,
depending on how she wanted to look at it.

Jade glanced at the clock and realized she had just
enough time to get dressed and make her favorite green
smoothie full of antioxidants before she had to leave to
teach her hot yoga class.

When she spun around, her eyes locked onto her
messed-up bed. The sheets were all askew, the comforter
half-hung off one side of the mattress. Her delicate throw
pillows were all over the floor and Cash's pillow still held
the indention from his head.

She never left her bed a total disaster. Even when she'd
taken a lover in the past, there hadn't been this reckless
abandonment and thrilling rush of arousal.

As if her sore body wasn't reminder enough of her
night, now Jade had a clear visual. She also had her torn
panties and bra still on her shower floor, just in case she'd
forgotten about what had transpired in there.

She had no idea what to think about sneaking around
with Cash. Could they actually pull it off? At what point
did they call it quits?

Questions laced with concern swirled through her
mind. If she agreed to this ongoing affair—and that was a
big if—there would be rules. There was no way in hell she'd
be sharing him with anyone else. No dates whatsoever,
and she knew Cash liked to date. She'd extend the same
courtesy if he was set on seeing her again.

Jade raked a hand through her hair, wincing when she

hit a massive nest of tangles. A hot mess was the downfall of tumbling into bed with wet hair, but hair maintenance had been the last thing on her mind last night.

Was she seriously considering a secret fling with the one man who drove her out of her ever-loving mind? What had gotten into her lately? In the span of a few days, she'd gone from loathing the man to craving his touch and actually aching for him.

As she went to gather her workout clothes, Jade couldn't help but wonder how many other women had gone down the fling path with Cash. The thought was absurd and immature because they were both adults and neither came into this as innocents. Still, was any part about their intimacy special, or did he legit just want her body until he decided they were done?

The more she thought about the idea, the angrier she became. First of all, he'd brushed aside her concern over his call, then he'd dropped that bomb just before waltzing out the door, like he had all the say-so here.

Jade jerked on her sports bra and yoga pants. If he wanted to do this fling in private, that was fine by her, but they would be playing by her rules—starting right now.

Chapter Eight

"You're not leaving, Dad."

Part of Cash wanted to let his father do just that. To just walk out of this rehab facility and wash his hands of the mess he'd put them in. But at the end of the day, his father was a broken man, and Cash couldn't just ignore his cries for help.

"I hate this damn place," Al Miller grumbled as he stared out the window of his room at New Hope Rehab Center. "I'm clean. There's no reason I can't leave."

Clean. How many times had his father proclaimed sobriety over the past . . . hell, too many years? He'd been clean this time for a month. But this was the fifth facility Cash had put his father in, and he wanted more than a month of sobriety before he called his dad "clean."

"You know exactly why you can't leave," Cash retorted. He crossed his arms and stared at the back of his dad's head. "You're staying here because you not only owe me, you owe yourself. You owe Mom."

His father spun around and pointed his finger like Cash was still five. "Don't you dare bring your mother in to this."

"Considering your self-destruction started after her death, I'd say she's part of everything in our lives."

Cash blew out a sigh and wished like hell he had a

sibling to help with this. Tanner and Jax were cousins, but
Cash wouldn't dare ask them to assist. They'd offered
many times over the years, but unless Al was passed out
cold and Cash needed help getting him from some bar or,
one time, a park bench, Cash tried not to call on them.
This was embarrassing enough without having other
witnesses.

"You promised you would stay here until I decided
you could leave," Cash went on. "Maybe you'll recall the
day you busted up my house in a fit of rage? Well, this is
your penance."

More like Cash had been scared shitless at the new
level of hell his father had slithered in to. There was no
more rehab where Al called the shots. This time Cash was
in charge, and he would be damned if he lost his father. He
needed that man back and would do anything to redis-
cover him.

"I said I'd pay for the damage," his father muttered as
he moved toward his rocking chair in the corner. "You
don't have to keep bringing it up."

"I rarely mention that day." Cash crossed to stand in
front of his dad. "But you need the reminder of why you're
not in charge anymore. Besides, what are you going to pay
me with? You haven't held a job in years, and you blew
through any savings you had a long time ago. I've already
fixed the door and the hole in the wall."

His father came back to his feet, putting them nearly
toe-to-toe now. Al Miller was a large, robust man. He'd put
up a good fight if he wanted to, and from the look on his
face, he was ready to throw down.

Cash fisted his hands at his sides and held his ground,
his eyes never wavering from his dad. He'd never laid a
hand on his dad, not even when he'd been pissed at all
the destruction he'd caused. This was still his father, and

respect had to count for something . . . perhaps his dad would see that one day.

"Why do you have to act like you're better than me?" his dad growled. "You think because you have your own business and your house and come and go as you please that you're somehow above me."

His heart cracked just a bit more, as it did every time he visited his dad. "I've never thought that," Cash defended, but purposely softened his tone. "If I did, I wouldn't waste my time or money on you. I want to see you better. But me wanting it isn't enough. You have to want a different life."

"I do," he all but yelled. "This is damn hard. It's easy for people like you to tell me to get better. Every day is a struggle. I want that next drink, that bottle of pills. That's the only thing that helps."

Cash took a step back and shoved his hands in his pockets. "Helps what?"

Al raked a hand over the back of his neck and sank back down into his chair. "Numb the pain," he muttered.

The pain of losing his wife. Cash knew his dad still hurt, but that was no reason to slowly kill yourself. Cash didn't know what he'd do if he lost his father, too.

Cash squatted down in front of his dad and placed his hands on his knees. "Mom wouldn't want you to do this to yourself. She wouldn't want you to grieve this way. You know as well as I do that she'd kick your ass if she could right now."

At least that got a half smile from his father.

"Forget the fact that I need my father back," Cash went on, silently cursing the clogged emotions in his throat. He had to be strong enough for both of them. "Do this for her memory. Do this because you're a better man than this. I know the real Al Miller is in there. That fighter I looked up to as a kid is still inside you."

His dad closed his eyes and shook his head. "I'm afraid he's gone, son. I don't even know who we'll find."

Cash refused to give up. No matter how easy that may seem or how difficult this road to recovery was, and it had been hell, Cash wasn't backing down. That wasn't how he was raised and that wasn't what had been instilled in him in the United States Air Force.

"I know we'll find Allen Miller," Cash stated with affirmation. "That's my dad, and I'll die before I see you give up."

His father looked up at him, weariness filling his eyes, dark circles heavy beneath. "Go on, Cash. I'm tired. I won't try to check myself out again."

Promises hadn't meant much over the past several years. Intentions were one thing, and his father was full of them, but intentions meant absolutely nothing.

"Go on," he repeated.

Cash rose to his feet and stared down at the top of his father's head. The man was only fifty-two years old, but he looked at least ten years older. The thinning hair, the extra wrinkles, the darkness that stared back at Cash, only reiterated the fact that his father had spiraled so far away from the man he used to be. Yet Cash held out hope, and no matter how small that thread was, he refused to ever let go.

"I'll call later to check on you."

His father merely nodded without saying a word. Cash hesitated but finally walked out and closed the door behind him. He stopped to speak to the charge nurse and then to the counselor before heading to his truck. Apparently, his father was making progress, but he also still lashed out.

Cash knew his father had run the gamut of emotions since the passing of his mother. Pain, rage, despair. Until

Al Miller got to the point where he wanted to wake up each day and make something of his life, Cash would continue to pay for a room here.

He made the hour drive back to Haven, and by the time he pulled into the gym, he was more than ready to lift weights, hit a punching bag, and get a good sweat going. The frustrations mounted, and he needed to work off some steam.

As if waking up to a call from his father's counselor wasn't bad enough, he kept replaying the past twelve hours with Jade. She wanted him, that was obvious, but she didn't *want* to want him. Cash had done flings before; he'd done one-night stands, but Jade . . . well, he wasn't sure what the hell category to slot her in. She was more than any of that, but he couldn't let her be.

She'd tried to give him the brush off and blame her actions on alcohol. Honestly, he'd expected better from her than to fall back on that lame excuse. There was no way he was going to let her shove their encounters aside like they meant nothing.

He hadn't been lying when he told her he wasn't done, but he would respect her wishes to keep things between them. At least they could agree on that.

Cash parked in the back of his gym and grabbed his duffel bag from the back seat of his crew cab. As soon as he pulled on the gym door, the sound assaulted him. The heart-thumping music was always upbeat and modern, to keep the younger crowd happy and pushing their workouts. Most people used their own music, but Cash couldn't stand the thought of a quiet gym.

He made his way to his office, not passing any employees as he went. Once inside, he locked the door and changed his clothes. The jeans and tee he'd been wearing yesterday needed to go. He pulled out a fresh T-shirt and shorts, along with boxer briefs and socks.

As soon as he changed, Cash took a seat behind his desk. The cell inside the pocket of his shorts vibrated. Cash didn't groan, but if this was New Hope again, he may just weep . . . or break something.

Cash pulled out his phone and took a deep breath. Interesting. He hadn't expected this.

"Hello?" he answered.

"I know you had somewhere to be, but you left rather abruptly after delivering such a bold statement."

He sat on the edge of his desk and crossed his arms. "Now, Red. I didn't think you'd be the type to get clingy."

"I'm hardly clingy."

He couldn't help but smile at the edginess in her voice. "No? Well, I must've misunderstood. Listen, I have a client due here anytime. We'll have to talk later."

"Don't you dare hang up—"

"See ya, Red."

He disconnected the call just as she let out a string of curses. Oh, she was such a good time. The woman just opened the door of opportunity to annoy her and he gladly stepped right through. She made it too easy to get under her skin. Besides, he wanted her to be just as off-balance as he was over this . . . whatever they had going on.

There was no appropriate label to put on what he and Jade were doing. The word "fling" seemed too juvenile, and they sure as hell weren't dating. No, she wouldn't be seen with him in public.

Even though he saw her side of that argument, he still wondered if she'd ever think they were on the same level. Joining her at her family's wedding was quite the eye-opener. They weren't just from money, they were most definitely in a whole other league.

Likely her family didn't do frozen pizzas or drink their beer from a can. The whole which-fork-for-which-meal was quickly shown to him by Jade during the reception dinner, but he didn't remember a damn thing. Wasn't a fork just a fork?

Cash pocketed his cell and pushed aside all the reasons they were different. Why was he even analyzing? It wasn't like he'd have to know her world, and she would never know his. Just the thought of her seeing how broken his personal life was had his gut tightening.

Relationships were out of the question for so many reasons. A shrink would get lost in all the broken paths inside his head. His mother, his father, his cheating ex-wife . . .

Cash was a walking country song, and even he didn't want to look too far into all the reasons he pushed people aside.

For now, though, he had clients to train, and with the mood he was in, he'd be working right alongside them. He needed the outlet.

An image of Jade in the shower with her hair slicked back and water droplets rolling down her skin flashed through his mind. That was definitely an outlet he could use, too, but that would have to wait.

Even though he left her frustrated and likely angry when he hung up, he'd also left her curious and wanting more. He may not know her well on a personal level, but he was more than aware of her personality. His Jade would come to him. There was no doubt about that.

Wait. *His Jade*?

No. She wasn't his. Jade would never be his, at least not permanently. Which was why he was going to enjoy her . . . for as long as it lasted.

* * *

After eight clients and handling a shipment of the new workout gear with his gym logo he was going to start selling, Cash was more than ready to call it a night.

He stared at the boxes lining the wall behind his desk in his office. He mentally went over the shelving and space he'd need to put out the new products tomorrow. He'd splashed the gym's social media pages with hints of what was to come. With his gym open for five years now, he wanted to do something to mark the milestone and offer his members affordable options.

"There you are."

A burst of red caught his eye, as did the angry tone. Cash pulled out his cockiest smile and turned to fully face Jade.

"Right here where I usually am." He crossed his arms and leaned back against the edge of his desk. "You look like you've already gotten your workout in."

And it took everything in him not to pull her to him and rip off her sweaty clothes. This was the Jade he wanted to see more of, not the one whose clothes were perfect or the made-up one at the wedding that he'd barely recognized. The new Jade he'd seen over the last few months, the one who started living for herself, had really become more attractive and intriguing than he should admit . . . even to himself.

"I've taught three classes today, two of those hot yoga." She held out her hands. "I'm gross, so just stay where you are."

"You're implying I'd ravage you here in my office?"

With a quirk of a brow, she mimicked his move and crossed her arms. "I won't put anything past you."

"Yet you came here," he reminded her. "So, what can I do for you?"

"We need to lay down some rules."

Well, that loaded statement sucked the enjoyment right out of everything.

"Rules?" he repeated, hoping she'd change her mind.

"If we're going to do this . . . thing." She waved her hand back and forth between them. "I think it's best to lay out rules so there are no issues when it's over."

Every single thing about her speech irritated the hell out of him. Cash rested his palms on the edge of his desk and forced himself to remain seated.

"First of all, I don't do rules," he informed her. "That's pretty much a relationship. Second, if you're already looking for this to be over, then end it now."

Jade remained still, staring and likely weighing her next attempt at controlling him. He wasn't backing down. He wasn't going to beg, no matter how good the sex was. There was no denying the fact that he wanted her, but he didn't play games or abide by anyone else's demands. Which is one of the reasons he worked for himself.

She turned and closed the door before facing him again. "Listen," she started, "I just want to know where I stand with you. If we're going to continue to sneak around, I want to make sure you're not seeing anyone else."

His lips twitched. "So, you want exclusivity to my body? As much as that sounds like a relationship, I can agree to that. Same goes for you."

Jade rolled her eyes. "Please. Nothing to worry about there."

"A sexy woman in a town where most people are married or just passing through, I'd say I have plenty to worry about," he corrected. "But we'll agree that as long as we're entertaining each other, nobody else is in the picture."

Jade nodded in agreement, but she said nothing else, nor did she move. Cash wondered why she hadn't just called or texted, but then his ego stepped in and assumed Jade wanted to see him.

"Pretty risky coming here," he added. "Unless you're here to discuss teaching those classes for me."

"No." She pulled in a deep breath, drawing his attention to the low scoop of her tank and the swell of her breasts over her sports bra. "Eyes up, Flex."

He obeyed but laughed. "Listen, I'm staying on my side of the room. At least let me have a little something."

"Focus."

He purposely let his eyes dip, linger. "Oh, I am."

Jade's laugh slid over him and had him feeling things he couldn't identify. How did she do that? Hadn't he told himself she wouldn't have control here?

"Would you rather teach thirty minutes away or five from where you live?" he asked. "Because I don't see why you won't do your classes here."

"You're stealing my game and throwing it back in my face?" She shook her head and started moving about his office. "You already know why. Originally, I wasn't working here because I was afraid we'd kill each other. Now, it's not smart because of, well, the exact opposite reason. Things will get messy when we decide we've had enough of each other and I don't want any awkwardness in my workplace. I've already been through that."

Cash refused to remain seated any longer. He caged her in with her back against the stack of boxes. Her eyes widened, but he didn't touch her. No, he kept a few inches between their bodies as he rested his hands on either side of her face.

"You keep bringing up when we're done with each other," he growled. "I haven't even begun to scratch the surface of what all I want to do with you."

Jade sucked in a breath and her chest brushed lightly

against his, but he remained still. "I just don't want there to be any confusion," she stated, tipping that defiant chin up a notch.

Without a stitch of makeup and her hair pulled back in some messy thing on top of her head, Jade remained poised and so damn sexy. Those emerald eyes continued to call him in deeper, which was absurd. He was never a man to go for the eyes first.

"Red, I'm not confused at all." He leaned forward just enough to dip his head and pull in a breath of her. "I know exactly where I stand and what I want."

Cash took a step in until he lined his body up with hers and she shivered against him. Her hands remained at her sides, but he knew that restraint was costing her.

"I didn't come here for this," she murmured.

He skimmed his lips along the side of her neck. "Didn't you?"

A knock sounded on his door and Cash muttered a curse, then stepped back . . . which was a good thing because Jax strolled right in.

Cash didn't have to look behind him to figure out that Jade likely had cringed and her face was completely flushed. But they hadn't been caught touching, which was a miracle because he'd been about a second from ripping those sweaty clothes off her and clearing off his desk.

"Hey, Jade," Jax said with a nod, then looked back to Cash. "Am I interrupting something?"

"Just trying to get her to work for me." Cash didn't hesitate, and opted for at least some of the truth. "She's still refusing."

"I have my reasons," Jade stated from behind him. "I'm done here, so I'll let you two talk."

Cash wanted to reach for her as she slid by him. He wanted to tell her to stay, that he'd kick Jax out, but that wouldn't fall in line with their plan of keeping this affair a secret.

Considering they shared a close unit of friends, this may prove to be more difficult than they thought. At least he was already having a difficult time because right now, he preferred Jade's company over his cousins'.

"Wait," Jax told Jade before she could leave. "It's actually good that both of you are here."

"What's up?" Cash asked.

Jax closed the door and plopped down on a short stack of shipping boxes. "The press release Jade created is supposed to run tomorrow in the local paper."

Cash wasn't aware she'd already written one up. They'd been a little too busy to discuss things they should actually be talking about.

"I emailed it to Livie between classes earlier," Jade stated. "Is something wrong with it?"

Jax shook his head. "Not at all. But I think this is a prime opportunity for us to really boost the marketing. We can use this time to gloss over the mishap and push for the exciting venture that will be the future of the airport."

"And how do you plan on doing that?" Cash asked.

From the corner of his eye, he could see Jade. Not once had she looked at him since Jax came into the room. No doubt she was mortified they'd almost gotten caught. Also no doubt he'd hear about it later — to which he'd remind her that she'd come to see him.

"I haven't talked to Livie yet, but I wanted to see what you all thought about doing a mock open house."

Confused, Cash shook his head. "What?"

"An open house," Jade reiterated louder, as if he hadn't heard. "A mock style would show residents exactly what the airport will look like, what we'll offer, what clients and customers can expect. Right, Jax?"

He nodded and rested his hands on his thighs. "I ran into Sophie Monroe, and she said she'd help and we could even use her real estate office to host the event."

Sophie Monroe had married Zach Monroe, one of the infamous bad boys of Haven. The Monroe brothers had re-vamped an old antebellum house and turned it into a women's-only resort and spa to honor their sister's memory. The guys had certainly had their fair share of issues to overcome, but they'd ultimately come together and were making a name for not only themselves, but also Haven.

Sophie was the top local real estate agent and was more than eager to see the town thrive.

"I think it's a great idea," Jade stated. "But you know you have to run this by the boss first."

Jax laughed. "I just let her think she's the boss."

Considering Livie's father was the original owner, most people would believe Livie to be the one with the final say. But Jax had been as close as a son to the man, and now that Jax and Livie were married, they made all the decisions together. Well, they made the decisions and then the financial backing team of Tanner, Melanie, Jade, and Cash threw in their opinions.

"I say we move on this," Jade proclaimed.

Cash focused his attention on her as she started speaking with her hands, and he watched as she shifted flawlessly from yoga instructor, to temptress, to business-woman within the next ten minutes right before his eyes.

She went on about contacts she had who could create a 3-D model of the finished product, then something about a kids' workshop to learn about aviation and a sample menu from the diner they planned to put in the renovated main building.

As each idea rolled off her tongue, Cash's admiration for her shot up. She was a beautiful, sexy woman; any man with breath in his lungs would agree. But she was brilliant. Jade's mind worked overtime, and Cash shot a glance to Jax, who also sat in complete amazement. There wasn't a doubt in Cash's mind that she'd been at the top of her game back in Atlanta. The firm that hadn't believed her regarding the sexual abuse wasn't worthy of her. He couldn't even imagine the paycheck she'd left behind, let alone the life she'd built. But he knew her well enough to know her integrity and reputation were much more important than any salary.

But Jade absolutely flourished here in Haven.

Flourish? Had he seriously just thought that word?

Yes. When it came to Jade McKenzie and the way she took charge with planning, she flourished. This was her element and he was rather impressed.

"I'll take all of that back to Livie," Jax said once Jade finished. "I'm sure she'll be all for it. Maybe you two can talk tomorrow and bring Melanie up to speed, get her ideas as well. I'll get back with Sophie on a time and day."

"Let me know," Jade replied. "I'll get my guy on that model of the airport ASAP, and I'll personally drive to pick it up."

"Perfect." Jax came to his feet and blew out a sigh. "Well, I'll be heading home. I just stopped when I saw Cash's truck still here, so I figured I'd discuss this face-to-face instead of text."

"I need to get going as well." Jade cast him a glance but quickly looked away. "Good night, guys."

"'Night, Red."

She walked out, and Cash grabbed his keys off the desk, ready to go home. Though the idea of leaving didn't hold much appeal now. He'd been much happier several minutes ago, when Jade had been panting against him and the evening held more promise.

"Tell me you're not screwing with her."

Cash jerked his attention to Jax, who stood in front of the door, arms folded and a narrowed stare shooting across the room.

"Screwing in which way? Figuratively or literally?"

Jax took a step farther into the office. "Don't. Livie will kill you if anything is going on between you and Jade. Damn it, man. Can't you just leave one woman alone?"

"Nothing is going on between Jade and me."

He'd never lied to his cousin before, but he had to respect the deal he'd made with Jade. He should probably stop to analyze the fact that he'd just put his temporary relationship with Jade over that with Jax, but those thoughts would probably scare the hell out of him, so he pushed them aside.

"Didn't look like that when I came in."

Cash shrugged. "Not sure what you thought you saw, but we'd been discussing her working here instead of a half hour away."

C'mon. Couldn't Jax just go back to his wife and daughter? Of all the times he didn't want to talk about a woman, this one ranked at the top.

"I know you, Cash." Jax continued to stare, as if trying to analyze Cash's every movement, every word, to uncover the truth. "Jade is sticking around Haven, at least for a while, and she's Livie's best friend. If the two of you start fooling around, things will be awkward for everyone when it ends."

Why the hell was everyone hung up on when this would end?

More importantly, why did those verbal concerns piss him off? He was the one who didn't want long term or anything resembling a relationship. Yet he didn't even want to consider giving Jade up.

Cash had to put his cousin's fears at ease. "I swear, man. Jade and I aren't dating or looking at messing with the harmony of the group. Is that what you wanted to hear? Don't bring this up again or the others will start wondering. There's no need to have Jade all angry, thinking I told you something."

Jax stared for another minute before nodding in agreement. "Fine. I believe you."

The weight of guilt settled heavily on his chest.

"You heading home, or do you want to head over to Taps?" Jax asked.

"I think I'm heading home. It's been a long day."

Jax narrowed his brows. "Everything all right?"

"Just the same old shit with my dad, then several things going on here. Nothing a cold beer and a good night's rest won't cure, but I plan on having my beer in the comfort of my recliner."

Jax started out of the office and Cash followed. He clicked off the light, shut the door, and locked it behind him. The music from the front of the gym continued a steady beat but still couldn't drown out the clanging of the metal weights.

"You know Tanner and I are always here if you need us." Jax fell into step with Cash as they stepped out the back door. "There's no need for you to always handle things on your own."

"Maybe not, but I'm more comfortable that way."

"And stubborn."

Cash shrugged. "Maybe."

The parking lot was bright with the overhead alley lights. Jax's old pickup truck was parked right next to Cash's black truck.

"I mean it," his cousin added. "Nobody would think

less of you if you asked for help. Tanner and I expect you to ask."

Cash turned when he got to his truck and slid his thumb over his key fob. "I've asked for help. Remember the plane in the field? There was no way in hell I would have been able to fix that on my own."

Jax rolled his eyes and pulled his keys from his pocket. "You know what I mean."

Yeah, he did, and that was what made this so much more difficult. Cash didn't want anyone else to have to clean up the mess in his life—including his father. *Especially* his father.

Cash may not have to do things alone, but he preferred them that way. Which was just another reason why he and Jade could never be more than a secret fling.

Chapter Nine

Jade circled the block for a third time and called herself all sorts of a fool. It wasn't her fault that her body had nearly overheated when Cash pressed her up against those boxes in his office. Apparently, she had zero control over her traitorous hormones and clearly hadn't gotten him out of her system yet.

Why couldn't she be attracted to an engineer or accountant or someone from another town? Someone who didn't push her buttons and enjoy the constant verbal sparring? Why did she have to be pulled toward the one man who irritated her, who mocked her fling rules, who was careless and had no qualms about turning her on and then ignoring her?

Jade slowed her car a block away from the white, one-story bungalow. Even his house was attractive. Did he do that landscaping himself? Because she was rather impressed with the mixture of colors and variations of greens in the shrubbery.

And she was totally stalling as she squinted and tried to see his house better from this distance.

Playing with fire. She was absolutely, 100 percent playing with fire. Common sense had long since vanished because Jade shut off her engine and grabbed her purse before she could talk herself out of this.

Haven was such a small town, she purposely pulled in front of a darkened home on this street and away from the lamplight. With her head down and hoisting her purse on her shoulder, Jade marched toward Cash's house like she had every single right to be there.

His porch light was on, so hopefully she wouldn't wake him. Perhaps she should've called or texted and given him a heads-up on her visit.

No, had she done that, she would've worried about his reply.

Considering he'd caught her off guard so many times, she figured it was time for a little payback. This fling, or whatever it was, should be fun and adventurous, spontaneous even. Had she ever had any real adventure in her life? The plane incident didn't count, considering that was terrifying.

She didn't stop at the bottom of the steps leading up to the covered porch. Jade marched right up and rang his doorbell like she hadn't a care in the world. Her heart beat so fast, so heavy in her chest, she wished he'd just answer quickly to get this anticipation over with.

Time seemed to be taking its good, old, sweet time, but likely she waited less than a minute before she heard the click of the dead bolt. In the next instant, the old oak door swung open to reveal a half-dressed Cash. He rested one muscular forearm on the doorframe and offered her a half grin.

"I'd say I'm surprised, but I'm not."

Jade narrowed her stare. "I can leave."

Without a word, Cash reached for her and pulled her inside. In the next breath, he had the door closed and her pinned between it and his firm, bare chest. This more than made up for his mocking greeting.

"I didn't see your car," he murmured as he barely brushed his lips back and forth along that sensitive area below her ear.

Her eyes nearly rolled back in her head. "I-I parked down the street."

"Is that right?" He nibbled at her earlobe. "Worried what someone might think if they see you here?"

"Why are you talking?"

More importantly, *how* was he talking? Her body had instantly picked back up where they'd left off in his office. Yet he seemed completely in control and in no hurry, which seriously grated on her nerves.

Cash eased back and stared down at her with that dark gaze that never failed to make her stomach clench. Only his chest touched hers as he raised one black brow.

"You didn't come to chat?" he asked. "Then why are you here, Red?"

The man seriously embodied frustration and sex appeal—a dangerous combination. He knew exactly why she'd stopped by and parked down the street.

Jade placed her palms on his chest, his taut muscles clenched beneath her touch. She pushed until he took the silent hint and stepped back.

She'd gone home and showered after leaving Cash's gym, but she'd only thrown on a pair of jeans and a sleeve-less, button-up shirt with a pair of sandals. It was nearly eleven o'clock now and she should be home in pajamas, making notes about the potential open house.

Yet she'd opted to put on normal clothes and pull her hair up into a topknot because she didn't want to take the time to dry it.

Silence settled heavily between them, but Jade kept her

eyes locked onto his as she reached for the top button of her shirt. With each one she released, she took in his clenched jaw, tight lips, flared nostrils.

"You're showing admirable restraint." She laughed when he remained quiet. "You're dying to rip this shirt and send the buttons flying, aren't you?"

"You've got about a second to finish before I take over."

As tempting as that was, she liked knowing she had some power over him. She thoroughly enjoyed watching him hang on by an invisible thread.

She shrugged from the shirt and let it fall behind her onto the floor. When she went for her pants, Cash swatted her hands away.

"I'll finish." He jerked at the button and slid the zipper down. "I don't know why you wore so many clothes when you knew you were coming here."

She shivered when his rough knuckles grazed her stomach. "Because I didn't want your neighbors seeing me naked."

"Next time just wear a coat. And heels."

Jade laughed when he hooked his thumbs in her panties and pulled everything down her legs. "I assume that's one of your fantasies?"

He dropped to his knees and lifted one foot. Cash slid off one sandal and tossed it over his shoulder before lifting the other foot and doing the same. Then he finished ridding her of her clothes.

"My fantasies?" he asked, remaining on his knees and looking up at her. "With you, Red, I have endless fantasies."

Another rush of arousal hit her at his low, throaty declaration. Never in her life would she have imagined this moment. Cash in complete submission before her, her plastered against the door, discussing fantasies.

"Cash."

The image they made seemed too intimate, too much.

"I only came here for—"

His lips quirked. "I know why you came here. I left you aching in my office when Jax interrupted. Would you have let me take you there? On my desk or against the door?"

The way her body throbbed right now, she'd agree to anything if he'd speed things along.

"Aren't you the one who's always in a hurry?" She was nearly to the point of begging.

Slowly, he raked his fingertips over the outside of her calves, behind her knees, circling around to glide on up her thighs. There was no way to control the trembling because she was too busy worrying if her legs would hold her up.

"Maybe I've been waiting on you to catch up."

When he removed his touch and came to his feet, she seriously about whimpered. "Catch up?" she muttered.

"I ache when you're not with me, so I think it's only fair you're just as hot."

She shook her head and tried not to explode. "I didn't come here to be analyzed or for you to play some ridiculous games."

Cash curved his hands over her hips and smiled. "I assure you, this is no game. But I do have something I want to show you."

"Your show better be a fast strip out of those running shorts," she warned.

Cash let out a bark of laughter before he bent over and lifted her over his shoulder. Once again, she was facing his back and upside down.

"Must you carry me like this?" she demanded. "I can walk."

"Your knees were a bit wobbly a second ago, so I thought I should help out."

"You can help out in other ways," she mumbled as she smacked his ass. "Where are we going? If you're trying to give me a tour of your house, you're doing a terrible job."

"We're going outside."

"What?" she shrieked, smacking at him now. "Put me down. I will not go outside completely naked for the entire neighborhood to see."

"Red, I promise I'm not about to share you with anyone, least of all the neighbors."

He stepped out the back door and eased her down onto her feet. Before she could lay into him about being completely exposed, not to mention still aroused, she gasped as she took in the sight.

"Oh my word," she whispered as her eyes tried to see all the beauty at once. "Cash, this is amazing."

The high wooden fence for privacy surrounded a deck of multiple layers, but in the center was a sunken hot tub. Steam rolled off it and looked so inviting. There were small, white pebbles highlighting the path from the porch to the deck. She'd admire the landscaping and such later, maybe in the daylight. Right now, she wanted in that hot tub and she wanted Cash to join her.

Without waiting for further invitation, Jade crossed the narrow space to the steps of the deck. She dipped a toe into the water, and tingles spread all over her.

Throwing a glance over her shoulder, Jade smiled and slowly eased down and let the warmth envelope her. "Care to join me?"

"One second."

He dashed back into the house, and Jade didn't know

what the holdup was now. She sank down onto one of the smooth seats beneath the water. After eyeing the key pad, she clicked the button for jets and groaned as the pulses hit her back. If she lived here, she'd never get out of this hot tub.

She closed her eyes and tipped her head back. Nothing relaxed her like a hot tub. She hadn't been in one for so long. Maybe she'd have to start making it a point to visit Cash more often.

The water splashed and waves rippled higher around her chest. She opened her eyes just in time to see Cash's very fine form disappear beneath the bubbles from the jets.

"What did you do?" she asked.

He smacked a foil packet on the edge of the hot tub and Jade pushed up out of her seat. Using her hands to guide her beneath the water, she ran into his thick thighs. The coarse hair on his legs tickled her palms, but she continued to ease up his body.

"You don't seem so grouchy now," he stated as he eased back against his seat. "I suppose we could've had a quickie in the entryway, but I figured someone like you would prefer this."

Someone like her. There was always that reminder that they were opposites. Well, he was the one always reminding her. Jade never felt that way, but he wouldn't believe her, and now wasn't the time to get into that argument.

Besides, they were having sex. They weren't looking to make lifelong commitments here. Their personal opinions really didn't matter . . . it was all physical.

"Would you rather have had me in your office or here in your hot tub?" She lifted her leg to straddle his lap.

"You won't let me answer 'both,' I'd definitely say here."

Jade smiled and looped her arms around his neck.

"Smart man. I'm a sucker for a hot tub. In fact, I'm already making plans to come back tomorrow night."

"Is that right?"

"Yes." She brought her chest even with his mouth, then leaned over to get the condom. "You might have to stand to get this on, you know."

"Or we could go without." He covered her breasts with both hands. "Your call, but I've never been without, and I get routine physicals."

Without protection? Wasn't that how Melanie got pregnant? Well, obviously that was exactly how that worked, but Jade was on birth control and she was clean, too.

"I'm protected," she told him. "Are you sure?"

He gripped her hips and eased her down until they were joined. Jade cried out, but Cash cupped the back of her head and pulled her lips to his. The privacy fence was only good for the view and she was making too much noise.

But how was she supposed to process how amazing, how perfect this felt? She'd never been without protection with a man before. This new level of euphoria warranted a scream.

The warm water covered them to their shoulders, Cash's arms wrapped around her, and there was a rush of pleasure like she'd never known. Why was every experience with Cash more than she'd bargained for? The man was a constant surprise in the most delicious, glorious way.

His hands slid beneath the water and then his fingertips were digging into her hips, holding her down while he shifted. The sensation had her body gearing up for release.

Jade tore her mouth from his and braced her hands on his shoulders. When she caught him staring, she closed her eyes. There was no way she could let this become too intimate. Exchanging facial emotions was almost like speaking a whole different language, and that whole gazing into each other's eyes couldn't enter in here.

Pleasure ripped through her and Cash's body went rigid beneath hers. Her fingertips dug into him as she stifled her cry. Water sloshed all around and over the edge of the hot tub.

Cash gripped her backside, then let his hands roam up her back until he cupped her neck with one, strong hold. He eased her down into the crook of his neck as she attempted to calm herself and come back to reality.

His heart beat heavy against her chest; his breathing rushed out in fast pants. Jade wasn't sure what to say or do at this point. As much as she wanted to keep the intimacy out of their sex lives, going without a condom was pretty intimate.

She didn't regret the decision, though. She trusted Cash, and perhaps the events that just had unfolded were a testament to just how deep she'd gotten. Getting so involved was more than a fling—she just didn't know if there was a proper term.

"I'd say that was better than my office desk."

The rumble of his voice vibrated through her. Jade smiled and lifted her head to see his face.

"A bit better," she agreed, then remembered the entire office incident. "Did Jax say anything after I left?"

Cash's eyes darted away for the briefest of seconds before coming back to her. Dread replaced the postcoital euphoria. She didn't think he'd betray her trust, but she'd put her stock in others before only to be betrayed.

Cash wasn't like that. Yet his silence was quite unnerving.

"What happened?" she demanded. "Did you tell him about us?"

Jade eased off his lap and sank down onto a seat on the other side of the hot tub. She knew she should've hung around and made sure there was no question as to why she was there. Cash had tried to blow it off when Jax came in, but Jade figured the guy talk didn't fully start until she was out of earshot.

Cash remained silent, and Jade wanted to reach over and shake him. Why did they only get along when they were having sex?

"Are you going to answer me?" she asked.

Cash stood up and stepped out of the hot tub. Water sluiced down his naked form, but she couldn't even take the time to appreciate the view. He stalked over to a storage bench along the fence and pulled out two towels. After he dried off and secured the towel around his waist, he laid the other towel on the edge of the hot tub.

"No, I'm not."

She stared at his back as he turned and retreated into his house. Of all the nerve. He just delivered a clipped answer and thought that would satisfy her curiosity?

Jade stood but shivered as soon as the night air hit her bare, wet skin. She quickly stepped out, dried off, and knotted the towel around her chest. Considering her clothes and Cash were inside, Jade marched straight toward the door.

As soon as she stepped in, she took in the spacious kitchen. Only the light over the stove was on and Cash was nowhere to be found. Maybe later she'd appreciate how classy and updated and nonbachelor his place looked, but right now, she was on a mission to find the man who frustrated her.

She moved through the dining area and took note of the hallway to the left, but she headed toward the front of the house, where her clothes were still near the front door. There was no way she could confront him half dressed.

Why was he acting angry? She had a right to know what happened after she left if the conversation involved her, didn't she?

Jade gathered her clothes from the living room floor. As she dressed, she glanced around at the sectional sofa and the wall-mounted big-screen television, and the main thing she noted was the lack of pictures. It didn't take much thought to instantly see the parallel to her own decorating. Even in Atlanta, she didn't have photos of her family.

And in that instant, she realized she wanted to know about his. Maybe this was bachelor pad motif, but she wasn't so sure. More like a man who wanted to be closed off from emotions.

Cash stepped from the hallway in black running shorts and a gray T-shirt with his gym logo on his left pec. She went over to the sofa and took a seat, because she wasn't about to walk out of here and leave things even more awkward. They could get along with their clothes on and she was going to prove it.

"Figured you'd be gone or on your phone, checking with Melanie and Livie to see if they'd heard anything about us," he stated. "But surely if I'd spilled all our secrets to Jax, he would've told his wife and then everyone would be texting both of us. Weird how none of that happened."

Hurt laced his tone and stirrings of guilt slithered through her. "I panicked, all right?"

He eyed her across the room but made no move to come any closer. Still feeling edgy from nearly getting caught in the office with Jax and the hot tub, which came too close to touching her locked-down emotions, Jade crossed her legs and laced her fingers around her knee.

"Always worried about appearances," he muttered.

"What?" she asked.

Cash motioned toward her. "You can't even relax on my couch. You parked down the street so nobody saw you come here and you flipped out at the idea that Jax and I discussed him finding you in my office."

She glanced down to the pale-pink polish on her nails. She'd removed Piper's purple work when she'd gone home to shower and she was feeling guilty about that, too.

Damn it. She *did* care about appearance.

"I want to blame my mother for this," Jade murmured without looking up. She rubbed her damp palms over her thighs. "Appearances were everything. How would you advance in your career or your relationships without putting your absolute best out there for the world to see and brag about? Even then, sometimes my best wasn't good enough."

Cash shifted, but she didn't dare risk glancing up. She'd opened a topic she never wanted to visit, but he deserved to know. She'd hurt him and that simply wasn't fair. He didn't deserve to be a victim of her warped childhood.

"My best went into my career and I was damn good at what I did."

She licked her lips, instantly tasting Cash. In some weird way, she drew strength from him. She wished she could be a little more relaxed and carefree. Those characteristics simply weren't in her, but when she was with him, she kept wondering why she felt more like herself than at any other time in her life. Maybe because there were no expectations and they both knew going into this that there was no ring on the finger coming at the end.

"Then, when my reputation and integrity at my job came into question," she went on, still staring down at her hands, "I thought my mother would support me, but she didn't even want me to use the family attorney for fear of more people finding out what happened to me. I was on my own. Which was fine; I managed and I succeeded. I guess I should be proud of myself for that. But I shouldn't have to prove myself to my own family."

The couch dipped beside her, but still she couldn't look at Cash. He may want to know more than she was willing to answer, and right now she was telling him more than she'd ever anticipated.

"I'm sorry for assuming you said something to Jax. We agreed to keep this private and I know you wouldn't lie to me." Jade couldn't stand the silence from him any longer. She chanced looking sideways at Cash. "Say something."

"Your mother doesn't deserve that title."

Jade waited for more, but then she let out a laugh. "No, I guess she doesn't, but I owe her. It's easy to get angry at how she's reacted to situations or things she says to me, but without her, who knows where I'd be?"

Cash narrowed his stare and shifted until he propped his knee on the cushion between them. He stretched his arm along the back of the couch behind her. The simple support he offered went a long way in letting her see this new side of him. Well, she was sure he'd always had his compassionate streak, but she'd never seen it before. Who knew of all the people in her life now that she was back in Haven, that she'd find solace in Cash Miller?

"You've said she saved you once before. What do you mean?"

There was nothing to be embarrassed about, but Jade had only told a handful of people. She was a grown woman; there was no reason to be ashamed of her parents' actions.

"I'm adopted," she explained.

Cash's brows raised as he reached and laid a hand over her arm. "So your mom and dad saved you from—"

"The system." Jade pulled in strength from his warm, firm touch. "I was just a few days old when they took me in. Lucky for them, my red hair and green eyes fell into place with their last name, though I'm more Irish-looking than they are."

She always thought that odd, but life was full of mysteries.

"My parents lived in Atlanta at the time," she went on. "I grew up with the best nanny, the best tutors, the best of everything except a normal childhood. I found out after I graduated that my parents were looking for a charitable statement."

"And you were it."

She glanced at him, stunned to see raging fire in his eyes. Jade took her free hand and patted the top of his. The last thing she'd ever wanted from anyone was pity. Life wasn't perfect and pain was simply a part of it.

"You look like you're ready to hit something," she joked, hoping to lighten the moment. "My life could've been much worse, you know. I could've fallen into the system and been bounced around from home to home. When I was little I used to lay in my room and cry when my mom would punish me for being out of order in front of guests. I used to think, would I rather be there in the palace lacking affection, or would I rather be in a foster home or orphanage living in scary conditions?"

Cash's lips thinned as he studied her. She realized she'd said too much, she'd let him in too far, and there was no way to take back what she'd revealed.

"That's why you always play the 'would you rather' game."

He didn't ask, he knew, so Jade merely nodded and

offered a soft smile. "It's just a reminder there are always choices. I went to college and took a job my mother loathed, which may be why she didn't help when I needed it. But I'm finally doing what I want, and this has nothing to do with my mother or my upbringing. I guess it only took me thirtysome years to figure out what I wanted to be when I grew up."

Cash didn't smile, even though she'd tried her hardest to get him to show some emotion other than rage.

Well, this had gone from sexy to intimate in a short time . . . and here she'd vowed not to let that happen. But talking about her path in life actually lifted some of the weight off her shoulders. For too long she'd let everything have a hold over her, and she was learning it was okay to be herself.

Cash inched closer, still holding on to her hand. "What about your birth parents?"

Jade swallowed. "Well, I asked about them once. I was told my biological mother dumped me at the police station. I have no clue if that's true or not, but it doesn't matter. I'm making my own life and that's all that matters."

He slid his fingertip along her cheek, pushing a stray strand behind her ear. "You're so damn remarkable."

Remarkable? She wasn't so sure about that. More like just trying to survive from day to day and not fail because she refused to fall back on her family for plan B. She was her own plan A through Z. She'd finally come to realize that happiness was what led to a full life. A padded bank account and the prestige of being labeled the best by peers certainly wouldn't keep her fulfilled, because all of that could go away in an instant . . . and in her case, it had.

Well, she still had nice savings to fall back on, but she'd also invested a hefty sum into the airport renovations.

"I'm sorry I assumed you said something earlier."

She turned slightly and rested her head against his arm on the back of the sofa. "I guess I was programmed for so long to worry about what people think and I just . . . I trust you."

Cash maneuvered his body, and in an instant, he had her turned and tucked against his side with her back to his chest. Jade settled in by stretching her legs out on the rest of the sofa. This entire evening may be shifting into a direction she wasn't comfortable with, because she really didn't want to share all her thoughts and feelings and insecurities. On the other hand, getting so much out so Cash saw where she was coming from and understood she'd never purposely hurt him was rather therapeutic. How did he make her feel so at ease when talking about the most uncomfortable topics?

The day's events, and her lack of sleep from the night before, caught up with her, and Jade attempted to stifle a yawn.

"I can't stay," she murmured, though her lids were heavy and she knew it was well after midnight.

"For now you can." He placed a kiss to the top of her head and kept his comforting hold around her. "You're exhausted."

"Maybe for a minute." She turned into his arm and inhaled the masculine scent combined with hot tub chemicals. "Just don't let me sleep too long."

"No, Red. I won't."

She took him at his word and let herself push away all worries of what this development would mean to their relationship. At this point, Cash had certainly entered the friend category . . . but why did she feel he was becoming so much more?

Chapter Ten

Cash wondered how he was going to work when he felt like hell. He had no clue what had come over him, but he also knew he couldn't just stay home. There was too much to do between the airport and the gym. His clientele had grown exponentially since he had started a ladies'-only lifting class.

He'd been watching the behavior of his members for a while and discovered that women were sometimes intimidated when they wanted to try something new. They often didn't venture into the area where the guys were lifting and joking around. So Cash had decided to set up a time in the studio part of the gym and taught lifting and technique in private. Those ladies ended up booking regular training sessions, which kept him swamped, especially once they were seeing results and their friends joined.

Cash had pushed through today, despite the lethargy and raging headache. He wanted to head to the airport to check on the progress of the renovations before heading home. He'd had a full day of clients and really just wanted to crawl into bed, but his broken-down plane came first.

He hadn't seen Jade in two days because she'd been teaching yoga and he'd been working nonstop as well. But part of him kept hoping she'd show up at his door in the dark of night again. He wanted another round in his hot tub with her, he wanted her to sleep in his bed and not just grab a few stolen hours on his sofa.

The other night, Cash had woken her up around five in the morning after he'd promised not to let her sleep long. He hadn't been able to help himself and had wanted her to relax. He'd been sitting there holding her and processing all she'd told him about her past, her childhood, her adoption . . . her coping mechanism of "would you rather."

Oh, she may not see her mind game as such, but that was exactly what she'd done when she'd played such a simple game with herself. That was how she'd gotten through the rough times.

And he feared there were plenty.

He wasn't sure who all she'd opened up to and revealed this pocket of information, but he knew Jade was mostly private about her affairs and personal life. Cash couldn't help but feel another click into place of their secret bond.

Cash pulled onto the airport lot and parked next to Jax and Tanner's trucks and killed the engine. He took a long drink from his water bottle before stepping out onto the grassy field they used for temporary parking.

The exterior siding of the main building had been removed and a new extension had been completely framed in, under roof, and new siding was going up all around. Stonework would be put on the front of the building along with stone columns extending up to the canopy for cars to pull under during bad weather.

The restaurant and gift shop would be located in the new addition, and those two draws would be a welcome sight to guests coming into their small town. Livie planned on featuring local talents in the gift shop, starting with

Sophie Monroe's pencil sketches. The woman wasn't only a master real estate agent but also a phenomenal artist.

The hammering and sawing echoed from the construction zone. Zach's workers hadn't touched the hangars yet, though all that needed to be done was some minor maintenance, and they'd be adding a few larger hangars to house bigger planes.

The runway would also have to be lengthened according to regulations to the size of aircraft they were going to cater to.

Cash rubbed his head and willed this damn headache away. He'd taken a couple of pills earlier to get rid of the nuisance, but nothing had changed. He hated to admit it, but his body was starting to ache all over now . . . and not in a good way.

He pocketed his keys and made his way to the open hangar door. Jax and Tanner stood near the broken Skycatcher and seemed to be discussing something Cash couldn't hear. When Tanner raked his hand over the back of his neck as Jax pointed and kept talking, Cash had a feeling whatever the chatter, it wasn't good.

"Are you staring it back to health?" Cash asked as he stepped up next to his cousins.

"That would be easier," Tanner agreed. "But we can fix it. The insurance company is dicking around with us, but we'll get the money owed once we jump through all their hoops and fill out all the online forms for the third time. We don't have a problem proving engine malfunction."

Cash swiped his forehead and cursed when his hand shook. Damn it. He was tired from running all over and not taking any downtime. That's all. He wasn't getting sick because, well, he said so. He didn't have time.

"I don't have any flights I have to take," he stated,

resting his hands on his hips and joining in the staring of the aircraft. "You have anything coming up, Tanner?"

"Nothing that can't wait," his cousin replied. "I'm trying to stick closer to home for Melanie because she may go into labor any day. She's not due for another few weeks, but the doctors have told her the baby is measuring big and . . . well, there were some other details you guys don't want to hear."

"Yeah, we're good on that," Jax stated, then slapped Tanner on the back. "And you may want to rest up on sleep now, because it won't happen again. At least, not for a while."

Cash listened to his best friends discuss babies and sleep patterns, and this was definitely one topic he was glad he had no clue about. Women, yes. Babies? Not so much.

Cash took a walk around the plane while the other two were still chatting like women. He assessed the damage to the fuselage and the landing gear. Not nearly as bad as it could have been. He still got a sickening feeling in his gut when he thought of how Jade could've been hurt or worse.

Maybe that whole near-death thing had opened both of their eyes and let them see each other in a different light. The true side of people always came out under the worst circumstances, and Jade had been strong and mostly calm, considering. Plus, she'd been tempted to kiss him, which made him wonder how long she'd had that thought in the back of her mind.

"Livie is on board for the mock open house," Jax called out, pulling Cash's attention from the plane and Jade.

Cash made his way back around the aircraft. "It sounds like a smart idea," Cash agreed.

Jax nodded and crossed his arms as he continued. "I spoke with her and she ran with the idea and immediately called Sophie."

"Good," Cash stated with a nod, ready to push even further with this new goal of theirs. They were getting closer to the dream becoming reality. "Jade had some good ideas the other night, too."

"Excuse me?" Tanner moved around Jax and laughed. "Did you agree with something Jade said? Did ice just form in hell?"

Cash refused to take the bait. "I can give credit where it's due. Jax heard her ideas, too. She knows what she's talking about. Just because we tend to irritate each other doesn't mean I'd undermine her when it comes to something this important."

There. That sounded good, didn't it?

He sure as hell didn't want them to question his statement, but he also knew Jade was being smart about the next steps they should make. Another reason he admired and respected her was her ability to exude intelligence. From her business sense to the witty banter she tossed his way, Jade was quite an amazing woman.

Cash rubbed his throbbing temple and focused back on the plane, hoping Tanner would drop the subject.

"Dude, you okay?"

Jax's concern had Cash shrugging. "I'll be fine."

"Well, you look like shit," Tanner added.

Cash turned to glare at his cousin but found both guys staring at him. "Would you two quit acting like my mother? I'm fine. Just tired, that's all."

"Your face is flushed," Jax pointed out.

Likely because he was feverish, which would explain the achiness. "I've been working out with clients all day."

"Get out of here," Jax commanded. "We don't want to catch whatever you have."

Cash didn't want to infect them either, but he also didn't

want to not help. "I wanted to check on the plane again, and I wanted to see how the renovations were going."

"I'll send pictures," Tanner grumbled. "Go home and go to bed."

Cash didn't have the energy to argue and didn't want to spread whatever he had—though he still held out hope that this wasn't anything more than lack of sleep.

"Maybe you should call your doctor," Jax suggested.

Shaking his head, Cash pulled his keys from his pocket. "Let's not get carried away. I'll be fine by tomorrow and then I'll be back."

A cell rang, echoing in the open hangar. Tanner patted his pockets and finally pulled out his phone.

"Melanie," he answered, sounding frantic. "You okay?"

Cash stared at his cousin, trying to get a read on what was happening. Was she in labor?

"Well, what else am I supposed to think when you call instead of text?" he exclaimed. "Yes, I'm aware. I'll be home in just a few minutes."

He disconnected the call and clutched his cell to his side.

"No baby?" Jax asked.

Tanner shook his head. "I promised I'd get the changing table put together today and she's holding me to it."

Cash never thought he'd want someone waiting at home on him again. He always thought answering to someone was no way to live, let alone put the stamp of love on the situation. But now that he was heading home and feeling like shit, he almost wished he had someone there for him.

"You're still here?" Tanner asked, turning his attention to Cash.

He held up his hands and stepped back. "I'm going."

After promising to return tomorrow evening, Cash headed back to his truck. He glanced toward the main

building, where the construction crew was wrapping it up
for the day. They'd been putting in long hours trying to
keep the project running on time. So far, so good.

By the time Cash pulled his truck into his drive, he
wondered if he should take a short nap right here to
muster up some energy to even get into his house.

Cash rested his head on the steering wheel for a moment
and closed his eyes. He could do this. He benched and
dead lifted more than most people weighed; surely he
could put one foot in front of the other, climb the four
steps to his porch, and get his ass inside. If he didn't make
it to bed, at least he could pass out on the sofa just inside
the door.

He fisted the keys and moved slowly from the truck to
the drive and up the porch steps. By the time he reached the
front door, Cash knew for certain the couch would have to
do. His heart beat fast, and he felt clammy and exhausted.
Maybe it was a good thing he didn't have someone at
home waiting on him. He was of no use to anyone right
now and there was no use infecting someone else.

Cash barely got the door closed and his keys and cell
placed on the end table before he practically crawled to
the sectional and fell face-first. His cell vibrated on the
table, but he really could care less about who needed him.

Damn it. Maybe it was about his dad again. Cash vowed
to look at his message in a bit; he just needed to rest for a
minute first.

In the back of his mind, Cash started calculating when
he'd need to get up and ready in the morning for his sessions, but then he realized tomorrow was Thursday, and
that was the one day he'd always kept blocked out for
office work and general business.

As he drifted off, he wondered if he heard his cell vibrate

again. He really needed to check the phone in case there was an emergency with his dad, the gym, or the airport.

In just a minute, he vowed again.

Jade slid her phone into her pocket and wondered where Cash was. She'd texted him twice, but he hadn't replied. Not that he needed to jump at her messages, and they certainly didn't have any plans for the evening.

Was it so wrong that she missed him? She could admit that and still keep an emotional distance, right? They were friends at this point, there really was no denying it, and they'd crossed some boundary last time they'd been together. He now knew her worries, her secrets, her past. He knew more than even Melanie and Livie. Jade had never disclosed her silly game to them and had only started it with Cash as a way to pass the time in the plane. But one conversation had snowballed into another, and now he knew the reason why.

Maybe that was what would keep this newfound friendship special. Because the intimacy would eventually come to an end. She wanted to keep him as a friend because she was well aware that having a friend you could trust was special.

Jade glanced at the clock and realized it wasn't as late as she'd thought. As she slid onto the stool at the kitchen island, she set her cell aside and opened her laptop. She wanted to get down some ideas for the open house before she forgot them all. She'd chatted with Livie earlier via text, but now that she was trying to get every thought down, Jade wondered if she was missing something.

Jade tapped on her cell and pulled up Livie's number. After putting it on speaker and laying the phone next to her laptop, she waited for her friend to answer.

"Hey, what's up?" Livie answered.

"I'm working on the notes for the open house. Did we decide on the afternoon or evening? I know we bounced around ideas, but I don't think we pegged down anything."

"Can I call you right back?" Livie asked. "I'm at the airport with Piper. We're getting ready to take Jax to dinner."

"Oh, sure. No problem." Jade tabbed down on her spreadsheet to the areas she'd remember. "You can even call tomorrow. I didn't mean to interrupt dinner."

"No worries," Livie replied. "I guess Jax wanted to go for drinks with Cash and Tanner, but Tanner had to go home and when Cash showed up he was sick. Jax said he looked like hell. Glad I get to be the stand-in for his buddies."

Her friend laughed, but Jade had blocked out everything except the fact that Cash was sick. Most likely that was why he hadn't answered her texts.

"Jade? Are you still there?"

Her eyes darted to the cell on the island. "I'm here. I'll call you tomorrow."

She disconnected the call in a rush and closed her laptop. Questions swirled through her mind. How sick was he? Did he need anything? Did he need her to help?

She had no clue, but she knew she couldn't leave him alone. She'd lived on her own long enough to know that being sick with no one to care for you sucked sometimes.

After searching through her cabinets, Jade made up a bag of necessities and grabbed her purse and keys. She didn't bother texting him to tell him she was coming.

Jade made it to Cash's house in less than ten minutes. All the exterior lights were off, but his truck was in the driveway. Gathering all her belongings, she stepped from her car and used the light from her cell to get up the curved stone walkway.

She knocked on the door, but there was no answer. Jade gripped the knob, thankful when it turned easily beneath her palm because she hadn't thought this far ahead and had no other way to get in.

"Cash?" she called softly as she stepped over the threshold and into darkness.

As she closed the door, she ran her hand along the wall for the light switches. She flicked one up, not realizing what it was connected to. The porch lights illuminated the living room without being too bright. The second she turned, she spotted Cash facedown on the sofa. He still wore his tennis shoes and his feet dangled off the edge of the couch. The back of his gray T-shirt was dark with sweat.

Jade dropped her things on the floor at the end of the couch and squatted down next to him. They were nearly face-to-face and she swept her fingertips across his forehead.

The cut from the rough landing was merely a scratch now, the black eye had vanished, and his thick beard covered his jaw once again. He looked back to his old self, only she'd never seen him so drained before.

She smoothed her hands through his unruly hair, pushing it back from his forehead and off the top of his ear.

"You must be an angel," he muttered without opening his eyes.

Jade smiled. "Your fever obviously broke because you're sweating, and you must be on the mend if you're flirting."

"I don't have the energy for any shenanigans tonight, honey." He attempted a smile, which looked ridiculous with his eyes shut and his cheek pressed into the cushion. "Just take care of me like I did you the other night."

Jade snorted. "I was half-drunk and you had sex with me in the shower."

"Right." He raked a hand over half his face. "I'll take a rain check on that shower sex. See what I did there?"

"I think you need to shut up and rest," she told him as she came to her feet. "Your flirting is getting worse. I'll take care of you, so just relax."

He was already snoring.

Jade continued to stare down at him another minute. She'd never seen Cash as anything but strong and resilient. The man wore pride like a second skin and would probably hate that she saw him like this. Once he recovered, he'd pretend he hadn't been bad, that he could've gotten along without her.

Maybe he could, but she didn't want him to. She liked the idea of nurturing him. As silly as that sounded, Jade had never really had anyone in her life who needed or depended on her. Perhaps her ego had become involved, because she refused to believe it was her heart. But Cash needed her right now and she wasn't going anywhere.

Jade gathered her things and headed to the kitchen. She got to work on making her homemade chicken soup. She never claimed to be a great cook, but she had accumulated quite a few healthy eating habits and formulated her own recipes over the years.

She also had started contributing to Melanie's popular blog, Mel's Motivational Musings. Her friend was a force in the online blogging world. Her popularity was beyond what any of them could have imagined when Mel had first mentioned starting a blog as a therapeutic way to get over her abusive marriage.

Jade was proud of her friend for consistently posting uplifting and motivational pieces to help women better themselves. And Jade was all too happy to add in a healthy recipe each month. This particular chicken soup was one of her favorites.

Talk about a wild night. Her lover was snoring with his broken fever, while she boiled chicken and wondered if it was too late for a cup of coffee.

Good grief. If this was how she was as a single woman, she'd hate to see herself as a married one. She'd be in bed by nine or some such nonsense.

Thirty minutes later, once everything was simmering on low in a pot, Jade headed back to the living room. Cash had rolled and now rested against the back of the cushions. His shirt had come up slightly and gave her a nice view of his washboard abs.

She'd run marathons, she'd worked out in and out of gyms most of her adult life. Seeing a well-built man was nothing new. Hell, seeing *this* well-built man was nothing new.

Yet each time she got glimpses of him, when she could let her stare linger longer than normal, Jade found herself being even more drawn to him. How ridiculous was that? Cash didn't see her as anything more than an itch to scratch. They were simply using each other in the most primal of ways.

Each time her mind drifted into that path of thoughts, Jade felt an uneasiness curl through her. She didn't know what was going on, but she didn't like the thought that either of them were being used. She also knew that everything between them went well beyond the physical.

Jade wondered what he'd say if she confessed that she thought of him as a friend now, or that maybe he had become much more.

Jade smoothed a hand down her hair and pushed away the silly thoughts. She'd been the one so adamant about keeping this fling secret. She'd put the rules in place, so changing them now would be a mistake and confusing.

Cash wasn't a long-term man and she . . . well, she doubted she'd be any good as a long-term woman.

She sat on the other end of his sectional sofa and waited on him to wake. After several hours, she went into the kitchen and put the soup in the fridge. Then she headed back into the living room, where he slept on.

A flash from the end table caught her eye. Cash's cell was lit up with a call. Who would be calling in the middle of the night?

As she got closer, she spotted the words "New Hope." She had no idea what New Hope was, but if he had the number in his phone, he must. This wasn't some random telemarketer or wrong number.

Jade glanced at him and contemplated waking him to take the call, but she opted to let him sleep. Jade grabbed his phone and headed back toward the kitchen as she answered. She didn't want to wake him by talking.

"Hello?"

"Oh, um, is Vincent available? This is Mary from New Hope regarding his father."

Vincent. The proper name didn't suit Cash, not one bit.

"He's actually not free at the moment," Jade replied. "Is there something I can help you with?"

"It's quite important I speak with him," the lady persisted. "His father has fallen and we are transporting him to Mercy Hospital."

Fallen? Jade didn't know what to do. Cash needed to rest, but this was clearly an emergency.

"I will make sure I find him and let him know." Jade didn't know the dynamics of Cash's relationship with his father, but he wouldn't just ignore him. "I'll meet you there."

"Make sure Vincent calls me," Mary stated. "I need to discuss some other matters with him regarding Al."

Al. That must be his father's name.

"I can give him a message," Jade replied. "If you want to let me know, I'll tell him as soon as he's available."

"I'm sorry, ma'am. I can only disclose this to Vincent."

Jade understood. She wanted to know more so she knew what she was dealing with, what Cash was dealing with, but she understood laws.

Once Jade disconnected the call, she quickly went to the browser on Cash's phone and looked up New Hope. She stared at the new information and was shocked his father was in a drug-and-alcohol rehab facility over an hour away.

Is that why he was so private? Was he ashamed of his father, or did he just want to handle everything on his own in that stubborn way of his?

Jade's mother wasn't part of her life because Jade had broken free, for the most part. But Cash's father wasn't present because he was away getting help for a real issue that had to be utterly heartbreaking for Cash.

"Snooping through my phone?"

Jade jerked around to find him leaning against the wall. Even with the pale skin, dark circles beneath his eyes, and beads of sweat dotting his forehead, the potency of that midnight stare affected her in ways she couldn't explain.

"I didn't think we were that far into our relationship," he added.

"I wasn't snooping," she defended.

Cash slowly closed the distance between them and held out his hand. "Just what did you find so enthralling on there?"

She placed his cell in his palm and watched his face as he glanced down to the screen. His eyes instantly darted back up to hers.

"Not snooping?" he mocked. "So at four in the morning,

you suddenly took an interest in a rehab facility? One that you obviously know I have ties to."

"You had a call," she stated, her heart beating fast. "They couldn't tell me much, but your dad fell and they're taking him to Mercy Hospital."

Cash swore under his breath, but his eyes widened as he instantly became more alert. "Who called? Mary?"

Jade nodded. "I told her I'd be right there. I wasn't sure whether to wake you or not, so I just looked up what the facility was because I didn't know what I was dealing with. My first thought was a nursing home, but—"

"He's an addict." Cash fisted his phone and swiped the back of his hand across his damp forehead. "Other than Tanner and Jax, he's all I have. Actually, I'm all *he* has."

Jade reached for him. She slid her hand just below his jawline, her fingers threading into his unruly hair at the nape of his neck. She stroked her thumb over the coarse hair on his jaw.

"I didn't know."

He nodded and stepped back, instantly putting that invisible wall between them. Clearly, the topic of his dad was off-limits, but she just wanted to help. Maybe they weren't as far into this relationship as she'd thought. They may have started out just physical, but she couldn't pretend they hadn't forged much deeper than that.

She'd shared so much of her life, maybe she was naïve to think he'd do the same.

"I can drive myself to the hospital," he told her. "I'm not feeling nearly as bad as I was."

He may be feeling better, but he looked terrible. "I'm just trying to help."

"You helped. I wouldn't have known they called."

Cash turned and headed down the hall toward what she

assumed was his bedroom . . . she'd never actually made it in there.

Jade followed but remained in the doorway. The king-size bed was a tangle of dark navy sheets and a charcoal duvet. There was a brown leather chair in the corner that held a stack of folded jeans. Her eyes scanned the room and landed on the chest of drawers on the opposite wall. There was only one decoration in the entire room, and that was the framed photo of a young boy sandwiched between a man and a woman. All three were smiling, all three appeared to be one unit.

No doubt this was Cash with his parents. Jade's heart hurt just looking at the image, but she wasn't about to bring it up when the tension and vulnerability was already so high.

Cash grabbed a pair of jeans from the chair and started changing his clothes, completely ignoring her. Jade didn't want to admit to hurt feelings; that was one trait she'd learned and actually used from her mother. Never would she let someone see if they'd damaged her in any way.

Jade straightened her shoulders and suppressed a yawn. It had been a long time since she'd stayed up all night and now that she was slowing down and not so worried about how sick Cash was, exhaustion was settling in.

"I made soup for you," she told him, trying to circle back to why she'd stayed to begin with. "It's in the fridge. I'll just clean up my stuff and get out of your way."

Wearing only a pair of unbuttoned jeans, Cash clutched a black T-shirt in hand and faced her. "Don't use that high-and-mighty tone, Red. We're past that."

She'd thought so, but maybe not. "I'm just letting you know. I'm glad you're feeling better."

Cash stared at her for another moment before he jerked

the T-shirt over his head and covered those abs he really should leave on display.

"I'm not trying to be a dick," he told her but made no move toward her. "There are just things I'd rather keep private."

Meaning he didn't want to open up to her, no matter that she'd spilled her own past and insecurities just the other night. Apparently, honesty and feelings only ran one way here.

Which was fine, right? They hadn't agreed to all the personal, deep-rooted emotions. They'd agreed to sex—secret sex.

Why was something so simple in theory actually more complicated than she'd ever anticipated?

"I understand," she told him and pasted on a smile she knew full well looked as fake as it felt. "I'll just get going."

She turned to go when he called her name. Jade stilled but didn't turn back around.

"I don't want you leaving hurt."

Jade flashed a glance over her shoulder. "I need to move my car before your neighbors see it. I was worried when I got here and didn't even think to park down the street."

His brows drew in slightly, his mouth tightened, and the pained expression that swept over his face nearly had her striding across the room. But she was nothing if not prideful . . . a default setting from her childhood.

"You were worried about me?" he asked, his tone low, almost surprised.

Jade held his gaze another second. "Hope your dad is okay."

She fled the room, not caring if her steps mimicked that of a marathon runner. She grabbed her purse by the front door where she'd dropped it and walked out. Whatever she'd left in his kitchen could wait, or he could keep it.

Right now, Jade just wanted to get home, where she could crawl into her bed alone and evaluate just what the hell Cash meant to her. Because it was clear they weren't on the same page anymore.

Chapter Eleven

Jade stood over Sophie Monroe's desk in her real estate office and surveyed the rough-draft pamphlets for the airport. There were six samples for them to choose from, but she couldn't pinpoint just one she thought was best. Jade liked portions of each and was calculating how they could be combined.

Of course, she could probably concentrate if she'd actually gotten a good night's sleep and hadn't spent the rest of the morning worrying about how she'd left things with Cash when she'd darted from his house.

How was his dad? Should she text and ask or just ignore and leave him alone now? He clearly didn't want to discuss his father . . . at least not with her. If he wanted her to know the status, he'd tell her.

"Zach said four women would never come to an agreement on what the final design should be," Sophie said as she took a seat at her desk.

Melanie sat in one of the armchairs opposite the desk and Livie sat in the other. They both leaned forward, inspecting the pamphlets.

"I'm sure we can come to some mutual agreement," Jade stated. "Clearly, you're the expert on this, Sophie."

"I just had these made up and used what I thought you

might want the public to know," Sophie stated. She pointed to one of the samples. "This one is my favorite as far as the layout and colors go."

Jade studied the classy white-and-black design before handing it back to Melanie and Livie. She grabbed another one with a navy-and-white design that she actually liked better.

"This one is still a timeless look," she muttered as she examined all sides. "I think I like the coloring better."

Sophie laughed. "That's my second choice."

"Well, hopefully we all don't like a different one," Livie stated as she reached for the one Jade held.

"Oh, no."

Jade's focus shifted to Melanie, who had dropped one of the samples and now clutched her rounded belly.

"What?" Livie demanded. "Don't tell me the baby. Do not say it. We haven't had your shower yet."

Sophie laughed but came around to the side of Melanie's chair and placed a hand on her shoulder. "Don't listen to her. Are you in pain?"

Melanie's eyes squeezed tight. "I didn't know if I'd been feeling contractions or not. I mean, this is my first baby. What do I know? But I keep getting them . . . and I'm pretty sure my water just broke."

Jade had zero experience when it came to babies and birth and labor, but she was positive breaking water was some warning to get straight to the hospital.

"Should I call an ambulance?" Jade asked.

"I can drive her," Livie offered. "Why don't you call Tanner and have him meet us at the hospital?"

Tanner. Yes, she could do that. Her hands shook as she shoved her hair behind her ears and tried to remain calm. She just needed to make a phone call; it wasn't like she was the one having the baby.

"I'm so sorry, Sophie." Melanie blew out a long, slow breath. "I really didn't mean to have my water break here."

Sophie leaned down and half-hugged Melanie as she patted her shoulder. "That's not something you had control over. Don't think a thing about it."

Jade crossed the spacious office to her purse on the accent table on the far wall. She dug for her cell and saw that she'd missed four texts from Cash. Unfortunately, she couldn't think about their rocky situation or reply to him right now.

She shot off a quick text to Tanner that Melanie was fine but to meet them at the hospital because she was going into labor. Jade hoped someone drove him because he'd be too nervous and anxious to drive himself.

"I'll drive Melanie's car," Livie said as she helped Melanie toward the door. "Jade, follow us in yours."

"Good luck," Sophie called after them. "Keep me posted."

Jade smiled as she shouldered her purse. "I'll call you later, and thanks again for helping with this project."

Sophie waved a hand. "I love seeing businesses thrive in our area. And you three ladies are going to be a force to be reckoned with, especially with Jax, Tanner, and Cash in the group. This airport will be one of the best things to happen to Haven."

"I couldn't agree more." Jade clutched her cell in one hand and her purse strap in the other. "Thanks again."

Jade stepped outside and instantly got pelted in the face with fat raindrops. She hadn't realized it had started raining while she'd been inside and her umbrella was in her purse. This weather would be hell on her hair. Her best friend's baby would come out and see Jade looking like Medusa . . . on a bad day.

By the time she got to her car, she was soaked and

shivering. That rain was freezing, but she wasn't going to run home first to change. She wanted to get to the hospital and be supportive for Melanie and Tanner.

Maybe she'd find a hair band in the bottom of her purse. Then she could pull it all back into a messy bun or something to tame the wild beast.

The closer she got to the hospital, the harder the rain came down. Thankfully, the new metal roof was on the main building and the new addition of the airport so everything was covered and safe from the elements.

Jade tried to park in the parking garage, but it was full, so she had to settle for a spot outside in the main lot. What did it matter if she got soaked now? She was already a walking disaster. Hopefully, Livie had dropped Melanie off at the door so she wasn't walking in this random, pop-up storm.

After several minutes, Jade finally found her way to the maternity ward, where Livie stood in the waiting area.

"You look like hell," her very dry friend stated as Jade stepped into the empty area.

"I take it you got in the parking garage?" Jade asked, taking a seat to dig through her purse for a hair tie.

"I did valet so Melanie didn't have to walk. I didn't want her coming in alone." Livie took a seat next to Jade and crossed her legs. "They just took her back to examine her and said they'd come get us in a bit."

Mints, pens, birth control, a lip gloss. Where the hell was a hair tie when a girl needed one?

"Where is she?"

Tanner busted into the waiting room looking like a frantic beast. While his navy police uniform was pressed and neat, his city medal shining, his hair was in all sorts of disarray, and not just from wearing his hat while on duty. Granted, his hair issue wasn't the rain, more like finger marks from raking his hands through it.

"They're examining her and said we could go back as soon as she's settled in a room," Livie stated. "Tell me you didn't drive yourself."

"Cash brought me." Tanner headed toward the double doors leading back to maternity. "How long did they say before we could go back?"

Jade listened as Livie came to her feet and tried to calm Tanner down, but her mind had drifted off the moment Cash's name was mentioned. Had he dropped Tanner off and then left, or was he parking the car? If he was here, they'd need to play it cool, which shouldn't be an issue, considering they'd left things pretty frigid.

She did another frantic search through her purse, because if Cash walked in here and she looked like—

"Hey, Red."

Damn. Oh, well. It wasn't like she needed to impress him, right? It couldn't be worse than the wedding hair . . . she hoped.

Jade closed her purse and pasted on a smile before looking up. "Flex."

That tempting mouth quirked in a half grin and she hated him instantly. He had gotten soaked, but instead of looking like the proverbial drowned rat, Cash managed to look even sexier than usual. How was that even possible or fair?

Oh, right. Because when his wet shirt clung to his body, it formed around taut muscles, and his dark hair glistened with the droplets. When her clothes were plastered to her, she took on the shape of a teenage boy, and in the next few minutes her hair was going to start drying in a nice, fuzzy frizz ball.

"Is something wrong? Why won't they let us back there?"

Tanner continued to stare through the narrow rectangular window as Livie stood at his side.

"Nothing is wrong," she assured him. "I'm sure had you been here first they'd have let you back, but it was just me. Give them a few minutes."

Tanner shoved both hands through his hair and laced his fingers on the back of his neck. "What if it's too soon? She's not due for a few more weeks. I know the doctor said the baby was measuring big, but does that mean everything is healthy?"

Jade didn't think Tanner was going to make it through this labor process. The poor guy was practically shaking, and if they didn't get him back there soon to reassure him that his wife and baby were okay, he was going to have a panic attack right here in the waiting room.

"Listen," Cash said as he stepped closer, "about the other night—"

Jade shook her head and darted her eyes to Livie and Tanner, to make sure they weren't listening. "Nothing to discuss."

"I shouldn't have been such a jerk," he went on.

"You were sick and worried about your dad." Why was she defending him? He *had* been a jerk. "How is he?"

"Fine."

Well, there it was. One simple word, a blanket word that should've covered so much yet told her nothing at all. Even with his apology for how he'd acted when she'd been concerned, he still kept her at a distance. His reaction shouldn't hurt because they'd never offered anything to each other, but the pain settled in just the same.

Jade came to her feet and set her purse in her seat. She smoothed her hair away from her face and ran a hand down the makeshift ponytail, then laid the wet strands over her shoulder.

"You left some things," Cash said. "Do you want to come by to get them later?"

Livie came back across the lobby and smiled at Jade, then her gaze went to Cash. "What's going on here?"

Jade's heart beat faster. Had Livie heard what Cash had just said? Why wasn't he being discreet? Didn't they agree to keep this affair a secret?

Cash stared at Jade another second before shifting his attention to Livie. "Just asking Jade if she wanted to come by to check the new studio I had remodeled at the gym. Perfect for yoga classes, and I'm up for adding a heated room for hot yoga. She just has to say the word."

Livie's brows dipped in like she was trying to decide what to believe. "You're still trying to get Jade to teach yoga for you?"

"He's relentless." Jade figured that was pretty damn close to the truth. "But even he has to realize what a bad idea that is."

"I think it's a great idea," Livie stated, then shrugged. "Sorry. I'd love to take your classes, but I can't always drive thirty minutes to get there."

Jade groaned, but before she could reiterate why she wouldn't join business forces with Cash, the double doors opened and Tanner all but flew through them. The young nurse simply laughed as he nearly ran her over to get to his wife.

"Room three," she called after him, then turned her attention to the rest of them. "Melanie said anyone could come back."

Livie turned and went back, then the nurse followed, leaving Cash and Jade alone in the waiting room.

"Are you staying?" she asked.

Cash took a step away and held up his hands. "I think

I'll just wait on the phone call or text when it's all over, and then I'll visit."

Jade grabbed her purse and slid it up onto her shoulder, still keeping a clutch on the leather strap. "Well, I'm staying. But the stuff at your house—I can get it another day. No big deal."

Cash opened his mouth as if he wanted to say something, but then he closed it and took another step back. Jade wished he'd say what he wanted, but when silence continued to grow between them, she pulled in a breath and turned away.

She'd almost hit the doors when he called her name.

"There are some parts of my life that are off-limits."

Jade dropped her gaze to the glossy floors and knew that statement had cost him a little bit of pride. But it had also opened a door, even if it was just a sliver, to something more.

"It's okay." She glanced over her shoulder and caught that dark stare. "You don't owe me an explanation about your dad."

"No, but I owe you an explanation about being a jerk."

The fact that he recognized he'd been rude was a huge step most men wouldn't take—or at least most men like the ones she'd dated over the years. But she and Cash weren't dating.

"Maybe you could come to my house and I could cook for you," he offered, shoving his hands in his pockets. "It's the least I could do."

Jade smiled and hated how her heart did a little flop at his offer. She couldn't let her heart start getting involved here—as if she needed to remind herself of that for at least the twentieth time. Emotional involvement combined with sex wouldn't be good in the long run.

"I'll text you a list of my favorite foods," she told him,

unable to resist temptation or listen to the sage advice she'd just given herself.

Cash let out a bark of laughter and nodded. "I'll be waiting."

He turned and headed out of the waiting area, leaving Jade to stare after him. She needed to wipe this silly grin off her face before she went back. There was no way to know what Livie had overheard, and if she saw Jade acting like a giddy schoolgirl, there would be no lying her way out of this one.

Exhaustion consumed her, but Jade had never been so happy. Melanie and baby Knox were happy and healthy. Even though he'd come into the world early, Knox had checked all the boxes of a full-term baby. There had been some chatter about having the due date wrong, but Jade had been too busy doting over him and stealing precious kisses on his soft little cheeks to listen.

And proud papa Tanner, well, he was adorable. Jade was positive his feet wouldn't touch the ground for some time.

Jade and Livie had decided to let the new little family have some privacy. Melanie had wanted her husband and best friends there for the birth. Jade had never seen anything like it, and part of her wondered if she'd ever have her own family, her own husband who looked at her the way Tanner looked at Melanie. There was something magical about being in a room when new life came into the world. There was a sense of hope and innocence, like everything would be just fine.

Jade climbed the old brick steps to her back porch and was thankful that Melanie finally had found her happy ever after. The marriage she'd been in before had been more like a controlling prison than holy matrimony.

Maybe that was why Jade hadn't found anyone to have in her life permanently. Growing up, she'd been in a prison of her own. If she found a man and considered marriage, she couldn't lose her freedom or herself.

She let herself in the back door and let out a yawn. Jade had lost so much sleep in the past week, between Cash and now Knox, but both were worth it. Thankfully, she didn't have a class to teach until this afternoon. Hopefully, she could catch a few hours' sleep so she didn't fall over while teaching hot yoga.

Jade let her purse drop to the kitchen island as she made her way toward the front of the house and the stairs. She had just enough energy to crawl up the steps and strip off her clothes before falling into bed.

Once she woke, she'd text Cash. She'd already given him the list of her favorite foods and honestly couldn't wait to see what he came up with for dinner.

At first she'd just been joking, but then she'd actually decided to see what he'd do with another nugget of her personal information.

Minor as it was, Jade couldn't help but wonder what was happening between them each time they exchanged pieces of themselves. The invisible string holding them together kept getting shorter and shorter, pulling them ever closer.

The knock on the front door startled her. Perhaps Cash couldn't wait for her to text and decided to come to her instead. Pretty brazen, considering it was broad daylight.

Thinking Cash may be on the other side of her door, Jade found she wasn't so tired after all. She crossed the living room and flicked the dead bolt, throwing the door wide with an exaggerated flourish to make him laugh. Only Cash wasn't her morning visitor.

"Brad," she gasped. "What are you doing here?"

"I want to talk."

Stunned by his rude, unannounced visit, Jade gripped the doorknob. She shifted her body to cover the gap between the door and the frame and didn't offer to let him come inside.

"There's nothing to talk about," she told him.

"I just want five minutes."

At one time she'd been attracted to Brad, but standing here now, she wondered what she ever saw in him. He was tall and lanky, his hair too fixed with a perfect part, his clothes too pressed and polished. Good grief, he looked like someone her mother would've chosen—which she realized was another black mark against him.

"No." Jade started to close the door. "Goodbye, Brad."

He put his foot in the door, and it was all she could do to stop herself from slamming it anyway, his polished shoe be damned.

"I made a mistake," he stated, his voice bordering on a whine. "Can I just come in for a few minutes?"

"She asked you to leave."

Jade glanced over Brad's shoulder to Livie, who stood directly behind him. Brad glanced back and forth between them but didn't budge.

"I just want to talk," he repeated. "I swear, I'll just be a few minutes and then I'll go. Just . . . just hear me out, Jade."

Livie narrowed her pretty blue eyes. "This is still my house and I'm telling you to get the hell away. You ended things when you decided to cheat with another woman and then humiliate Jade in public."

What a friend to bring that back up. As if Jade could

have forgotten the spectacle at Taps, where Brad had had his new arm candy and proclaimed she was better in bed. The man had been drunk and completely out of line. And, to be honest, he was the one who was bad in bed, but she'd been a lady and refrained from voicing her thoughts.

Livie pushed forward. "Now, if you'll excuse us, I'm here to see her."

She wedged herself between Brad and the door, and a quick shoulder move threw Brad slightly off balance. Once Livie stepped inside, Jade closed the door on his confused face.

"What on earth did he want?" Livie asked as she stepped into the living room.

"He said he made a mistake." Jade sent the dead bolt back home and turned to lean against the door. "I'm not sure if he was referring to the fact that he cheated on me or that he publicly embarrassed me, but I'm glad you came when you did. I was running out of patience with him. Why aren't you home sleeping?"

Livie reached into her pocket. "You left your phone in Melanie's room."

She'd been so tired, she hadn't even noticed it wasn't in her purse when she'd left. "Thanks."

Jade started to reach for it, but Livie moved back. "Interesting messages from Cash this morning."

Oh no. No, no, no.

Jade's breath caught in her throat, her heart started beating even faster, and she was nearly too tired to try to come up with more lies.

What had he texted? She was afraid to ask and even more afraid that Livie was going to tell her anyway.

Jade refused to act like she knew what her friend was talking about until, well, until she knew what she was talking about.

"I didn't sneak into your phone, but your phone was vibrating on my way out of the hospital." Livie tapped the screen and held it up for Jade to see. "Something about dinner, then a session of hot yoga just for the two of you, and then he got descriptive about chocolate cake and where he'd like to put the icing."

Jade's heart sank and she had to fight to keep her mouth from dropping. First of all, every bit of that sounded like a lovely evening he had planned. Chocolate cake had been on her list of favorites, and she had to give him props for the creative uses.

Second of all, she wanted the floor to open up and swallow her. There was only one way out of this and that was to feign ignorance straight to her best friend's face.

Jade pasted on a smile and waved a dismissive hand. "Please, you know Cash. He's always flirting and being bold with his words. It's no secret he wants me to teach yoga at his gym. Apparently, he thinks flirting is the way to win me over."

"Flirting?" Livie repeated with a laugh. "Flirting is a smile or a compliment on your beauty. Offering to smear chocolate icing on your—"

"I get it." Jade put her hands over her ears because she simply couldn't hear Cash's fantasy come out of Livie's mouth. "Cash never does things halfway, does he? I'd hate to see how he interviews other employees."

She laughed as her hands dropped to her sides. Livie still held the phone away and didn't look convinced. Time to pull out her best acting skills, which were nearly non-existent unless you counted the time she'd played the tornado in her third-grade rendition of *The Wizard of Oz*.

"Listen." She made sure to keep her eyes locked on her friend, because if she glanced away or fidgeted, Livie would know Jade was lying. "I know what this looks like, but do you honestly think Cash and I would mesh? You've seen us together, right? We argue and annoy the hell out of each other."

Until their clothes fell off, and then they got along quite well.

Livie pursed her lips, narrowed her eyes, and ultimately handed over the phone. "I suppose not. I'd like to think if you had a crazy hot affair going on, you'd at least say something to Melanie and me. Even if it was Cash. Hell, *especially* if it was Cash."

"Of course I'd tell you guys," Jade agreed, though the heavy dose of guilt settled uncomfortably on her shoulders.

She pocketed her phone and immediately felt it vibrate. No way was she going to look at the thing while Livie was there. If he started in on any more sexual options for chocolate icing, she'd likely start moaning.

Jade never lied to her friends. She actually prided herself on always being upfront and honest. But if she said anything now, that would be betraying the pact she and Cash had made.

Since when did she put a man before her very best friends?

"Do you want me to stay in case Brad comes back?" Livie asked.

"Oh, no." Jade shook her head, knowing full well her friend would stick around. "He's harmless, just annoying. You go on home and rest. I wouldn't even hear if he came back because I'll be upstairs asleep."

Livie let out a yawn and headed toward the door. "If you need me, call. Or call Jax. He's at the airport because the new heating and cooling units are being installed today."

"I'll be fine," she assured her friend just as the cell in her pocket vibrated again. Relentless man. "I'll text you later and we can figure out what to do about this baby shower we were supposed to have in a few days."

Livie laughed. "I guess Melanie and Knox can both attend."

Jade held the front door open and let Livie out. "Oh, wait," Jade said.

Turning back around, Livie raised her brows and grinned. "You want to confess something? Maybe about Cash?"

"Not likely. I want to discuss something with you when we're both not sleep-deprived." Jade stepped out onto the porch with Livie. "It's about the house."

Her friend's blond brows drew in. "You're moving? I don't have the energy for this now. Please tell me you're not leaving Haven."

Jade reached out and grabbed Livie's hand, giving it a reassuring squeeze. "No, I'm not moving. Actually, the opposite. I wanted to discuss buying your house."

Livie's eyes widened. "What?"

"I think I want to stay in Haven. You know, reset my roots." Jade dropped Livie's hand and shrugged. "Definitely something we can talk about later. And if you don't want to sell, I completely understand."

Livie's eyes misted. "If I sell my childhood home, I can't think of anyone else I'd want living here."

A bit of weight lifted off her shoulders. Jade hadn't even realized how much she wanted this until now. She'd been tossing the idea back and forth in her mind, but she figured she'd mention it and just get a feel for Livie's stance. Now that she knew, Jade truly wanted all this to work out. Coming back home wasn't always easy, but she had a good feeling she'd made the right decision.

Jade wrapped her arms around Livie. "Thank you."

She eased back and tipped her head from one side

to the other to relieve some tension. "Now, go on home. We'll talk later. Just discuss with Jax what a fair price would be."

Livie nodded. "You'll get the family discount."

Their friendship was stronger than that of most sisters, but Jade wasn't going to let Livie discount her home. She wanted to be fair, so she'd probably get Sophie over here to give her an idea of what she should offer.

Once Livie had gone, Jade closed and locked the door. As she climbed the stairs, she pulled her cell from her pocket. She tripped over the last step and nearly fell into the hallway as she read Cash's latest messages.

He'd incorporated all her favorite foods all right. Each one on a different body part and in different rooms of his house . . . including the hot tub.

Well, that man certainly had quite the erotic imagination—and she was one lucky woman.

Had Livie seen these, there would be no denying what she and Cash had going on. Jade would have to be more careful if she wanted this affair to remain undisclosed.

Scrolling through the messages, Jade smiled as she reread each one. But she didn't reply. He deserved to wait on her response after getting her in a bind earlier. Technically, leaving her phone behind was Jade's fault, but the timing of his messages couldn't have been worse when the cell had been in Livie's possession.

Besides, she didn't have the mental stamina to start this conversation. She needed sleep, and dealing with Cash would require her to be at her best.

No one challenged her like he did; nobody ever had. The allure of a secret affair with someone who made her feel giddy and reckless was too exciting to end it. Jade was certainly in no rush to call it quits, which meant she'd have to hone those acting skills before she ruined a good thing.

Jade sank down onto her bed and swiped a hand down her face. First she got involved in a heated affair she didn't want to end, then she was talking about buying a house in her hometown.

If she had more energy, she'd start analyzing everything from every angle. Jade toed off her shoes and fell back onto her mound of pillows. She stared up at the draped sheers over the canopy.

Would she rather be back in Atlanta making seven figures and being taken for granted in a thankless job, or would she rather make significantly less living in her hometown, where she was risking everything by investing not only her money but her time and emotions in an airport?

More importantly, would she rather find someone to settle down with or would she rather continue on with a man who made her feel alive for the first time in her entire life?

Jade smiled, knowing everything she'd decided was worth the risk. The permanent move *and* the temporary man.

Chapter Twelve

Cash wasn't sure what had come over him as he pulled into the lot of another gym thirty minutes outside of Haven. Why in the world did he let his hormones make decisions? Hadn't he learned his lesson from his ex-wife?

Obviously not, because he was gearing up to take his first-ever hot yoga class. Maybe if Jade saw he was serious about getting her to work for him, she'd reconsider. This was purely business. Never let it be said he wasn't persistent.

After grabbing his water bottle, Cash stepped from his truck and pocketed his keys. He'd been to this gym years ago, before he opened his own. There had been several on his research tour when he was scoping out ideas to start up his dream business.

Cash never looked at other gyms as his competition. He wasn't in the business to get rich or scheme people into diets that didn't work. No, he legit wanted to help people better themselves and live healthier lives.

He couldn't pinpoint what made him want to be a gym owner and trainer. Cash had always just enjoyed lifting weights and working out. He'd found no better therapy as he'd gone through the divorce and the ongoing issues with his father.

Added to that, there was something to be said about people who consistently saw one another in a setting where everyone was trying to improve. It was like a bond that only that group could understand, and many of his clients had become friends. The people he saw and worked with every day were folks he genuinely cared about.

Maybe that was something he and Jade had in common. She seemed to love teaching this class and he'd heard her talk of marathons in the past. Someone who cared about their body was pretty damn sexy.

Though Cash never put a woman's worth on what she looked like. Health came in all different sizes and shapes. Someone could be healthy and weigh much more than an unhealthy person. Just taking pride in their appearance was what Cash found to be a total turn-on.

And Jade seemed to check off nearly every box in that turn-on category. Oh, she claimed she hated her body because she thought she was too flat-chested and her hips were too wide, but he couldn't find a damn thing wrong with her, and he'd definitely taken time to explore.

When Cash stepped into Fit and Trim, he was immediately greeted with a welcome from the young guy behind the front desk.

"I'm here for the yoga class," Cash stated, resting his water bottle on the counter.

The young man laughed. "You're brave. I tried that once and nearly passed out. But good for you."

Fabulous. Just what he wanted to hear. Despite the warning, Cash was ready to tackle something new and convince Jade to work for him, so taking an hour to admire her wasn't a bad way to spend his afternoon.

When Jade hadn't responded to his detailed dinner and dessert messages, Cash decided to see her another way. Besides, shouldn't he check this out for himself instead of taking other people's word for how amazing these classes were?

Hot yoga classes were growing more and more popular in the area, and he wanted to keep his gym thriving with new and fresh ideas. The fact that Jade could be there as well added the proverbial icing on the cake.

Their physical relationship aside, Jade would be an asset to his business. Now he just had to continue working on convincing her.

Cash paid the one-time fee for the class and headed in the direction the young man pointed. He put his shoes, socks, keys, and cell in a locker in the changing room and grabbed a towel from the bin as he followed the signs to the back of the gym, where the classes were located.

He found the large steel door at the end of the hallway and wondered just what he'd experience on the other side. Passing out in front of Jade and a full class wouldn't bode well for his self-esteem.

Cash turned the handle and slowly opened the heavy door. The hot studio was . . . well, hot. His first deep breath in was quite stifling, and just stepping inside was enough to melt the shirt off his back.

A little sweat never hurt anybody, but this was going to be quite a different experience.

There were blue mats lined up in two neat rows on the dark wood floors. Some of them had orange balancing blocks, others had towels and water for people already claiming their spots. Cash wasn't sure if he wanted to be up front to watch Jade or in the back, where he could hopefully go unnoticed. All of the heat aside, he had never done yoga in his life and he had no doubt he would stand out as a newbie. He just hoped he didn't fall and knock over the others like a row of dominoes.

For the first time in Cash's life, nerves settled in deep.

Cash closed the steel door behind him and spotted Jade across the room, chatting with another lady. He didn't want to alert her to his presence, so he quietly made his way to a mat in the back corner.

He set down his bottle and unfolded his towel, laying it like the others were. Sweat already trickled down his back.

How long was this class again? An hour? He should've brought a gallon of water to stay hydrated.

"New here?"

Cash glanced to the middle-aged, petite lady beside him. "Is that obvious?"

"No," she replied. "I'm just at every class Jade teaches and I didn't remember seeing you before."

His eyes darted over the lady's shoulder and noted Jade had moved on to talk to someone else, moving closer to him now.

"Yes, I'm new." He returned his attention to the woman. "I'm a gym owner in Haven and thinking of adding some hot yoga classes. Thought I'd check it out for myself."

No need in mentioning he was trying to steal Jade away from this place. For now, though, he wanted to make it through the next hour.

"Okay, let's get started," Jade announced. "We have a full class—"

When she turned, her eyes locked on to his, and Cash merely smiled. Damn it, she looked good in her black sports bra, oversize bright-blue tank scooping down on the sides for him to see all that creamy skin . . . skin he'd explored over and over. She'd pulled her hair over one shoulder in a side braid. The black spandex capris hugged those hips she always complained about. Cash wasn't complaining about anything going on right now.

Jade tipped up her chin as a slow grin spread across her face. Dread overcame him, because he'd seen that smile before. Jade wasn't going to make this easy for him, not that he expected her to, but if he was going to make it through this next hour, he'd have to bring his A game.

"We have a few new people today," Jade went on as she walked to the front of the class to stand in front of the wall of mirrors. "Which is perfect because I have a few new moves I'm implementing, and everyone will be on the same level."

Same level? Not likely. New moves or old moves didn't much matter to him because he wasn't sure he could do any of them. Still, he wasn't going to admit defeat, no matter what she threw at him.

The slow music started and Jade stood before them with her hands at her sides.

"Palms forward, toes touching, and heels slightly apart," she said in a calming voice. "Let's start breathing in and out of our nose to get our body warm."

Body warm? Check.

"Close your throats," she went on in that tone that made him think of a smooth bourbon. "Rid your mind of everything that doesn't serve you. We want to focus on our health, both mind and body."

The song playing was a familiar '90s rock tune, but it had been slowed down to a relaxing tempo, and Cash was surprised he rather enjoyed this version. Maybe she'd give him her playlist when they were alone.

"Mountain pose. Turn your pinkies in toward each other."

Cash followed as everyone lifted their hands overhead.

"Baby backbend. Make your arms into goal posts," Jade stated as she went back to the front of the class and joined in the poses. "Really arch that back and push your hips forward. Gaze up to the ceiling."

Okay, this was a good stretch. Jade led them through several more movements to stretch, and he had a sense of relief that he'd been able to do everything so far. Five minutes down, only fifty-five to go.

"We're going to be moving into our flow segment."

Jade's eyes darted to his and she smiled. That smile sent a punch to his gut. She was in her element and absolutely thriving. He wondered if her mother ever saw her like this. If her mother ever cared to see how amazing Jade truly was when she was doing something she loved.

The next movement Jade called out seemed easy enough . . . until he tried it. Cash attempted to balance on one foot, lean one arm out parallel with the floor, reach behind him to grab the inside of his foot, and then lean farther. What the hell?

"Standing bow pose should be giving you a nice stretch throughout your body," Jade said. "This will keep your legs strong."

Not if he fell over and broke one.

Cash stepped out of the pose and took a deep breath before trying once more. As he stared at his extended hand, he spotted Jade's eyes in the mirror. She didn't smile but merely quirked a brow. Like hell he'd show weakness. He would get through this class or die trying.

Had someone turned the heat up even more?

Sweat rolled down his forehead and his shirt clung to his back. Jade issued another set of poses and said something about "flow," and if he'd had the energy, he would've laughed. There was no flowing. At best, Cash stumbled and jerked through each movement.

Something, something eagle pose didn't seem too difficult. He certainly felt the stretch and his concentration grew deeper as the class went on.

Then they moved to the floor, and the next thing Cash knew, everyone was on their head and their knees rested on their elbows in what Jade called "crow pose."

He thought for sure he'd make a fool of himself, but Cash used every bit of his upper body and core strength and slowly got into position. As he tightened every muscle, he closed his eyes and concentrated on breathing.

"If anyone wants to try moving on to extending your legs straight up, let me know," Jade said. "I can talk you through it or help you get into position."

He heard her soft footsteps swipe across the floor as she moved around. Cash's ego wouldn't let him remain still. He gritted his teeth and started to move his legs, but his balance wobbled a second before familiar hands gripped his ankles.

"You've got it," Jade told him as she assisted him into position. "Tighten your glutes."

She released him, and he was surprised he was able to stay in hold. "Perfect," she whispered.

Then she stepped away, and he heard her assisting someone else in the class. Her soft tone combined with the pale lighting and the slow music no doubt was key in the concentration.

Cash had just grown comfortable and confident when a cramp attacked his glute and sabotaged his perfect form, and he fell over onto his back.

Thankfully, he landed on his mat and didn't hit anyone around him, but still, humiliating yourself was rather painful.

Cash swiped his hand across his sweaty forehead and caught Jade's eyes across the room. She smiled but didn't say a word.

When Cash grabbed a quick drink and settled back onto his mat, the lady next to him came back down from her own pose and sat on her heels.

"Don't worry," she told him as she shook her head.

"We've all done it a time or two. You're officially part of the group."

Cash laughed. "Glad I passed the initiation."

The final portion of the class went on a little calmer, but by the end, Cash worried he wouldn't be able to walk later. He was used to heavy weights, not so much stretching his muscles and pushing himself to hold poses for long periods of time.

During the cooldown, Jade had them lie on their backs, palms up to the ceiling and eyes closed. He was all on board with that pose. Her feet shifted over the floor, but he didn't open his eyes. Suddenly, her fingertip tapped between his brows, then her hands gave a subtle massage to his temples, then feathered away, and she was gone.

Whatever oil or liquid she'd used on his head and shoulders smelled like her. He always associated this scent with Jade, and now he knew why. Was this jasmine? Whatever it was, Cash was totally getting turned on.

After they came back to a sitting position on their knees, they bowed down to the mat to end class. Jade dismissed them and promised to see them in two days.

As much as Cash wanted to get out into fresh air and peel off his shirt, he took his time in putting his soaked towel in the bin and rolling up the mat. Once the room was cleared out, Jade closed the door, only leaving it slightly ajar for the cooler air to creep in.

"Not a bad start, Flex."

Jade reached up on the shelf in the corner and grabbed a clean towel. When she turned, she tossed it his way. Instinctively, Cash snaked out his arm and caught it.

"That's a damn hard class, Red." He mopped the sweat off his head and swiped the back of his neck. "I don't know if the poses or the heat was worse."

Jade laughed as she reached for her bottle of water.

"So, would you rather a room at one hundred three degrees for sixty minutes or regular yoga in air-conditioning for ninety minutes?"

So they were back to the game? Fine by him. He liked how they had this little bond on top of their secret affair.

"I'd take the heat," he told her. "Some of those poses kicked my ass."

Jade clutched her bottle and crossed the room. "That's what happens when you only lift and don't stretch. Your muscles are short."

Cash nodded. "All things I'm aware of. Which is one reason I'm here."

Jade stopped in front of him and grinned. "And what other reason did you have for coming here?"

"Maybe I'm still trying to convince you to work in my gym."

She nodded and crossed her arms, the innocent movement doing amazing things to her chest. Cash's eyes focused on the droplets of sweat disappearing into the valley between her breasts.

"Eyes up here, Flex."

Cash obeyed. "You didn't answer my texts."

"No, but Livie almost did."

From the hard set of her eyes and her firm tone, he knew she wasn't kidding. Damn it.

"I left my phone in Mel's hospital room," Jade went on. "When Livie followed me home, she helped me get rid of Brad and then was all too—"

"Brad?" Cash didn't like that bastard one bit, and he sure as hell didn't like him near Jade. "He was at your house?"

Jade took another drink and then capped her bottle.

"He's not important, but yes, he showed up at my house. Anyway—"

"No. Don't move on." Heat forgotten, Cash rolled the towel and hung it around his neck. "What the hell did he want?"

Jade rolled her eyes. "I should've never mentioned that."

"You should've mentioned it before now," he growled.

"It was just this morning, relax."

He flexed his fists at his sides, but remained silent. Anything he said now would come out sounding like a jealous boyfriend. Besides, Jade was a big girl, and he trusted that she could handle herself. He just didn't like that she'd had to.

"As I was saying," Jade continued, "Livie had my phone, and when your texts popped up on the screen, she was a little shocked."

Cash smiled and reached up to grip the two ends of the towel with one hand. "Why is that? Do you have me listed under Hot Shower Sex?"

Jade swiped stray, damp hairs from her forehead and laughed. "Not hardly, stud. Obviously I have your name or she wouldn't have known it was you. But she did see the icing comment."

Oh, that was a good one. In fact, he'd already ordered a chocolate cake and had it in his kitchen. He could cook, but he drew the line at trying to bake. He really should've asked for extra icing . . .

"Would you get that shitty grin off your face?" she scolded. "I'm being serious."

"Oh, I was serious about the icing."

Jade swatted his arm but continued to smile. "Do you even care what I said to Livie?"

Cash shrugged. "I trust you handled the situation however you thought best."

Her green eyes narrowed. "You're really that trusting?"

"Not normally," he countered. "But I trust you."

Jade stared at him another minute, pursed her lips, and then muttered something and walked out of the room. Confused, Cash followed.

The cool blast of air hit him hard as he stepped into the hallway. Before he could take another step, Jade whirled around on him.

"I can't believe you're that easy," she declared. "I jumped all over you the other night and you just . . . just . . ."

Cash crossed his arms over his chest and glanced down the hall to make sure they were still alone. He took a step closer and stared into her disbelieving eyes.

"Red, I was married to a woman who lied to my face without thinking twice. The fact that you were worried the other night, even though you handled it wrong, tells me that you recovered and managed today just fine."

Jade's eyes widened as she stared back like he'd lost his ever-loving mind. "You know, that's pretty sexy."

"Excuse me?"

"The way you defended my actions when I was hard on myself," she explained. "It's pretty hot."

A smile spread across her face and she started to reach for him, but pulled her hand back as someone came down the hall, then turned into another studio room.

He hated this. He didn't want to worry they were in public. When she wanted to touch him, he wanted her to have that freedom.

So did that mean he wanted a relationship? Hell, maybe he did, but he wouldn't say anything. At least not for now. He had to make sure his thoughts weren't skewed by great sex.

"You wanna come to dinner about seven?" he asked, more than ready to get some alone time with her.

She reached up and slid the towel from around his neck. "Let's make it seven thirty. I have a few things I want to do."

Cash raised his brows. "More important than dinner and sex?"

Jade laughed. "Well, I want to go by the hospital to see the baby."

Cash nodded. "I think I'll wait until they're home."

A group of ladies turned into the hallway. Their laughter preceded them, then faded as they went into the side room.

"I don't like not touching you," he whispered.

Her eyes flared wide. "You'll touch me later."

"I'm counting on it, Red."

She offered him another saucy smile. "See you in a few hours."

Cash let her head out of the hall first before he headed to the men's locker room. Each time they were in public together or around their friends, Cash was finding that not acting on his feelings was becoming harder and harder.

Maybe he'd need to think more about this relationship thing. Perhaps he should also get a feel for what Jade thought, because he wouldn't lay his heart on the line again unless he knew it wouldn't be handed back to him in pieces.

"And Livie has ordered four dozen petit fours, all white with little blue clouds."

Jade sipped her glass of wine and sat back in the patio chair as she stared across the table at Cash. He'd made her an amazing dinner of grilled chicken with fresh vegetables and a salad that had nuts and strawberries, and he'd even chilled her favorite Riesling. She knew for a fact he'd had to drive to get this bottle because the Quickie Mart in Haven carried two types of wine: cheap red and cheap white.

"You're not even listening," she stated.

Cash sat sideways in his chair with his arm resting on the back. He'd been staring at her weirdly all evening. He hadn't once cracked a snarky joke or made good on any promise from his blatant texts.

"Is something wrong?" she asked. "Is it your dad?"

He sat up straighter. Any time she mentioned his dad, Cash seemed to jump right out of any other thought.

"Dad is fine, considering." Cash shifted to lean forward and grab his beer bottle. "Did you enjoy dinner?"

"You know I did. These are some of my favorite things."

Cash nodded, then took a long pull of his drink. "How were Melanie and Knox?"

Jade set her glass on the table and leaned forward on her forearms. "I literally just spent the last ten minutes discussing my visit and the baby shower Livie and I are throwing this weekend. What's up, Flex?"

He stared down to the label on his bottle and started picking at the corner that had come loose from the condensation. Jade waited, wondering what was on his mind, but more wondering how she could get back the Cash she'd been with only hours ago.

"Too tired from the yoga?" she joked, hoping to put a smile on his face.

Nothing. He continued to pick at the damp paper.

"Do you ever want something and then, when you get it, your goals immediately change?"

His question threw her off. Something had been eating away at him and she wanted to help. Wasn't that what friends were for?

"I have a feeling we're not talking hypothetically."

Now his dark eyes did dart up to her, and Jade found herself frozen. Whatever he was thinking had something to do with her. The way he looked at her across the table like . . .

No. He wasn't looking at her like anything. He only wanted her in the hot tub again, that's all. Cash wasn't getting emotionally invested.

"I want you to have everything," he murmured. "Part of me feels like this fling . . . maybe it's not fair to you."

Had she taken a drink of her wine during that deliverance, she would've choked. Vincent "Cash" Miller was pulling the gentleman card right in front of her eyes. The man who flirted with every breath, the man who didn't hesitate to get her naked and in the shower when she'd been a sip away from drunk, was sitting here telling her she basically deserved more.

More than what? Because she was having a good time with the way things were going.

"Are you telling me you don't want to do this anymore?" she asked.

Because if that were the case, she'd have to respect his decision, but she didn't have to like it.

Cash shook his head. "That's not what I'm saying at all," he clarified. His hand stilled on the bottle. "I'm saying the exact opposite."

The exact opposite, as in . . .

Oh, wait. Jade reached for her wineglass and finished it off. She couldn't have heard him right. Cash was actually considering a relationship?

"Cash—"

"Crazy, right?"

He let out a nervous laugh. But Cash didn't get nervous . . . did he? All this was such new territory, she wasn't sure how to respond, or if he'd fully thought this through.

"I don't even know what to say," she mumbled as she stared at her empty glass. She'd love another, but she definitely needed a clear head for this conversation. "What exactly do you mean? You want a relationship? Like in public?"

He stared at her another minute before he picked up his bottle and cleared his throat. "You're right. We should keep things as they are. Forget I mentioned it."

When he scooted his seat back, Jade came to her feet first. "Oh, no," she demanded as she pointed across the table. Cash didn't move. "You don't get to do the whole passive-aggressive thing with me."

A corner of that wicked mouth kicked up in a grin. "I wouldn't dream of it, Red. I just laid a question out on the table and then took it back. Simple as that."

Simple? He thought mentioning a relationship with her was simple? Nothing about their setup was easy, yet she refused to let go. But a relationship? That word elicited a bit of panic, she wasn't going to lie.

She'd dated over the years, she'd even had a couple of boyfriends who were somewhat serious. None she ever thought of as long term. But Cash? He was a good time, no doubt about that. She honestly wasn't sure either of them were capable of a solid relationship, and two people floundering through the process didn't seem like a smart idea.

"Listen, I didn't initially invite you just to discuss this." Cash slowly came to his feet and rounded the table until he stood mere inches away. "But after not being able to touch you or even kiss you without thinking who would be watching, I thought we were both being cheated."

Jade reached out and laid a hand on his chest. "You're being logical on me. I didn't expect that."

Cash tipped his head and shrugged. "I'm more than just a pretty face, Red."

She couldn't help but laugh as she looped her arms around his neck. "Always so modest," she murmured against his lips. "How about we work on that chocolate cake and then rinse off in the hot tub?"

He palmed her backside and jerked her hips to his. "Sounds like you're being logical now."

When he covered her mouth with his, Jade realized they hadn't resolved anything really. His question, though he claimed to have pulled it back, was still out there, hovering in the air. She couldn't ignore it, and neither could he. At some point, they were going to have to figure out what all this meant, because now that he'd thrown down that gauntlet, she had to decide whether or not she should pick it up.

Chapter Thirteen

"Who's going to eat all these petit fours?" Jade asked as she surveyed the food table decorated in blue fluffy tulle to mimic clouds.

"I'll take them!" Piper raced to the table and stared up at Jade. "Can I?"

"I'm not sure Livie will think that's a good idea," Jade replied, tapping the adorable blonde on the tip of her nose. "But maybe you could take a couple and share them with your dad."

Melanie had taken Knox to the bedroom to nurse him while Jade and Livie cleaned up after the successful baby shower. They'd opted to have the event at Tanner and Melanie's house because that was easiest for Mel with the new baby.

"The trash is all out and the kitchen is clean," Livie said as she came back into the living room. "Don't even think of touching those cakes, young lady."

"I hope you're not talking to me," Jade joked.

"Jade said I could take a couple and share with Dad." Piper reached out and snagged two, then turned to Livie. "I promise to share."

Livie nodded and blew out a sigh. "That's fine, but let's get a paper plate to put them on so you don't have them all over my car. Jade, you can take the rest. I don't care where you take them, but they aren't going to my house, and Melanie said she didn't want them either."

Of course. Everybody was suddenly aware of their waistlines and Jade was stuck with the goodies.

She put the rest of the petit fours in the box they'd come in. What was she going to do with all of them? There were almost two dozen tiny cakes.

And looking at all that icing had Jade thrust back to last week, and chocolate cake and Cash's talented hands and mouth.

They still hadn't discussed a full-blown relationship. They both had gone on about their ways, keeping everything secretive where she'd sneak to his house and stay late, then leave before morning.

But she hadn't been able to shake that moment when he'd looked so insecure, so vulnerable when he'd voiced his thoughts about wanting more. No, he hadn't necessarily said that, he'd said she deserved more. Jade truly believed he meant that. She worried he felt he wasn't offering enough, but she'd never asked for more, and she certainly didn't expect it.

Cash was everything she needed at this moment in her life. He made her laugh, challenged her, threw her off guard in all the good ways, and was a complete gentleman in the midst of all that.

Melanie came back into the room holding a swaddled Knox. "Well, he's asleep again. Eat, sleep, poop. Babies have a simple cycle."

Jade put the bakery box on the table and glanced at her friend, who was still glowing over being a new mom. Mel and Livie had both found love and were mothers, and Jade couldn't help but wonder about her own future and whether motherhood would be on her path of life.

"Hey, you okay?" Melanie asked. She shifted to stand closer to Jade as she patted Knox's back. "You looked lost in thought."

Jade put each of the cakes back into the box. "I'm fine. Just thinking how much stuff you got. I can't believe one little person needs so many things."

Melanie glanced into the corner of her living room that was piled with boxes and clothes and toys and books. There were even little totes with Knox's name embroidered on them, which was seriously impressive, considering people had had less than a week to get those gifts together.

"It's a bit overwhelming," Melanie agreed, glancing down to the sleeping baby in her arms. "But he's so worth it. I never knew love like this."

Jade's throat clogged with emotion. She couldn't help but wonder what her birth mother had been like. Had she not wanted children at all, or had she been forced to give up her child? Maybe she couldn't afford kids and just wanted a better life.

At one time, Jade had thought about finding her birth mother but opted against it. She didn't want to intrude on someone's life who maybe didn't want the reminder from the past. Besides, Jade had a good life, she'd turned out just fine. Her mother may not have been the most loving—at all really—but Jade's nana was absolutely everything.

"Can I take baby stuff to the nursery room?" Piper came bouncing back into the room and headed straight to the toys. "I want to make it pretty for him."

"Honey, maybe Mel wants to do that," Livie said as she followed her daughter to the corner.

"She's fine." Melanie crossed the room and leaned over to where Piper was digging through the new toys. "You

can take whatever you want to Knox's room. That would
be a big help."

Jade had just put the lid on the box when her cell
vibrated in the pocket of her sundress. She'd been careful
to keep track of her phone, especially when she was with
others. Anytime she'd been in public, she'd made sure to
keep it in a pocket; she couldn't risk anyone seeing her
texts again.

As Piper and Livie carried things down the hall to the
nursery, Jade pulled out her cell and glanced at the screen.

> Your mother wants to come for a visit. I've tried
> holding her off, but . . . heads-up!

Jade read the message from her nana three times and
still couldn't process it. Why did her mother want to visit?
She hadn't shown interest in Haven since she left after
Jade's graduation.

Piper's giggle filtered down the hall, and Jade glanced
back to Melanie, who had taken a seat on the sofa and was
smiling down at Knox. Jade fired off her own frantic text,
because she didn't want her mother here.

> What does she want?

She slid the phone back in her pocket and finished
cleaning off the table. The box of pastries went into her
trunk and the tablecloths and décor were put into a storage
tote and placed by Livie's car.

Jade checked her phone again, but nothing. Nana
couldn't just drop that warning and then not give an explanation. Jade wondered why her mother hadn't bothered

calling or texting herself. Or maybe she was just discussing it and Nana had overheard.

Regardless, the fact that a trip to Haven was on Lana McKenzie's radar didn't sit well with Jade.

While she had her phone in hand, Jade pulled up Cash's. She squinted against the late-afternoon sun toward the porch and noted she was still alone.

> Would you rather me grab some wings and sandwiches from Taps or do you want me to get something to put on the grill?

She waited a minute, but he didn't respond, so she slid her phone back into her dress pocket and headed back into the house to tell her friends goodbye.

She and Cash didn't have set plans, but they never did. They'd just formed some unwritten pact that they'd spend every evening together. Dinners turned into conversations, and that rolled right into intimacy. Jade wasn't sorry they'd found their rhythm. Cash seemed just as happy as she was and, so far, none of their friends had a clue.

Jade stepped back into the house and ran right into Piper. The stack of little cardboard books clattered to the hardwood floor.

"Oh, honey, I'm sorry." Jade squatted down to help Piper gather the mess. "I didn't even see you there."

"Because I'm short and you're tall," Piper explained, as if that were the only answer.

Jade reached out to grab a book and her phone slid out of her pocket and vibrated on the floor. She picked up the book and reached for her phone, but not before Piper glanced over.

"Uncle Cash," she yelled. "Can I message him back?"

Jade risked looking over her shoulder, and of course

Livie stood there with one brow raised and her arms crossed over her chest.

"What?" Jade asked. "Don't give me that look."

Piper picked up the phone and waved it in Jade's face. "Can I?"

"Not right now," Jade answered, taking the phone. "My battery is running low."

Great. Now she was not only lying to her friends, she was lying to a little girl. She knew lies snowballed into a colossal disaster. She'd seen firsthand when she'd worked in Atlanta at the advertising firm and her jerk coworker tried to weasel his way out of getting caught sexually harassing her.

Not that Jade was in any way harming anyone, but still. Lying was wrong and she knew better.

Yet she couldn't stop herself. She didn't know what her friends would say. If they disapproved, she'd have to lie anyway, because she wasn't done seeing Cash. If they approved, she'd have to keep reminding them that she and Cash weren't an actual couple. They were just having fun.

Jade stacked the last of the books and came to her feet. "Here you go," she said, handing them over to Piper. "Once I get my phone charged, I'll tell Cash you said 'Hi.'"

"Tell him I have a friend at school and she needs a dad."

Livie rushed forward. "What is it with you trying to play matchmaker? Your friends' parents can find their own dates."

Piper frowned. "Well, they haven't yet. And if your friends marry my friends, then we can all be one family, and I can see my friends even more."

In the mind of a five-year-old, that was pretty logical thinking and a simple fix. In reality, there was no way in hell Jade was going to stand back and watch Cash date another woman.

Which some might say was a good indication that she was in deeper than she'd intended, but she didn't think so. They were merely not done having fun yet, that's all. Besides, they'd agreed to exclusivity.

And what was she even thinking this for? Piper wasn't actually going to set Cash up on a date.

"Go on and put those books in Knox's room," Livie ordered. "And make sure they're nice and neat. Take your time."

Once Piper was out of sight, Livie turned and leveled her gaze. "Seriously. What's going on with you and Cash?"

"What?" Melanie exclaimed from the couch.

Jade glanced her way and shook her head. "Don't listen to Livie. She's reading too much into this."

"Am I?" Livie retorted. "First there's the rather descriptive texts about food and your body and what he'd like to do with both, and now he's texting you again. Care to share with the class what he said?"

"What's going on?" Melanie exclaimed as she slowly came to her feet and crossed the room. "I'm busy having a baby and you and Cash are, well, busy doing other things."

"No, that's not it at all," Jade insisted, though that was exactly the case.

All of this had snowballed into more than she was willing to get into. She put her cell back into her pocket and crossed her arms as she shifted her focus directly to her friends.

"Listen, Cash texts me now and then." Truth. "We annoy each other, but we've learned to just deal with it because we're so opposite." Truth. "But nothing is going on. Nothing." Lie, lie, lie.

Jade didn't back down, she didn't look away, and she sure as hell didn't smile. If her friends ever found out that she'd lied to them . . . well, they could never find out. She loved Mel and Livie with her whole heart and considered them family, closer than any sisters she ever could've had.

When they remained silent, Jade forged on. "He still wants me to work at his gym. In fact, he came to my class over in Olive Hill last week."

Melanie laughed, but when Knox stirred in her arms, she started swaying back and forth and patting him again.

"I so wished I could've seen that," Melanie said in a softer tone. "How did he do?"

"Not bad, surprisingly." Jade was still impressed that he'd come all that way and tried everything, succeeding at most of it. "He's persistent. I know he has the clientele; I just worry what will happen when we irritate each other one too many times and I can't work there anymore."

Livie smoothed her blond hair over one shoulder and clasped her hands together. "I don't think that will happen."

"You're joking," Melanie said as she turned to Livie. "Have you been in the room with those two? They pick at everything."

Livie shook her head. "They're both professional and passionate about what they do. I actually think, business-wise, the move would be smart."

"So you're Team Cash?" Jade asked.

"I am," Livie stated with a smile. "You could always offer a class at his gym one day a week. See how it goes."

She could, but that would mean more time with him in public, and they really needed as much privacy as possible. Cash had told her he had a difficult time holding back his feelings when they were out in the same place. Jade couldn't lie: it was quite difficult to see him, talk to him, but not touch or kiss him.

"I'll think about it," Jade said after a minute.

Then she shifted the conversation because she couldn't handle more Cash talk and because there was other business to attend to.

"Sophie said the pamphlets are done," Jade told them. "Even though they were shipped to her office and we're holding the event there, I wanted to see them beforehand. I'm going to pick them up tomorrow, and I'll make sure you guys see them first. Sophie also has a nice stand we can set them in for the open house."

Via text over several days, they'd all managed to narrow down the design. Thankfully, a small printing press in town made their order top priority for a small fee, and the marketing portion was in full swing. They had the fliers advertising the open house and the pamphlets to hand to each guest who came through the doors. Plus, several online ads and their own social media page were set up, thanks to Melanie.

With her resources, hopefully this new business venture would take off. Online marketing would be key in spreading the word. Also, Melanie had written up several option statements to send out to film crews, film agents, and some HR companies in LA. Maybe nothing would come of the informative letters she'd drafted and sent, but perhaps they would lead to bigger things.

"Perfect," Melanie replied with a wide smile. "I can't wait for this mock open house. I really think it's going to be a success and generate even more buzz around the grand opening."

That was their hope.

"I also talked to my friend in Atlanta, and the 3-D

model is nearly done, so I'll head there over the weekend and get that."

"Liam Monroe has graciously offered to donate baked goods and some finger foods for the event," Livie added. "Which will also help out their business, but that was so generous."

Liam Monroe and his brothers' women's-only resort and spa was in memory of their late sister, who'd had those plans in mind. The guys had been extremely successful, and Liam was not only the cook at the resort but also ran the café they'd opened just last year. The café was open to the public, but the resort always seemed to be booked months in advance.

"Sounds like this is all coming together," Jade stated.

Her cell vibrated in her pocket once again. Whether it was Nana or Cash, either one would have to wait. There was no way she'd risk pulling out her phone again, not when she'd just gotten them on another topic.

"Only ten more days." Livie beamed. "It's really all happening."

Her voice cracked on that last word and her eyes filled. "Sorry. I just wish Dad was here to see all this unfolding."

Jade reached out and wrapped her arm around Livie's shoulders. "I'm sure he's looking down on you and Jax and he's so happy you guys not only found happiness with each other but also are taking his business into a new era."

Livie nodded and swiped beneath her eyes. "I'm a bit emotional," she said, glancing from Jade to Melanie. "This probably isn't the right time to announce this, but—"

"They're all fixed," Piper exclaimed as she skipped back down the hall. She stopped and stared up at Livie. "Why is she crying?"

Jade stared at Livie as well, because she'd been about

to say something and then stopped. She glanced at Melanie, who had wide eyes and a big smile.

"Tell me it's what I'm thinking," Melanie said and wiggled Knox in her arms.

Livie nodded, but looked down at Piper. "There's so much going on right now, and with everything still so new, we're just taking it day by day before, well . . ."

It was all Jade could do not to explode and scream and wrap both arms around her friend.

So she pulled back and nodded, but couldn't prevent the smile from overtaking her. "I understand. You guys are smart and so lucky."

Livie nodded. "We definitely are."

"Well, this is all so exciting," Melanie stated. "And there's never a wrong time to discuss . . . um, airport renovations."

"I'm going to be a pilot when I grow up," Piper said, then took off with her arms spread wide as she mimicked a plane. She raced through the living room and down the hall.

"How far along are you?" Jade whispered. "I assume Jax knows?"

Livie nodded and glanced toward the hall, then back to her friends. "I'm nine weeks and I just told him a few days ago. But with Melanie delivering and the shower, I didn't want to ruin her moment."

"This definitely does not ruin anything," Melanie countered. "Happy news always comes at just the right time."

Livie laughed and shook her head. "When I told him, he was so happy. Then he wanted to know if he was getting another plane. Always the smart-ass, but I love him."

Jade couldn't be happier for her friends. When Livie had proposed to Jax, she'd bought him a plane. It was no wonder the man wondered what his next gift would be.

Her phone vibrated again just as Piper came back down the hall, still in plane mode.

"I really need to be going," she told her friends. "I'm so happy for both of you. Really. The move here has been the best decision we've ever made."

"I agree," Melanie said.

Livie wrapped one arm around Jade's shoulders and her other arm around Melanie's. "I love you guys. I don't know how I could do all this without you."

"Well, you won't have to find out, because we're not going anywhere," Jade said as she leaned her head against Livie.

Livie shifted back and dropped her arms. "Which reminds me, Jax and I came up with a price if you're still interested in the house."

Jade nodded. "I am."

"Great. How about I swing by later and we talk?"

Considering she wouldn't be home later, that would be a problem, but she couldn't exactly tell Livie that.

"I need to run a few errands," Jade replied. "Let me call you when I get home. That work?"

"Sure thing."

Jade said her goodbyes and even snagged a hug and a kiss from the minipilot before she headed out. Not until she was safely in her car did she pull out her phone and check her messages. Both Nana and Cash had replied. Her mother was indeed planning a surprise visit and Cash said he had dinner for them.

Jade pushed aside the thought of her mother coming to town; maybe she'd outgrow the idea.

Instead, she focused on Cash and told him she was running by her house first and then she'd be right there. He'd made dinner for her even though he'd worked at the gym that morning and had gone to the airport to help lay the new flooring. Anyway they could cut corners and save money, they were doing it. So the guys all had been there during the baby shower.

Jade went straight to her house and gathered a few things. Just because he'd made dinner didn't mean she couldn't make dessert. She'd seen something on Mel's blog the other day and had thought it sounded perfect for an evening out on the patio with a glass of wine.

Cash had been keeping her favorite stocked in his fridge because she'd been there every night. Their routine worked for them, and as the sun started sinking on the horizon, Jade couldn't help but wonder if she did want more. Maybe Cash had been on to something when he'd mentioned a relationship. Maybe they could give it a try.

Nerves raced all through her as she put her wine and ingredients for dessert into her canvas shopping bag. What would he say if she confronted him and told him she wanted to go for it?

Jade had to suppress a giggle as she headed toward her back door. A giggle. How juvenile and girlie was that? She never giggled, let alone over a man.

But Cash was different, and if anyone warranted a schoolgirl-crush giggle, it was that man.

Just as she hoisted the tote up onto her shoulder, the doorbell rang. Jade froze. There was no way her mother could've gotten here so fast from Atlanta. So who was at her front door?

If Brad thought he could just drop by whenever, she was going to have to set him straight once and for all.

Jade sat her bag, purse, and keys back on the island, then headed down the hall toward the front door. With the porch lights on a timer, the front of the house was already lit up. She couldn't tell who was out there as she got closer.

Sneaking toward the sidelight, Jade shifted so she could catch a peek of the visitor.

"Hurry up before someone sees me," Cash yelled through the door.

Jade quickly reached for the dead bolt and jerked the door open. "What are you doing here?" she scolded as she reached out and grabbed his shirt to pull him inside.

He held a large brown bag in one hand and had a white plastic bag hanging from his other arm. "Relax," he told her. "Nobody saw me."

For the first time since she'd known him, Cash had on a black baseball hat with his gym logo right in the front. The bill had been pulled low to shield his eyes. Something about the unruly hair sticking below the hat and the dark beard made him seem even more mysterious and sexy. There was something rugged and careless about this look.

Suddenly, Jade wasn't so hungry anymore.

Chapter Fourteen

Cash had taken a chance coming here without telling her, but he'd been out getting food when she said she was running home, so . . . here he was.

And that look in her eyes had him feeling pretty confident in his decision.

"I do like the way you're looking at me, Red, but can I set this stuff down before you ravage me?"

Jade rolled her eyes and motioned toward the hallway. "You know where the kitchen is, and I wasn't going to ravage you."

"No?" he asked, easing past her. "Those traveling eyes and the way you licked your lips must not have gotten that message."

He headed to the kitchen and put everything on the dining table. "I wasn't sure what you wanted from Taps, so I grabbed a little bit of everything."

Jade stepped up beside him and crooked a finger over the edge of the brown bag. "If that's their beer cheese and warm pretzels, I'm going to be the happiest girl."

"I hear it pairs well with tiny baby shower cakes."

She stopped looking in the sack and turned those sultry green eyes on him. "Where did you park?"

Again with the worrying about who would see. He was

used to this game. He didn't like it, but this was part of the deal.

"I parked against the garage in the alley behind the house," he told her. "I couldn't get your gate open with my hands full or I would've just come to the back door."

Jade turned and tapped the bill of his hat. "I like this. You look . . ."

Cash quirked a brow, waiting on her to finish.

"I don't want to give you any more compliments," she said on a laugh. "You already think enough of yourself for both of us."

Cash shrugged. "I wasn't going for any type of look when I threw this on. I had it in the truck, and when I left Taps, I put it on so I could, hopefully, walk to your door and not draw too much attention."

"Yet it has your gym logo on it," she reminded him.

Cash snaked his arms around her waist, settled his hands on her backside, and pulled her in to him. "If someone was close enough to see the logo, they'd be close enough to see my face."

Jade scowled, then rested her hands on his chest. "I suppose," she said, looking at where her hands rested before finally looking up at him. "I know you just bought all this, but I was wondering something."

"What's that?" he asked as he leaned in just a bit closer.

A smile spread across her face, and he wanted nothing more than to kiss that pale pink lipstick off those full lips.

"Would you rather take the food upstairs to the bedroom or just have your wicked way with me here?"

Cash's body stirred at her options. "Either way, the food is going to wait."

"That's a given."

His fingers were already moving, gathering her dress

and bunching it up. "I'm not so sure I can make it upstairs. I had to walk so far from the car to get here."

Jade slid her hands beneath his shirt, her fingernails raking across his abs and around to his back. "You do look tired. You've worked so hard all day and you managed dinner. I think you deserve a reward."

"Oh, I definitely do," he agreed.

Jade laughed again. He loved that sound. Loved even more that he was the one who elicited such happiness.

In a fury of hands, clothes fell to the floor, and Jade's wide smile and bright eyes only added to the playfulness. Cash couldn't believe Jade stood in her kitchen completely naked. Before getting intimate with her, he never would've guessed her to be so carefree and spur-of-the-moment.

Of course, maybe he brought this side of her out.

Cash kicked aside the pile of clothes and shoes and grabbed the back of a kitchen chair and took a seat. He stared up at the most beautiful sight.

Jade gloriously reveled in her perfect shape, her dark red hair spilling over her shoulders, a flush to her skin from arousal.

"I like how you look at me, Flex." She took a step forward to stand between his legs. "Makes me wonder what's going on in that mind of yours."

He gripped her hips and eased forward to slide his lips across her abdomen. Jade's fingers threaded through his hair.

Without a word, he guided her closer, gripping the back of one thigh and then the other until she straddled his lap.

Cash slid his hands back up over her hips and settled on the dip in her waist. He shifted in the chair and tipped back his head, making sure to keep his attention solely on her.

Those delicate hands came to his shoulders as she

locked eyes with him and slowly lowered her body until
they were joined.

Her sharp intake of breath and the arch of her back as
she stilled against him had Cash sliding his hands on up to
cup her breasts. The moan escaped her and added fuel
to the raging fire.

He jerked his hips, and Jade started working with him,
then she leaned down and covered his mouth. Cash freed
his hands from between them and reached around to hold
on to her backside. The way Jade could make love to his
mouth, his body, and still make him want more was absolutely insane. But there had never been a moment since
he'd started seeing her secretly that Cash ever felt he had
enough. Every second with her left him aching for more.

The ends of her hair tickled his hands. He gripped her
body with one hand and reached to fist a handful of that
thick hair. He gave a slight tug until she lifted her mouth
from his. He pulled slightly more until she arched further
against him, offering up her breasts at the perfect level.

Cash wasted no time in covering one nipple. Jade cried
out, her hips working faster against him, her fingertips
digging into his shoulders.

She panted his name, something else he'd never tire of
hearing. When her entire body tightened, Cash lifted his
head and stared up at her, not wanting to miss a moment
of her passion, her release.

Just watching as she squeezed her eyes, bit down on her
lip, and continued to work that sweet body against him
had Cash losing complete control and following her. The
climax overtook him, but he never stopped looking at her.
Finally, she brought her gaze to his, and there was something he saw that he hadn't before. Something he couldn't
label, but his body still shook with tremors and he was
floating in that postcoital state.

Jade wrapped her arms around him and leaned down over him, resting her cheek against the top of his head. Her breathing came out in erratic beats, right in rhythm with his own. Her heartbeat thudded against his chest and sweat dampened her skin.

She started to shift, and that was when he heard it. A crack from beneath him. Another crack echoed through the room, and before he could push her off, the chair beneath him gave way and dumped them both to the floor.

Cash instinctively wrapped his arms around Jade, but her laughter in his ear was a clear sign she was fine. His ass, on the other hand, was not.

"Are you all right?" she asked between fits of giggles.

He shifted beneath her, careful not to let any of the broken wooden chair scrape his very important, *very bare*, parts.

"I'm fine," he grumbled.

Jade eased off him and moved aside as she sank onto her heels and rested her hands on her thighs. "Wow. I can honestly say you've been quite a few firsts for me."

Cash lifted himself up and turned to see the splintered chair. "Oh yeah?" he asked, then turned his focus back to her. "Such as?"

Her hair was a complete wreck, that lipstick he'd vowed to kiss off had vanished, smudges of mascara had settled beneath her eyes, but she continued to smile as if this were the greatest moment of her life.

"I've never broken furniture before," she claimed. "I never had near-drunken shower sex, a secret fling, or been in an emergency landing. I've also never introduced any guy to my mother. I'm not sure if that makes you lucky or cursed."

He listened to her ramble on. They sat on her kitchen

floor totally naked with broken chair parts around them like this was a perfectly normal way to carry on a conversation.

Once she was done ticking off her boxes of firsts with him, Cash got to his feet and extended his hand to help her up. He made sure to angle her away from the splinters of wood that had shot across the floor.

"I hope this wasn't an antique from Livie's great-grandmother or something," Cash said.

Jade laughed again. "It wasn't, but I do believe it's been here since Livie was a kid. Not an heirloom, though."

"Where's the broom and I'll get this cleaned up?"

Jade glanced around the floor, then went to retrieve his clothes. He thought she was gearing up to kick him out, but she slid the T-shirt over her head and handed him his running shorts.

"I can't concentrate when we're both naked," she told him.

He raked his eyes over her very fine form. "Well, I can't concentrate when you're wearing my clothes."

She rolled her eyes and shook her head, then tiptoed carefully around the island and to the hallway. Jade got into the closet and pulled out a trash bag, a broom, and a dustpan.

"I can get it," she told him. "Why don't you take the food over to the counter? I have paper plates, or we can eat out of the containers."

He met her at the entryway and took the cleaning items from her hands. "I'll get this and I can bring you the food. Go in and have a seat on the couch. Or go on up to the bedroom. I kind of like the idea of eating in that fancy bed of yours while you're wearing my shirt."

Jade's face flushed once again. "I'll let you clean this, but I'll get the food and take it upstairs."

"There's wine and beer in the plastic sack," he told her as he started gathering the large pieces of the chair.

"My sack on the island has those cakes and some wine. Bring it when you're done."

He threw a glance over his shoulder. "That's going to be quite a bit of food and drink. How long are you planning on keeping me up there?"

Jade flashed him a naughty grin. "Would you rather keep up your stamina or not be able to fulfill my needs because you need sustenance?"

His body already started stirring. "We'll take all of it," he commanded.

As she gathered everything, Cash finished bagging up the pieces and sweeping the smaller splinters. Jade's cell chimed on the island just as she'd gathered everything in her hands.

Cash leaned over to stare at the screen. "It's Livie."

Jade's eyes widened. "I told her I'd call so she could come over. Damn it."

"I can hold the phone to your ear," he offered. "I won't say a word."

Jade nodded, and Cash picked up the phone, swiped the screen, and held it up to her ear.

"Hey, Livie," Jade said, the smile on her face strained, but the happiness came through in her tone. "I forgot to call. I've been busy."

Jade stared at him as she listened to her friend. "Actually, tonight might not be the best. My stomach is cramping something awful."

There were things Cash didn't need to know, and even

though she was lying, he still didn't want to hear about stomach cramps.

"Yeah, I think I'm just going to go to bed early," she added.

Cash wiggled his brows and smiled. When Jade mouthed *stop*, he couldn't help but do it again. She pursed her lips to keep from laughing.

With her full hands and her attention focused on Livie, Cash couldn't help but have a little more fun—and she was standing there in his shirt, so how was a man to resist?

Cash reached out and slid a hand up the side of her thigh and beneath the hem of the shirt. He glanced up to see her eyes widen, laughter and passion colliding in her gaze.

"Listen, Livie, can I call you tomorrow? I need to get to the bathroom."

Cash narrowed his eyes and Jade stuck out her tongue. "Okay. Bye."

Cash pulled the phone away and disconnected the call. "You're gross."

Jade merely laughed. "I had to do something to get her off the phone. You said she wouldn't know you were here."

"No, I said I wouldn't say anything, and I didn't." He set the phone back on the island. "You'd better get upstairs before I decide to lay you out on this island. I'd hate to break that, too."

Shaking her head, Jade headed toward the staircase off the kitchen. This old, Southern home was quite stunning and had aged well. Cash loved the charm and simplicity of the place.

He loved watching Jade's body shift beneath his shirt even more.

As much as he'd teased her about the call with Livie,

another part of him hated that they were being so deceitful. What had started in Nashville as fun and flirty had filtered over into their daily lives. They weren't just hooking up randomly every now and then; they were in a relationship.

Whether she wanted to admit it or not, whether either of them were ready for what this meant, there would be no dancing around this bold fact for much longer. Because as much as they tried to keep this about sex—and they'd done a stellar job at that—so much more had happened. Each day seemed to bind them closer and closer.

Cash took out the trash, thankful the can was just off the porch of the fenced-in yard where nobody could see him. Then he carried out the larger pieces that didn't fit in the sack.

Once he'd locked the doors, front and back, he grabbed her bag and her cell. He mounted the back steps toward her bedroom. Night had fallen, and he just wondered if this would be the night they made it all the way through without a walk of shame before the sun came up.

Empty boxes lay open all over Jade's king-size bed. Her stomach was full and she was starting to feel the warmth of the wine. Combine that with the man across from her staring back like she was his entire world and Jade considered herself pretty damn lucky.

She didn't know how her life had circled back to Haven and now to Cash, but she wasn't the least bit sorry.

"You look like you're about one glass away from great shower sex," Cash stated as he flashed that naughty grin.

"I don't think you'll need to give me anymore wine to get me in that shower," she replied, taking the last sip from her glass. "I'm pretty easy when it comes to you."

One dark brow quirked. "Is that right?"

Jade shifted and set her glass on her nightstand, then turned back and started gathering their garbage and putting it back in the brown bag.

"That was probably the best meal I've had in a long time," she told him. "I'm kind of glad you decided to surprise me here."

"Despite the broken chair?"

Jade shot a glance his way. "Even with the broken chair."

He picked up his own mess, and once they had the bed cleared off, Cash reached for her hands and tugged her until she sat closer to him. She extended her legs to rest over his thighs and trail behind him.

"I've been thinking," he started, hating the nerves in his stomach or the fact that he was risking too much by bringing this up. "I want to tell you about my dad."

Jade's eyes widened. "That's not where I thought you were going when you pulled me over."

"Yeah, well, you bring out a different side of me."

And she did. He'd never wanted to tell anyone about his father. Not that Cash was embarrassed, but he did have pride, and he also wanted to protect his dad. The man didn't want to be trapped in his own living hell. He hadn't purposely set out to destroy years of time with his son, but he'd done it just the same.

She reached up and framed his face with her delicate hands. When she made such sweet, simple gestures, Cash couldn't help the stirrings that shifted through him. He couldn't help but wonder where they were going and what she wanted to come from this.

"I'll listen to anything you want to say," she told him, her eyes holding his. "But don't feel like you have to."

Cash reached up and circled her wrists. He knew he wasn't obligated to tell her anything; she'd offered to help the one time, but she hadn't pressed.

"My mother passed away in a car accident when I was young," he started. He didn't release her, as if holding on to her gave him the extra boost of strength he needed. "When it was just Dad and me, I thought we did okay. But each year that passed, I started seeing him decline. I didn't realize at first what was going on. Maybe I was too busy with my life and selfishly didn't want my dad not to be perfect hero material. I don't know. But one day he didn't show for one of my football games, and it was senior night. When I got home, I was so pissed. As soon as I stepped through the door, though, I found him passed out on the sofa with an empty whiskey bottle at his feet."

He could still see the image, still feel the fear and rage in that seventeen-year-old boy.

"For a split-second, I didn't know if he was dead, too," Cash went on. He glanced down to where the hem of his shirt hit Jade's bare thighs. "The booze became a problem, until one day I realized there were bigger problems."

Pulling in a shaky breath, he glanced back up to her and eased her hands between them as he held on. "He decided the alcohol wasn't numbing the pain enough, so he added in a few painkillers here and there. Anything to help him cope. Her birthday, their anniversary, the date she died . . . he had a reason for needing his pills on any given day."

Unshed tears formed in Jade's eyes, but she never looked away. She sat there, dressed in his shirt, wrapped all around him, taking in his pain.

This was why he wanted to let her in. Jade was part of him, she was his soul, his heart. There was no use trying to ignore his feelings because everything in him loved this woman.

But if he dropped that on her now, he figured she'd scurry right off this bed and put up some protective shield.

So he kept the thoughts to himself, and because he needed her, he needed her support. Besides, he needed to get used to love. He'd thought he'd been in love once, but that had turned out to be a lie because what he felt for his ex was absolutely nothing compared to all the feelings he had for Jade.

"You know I was married once," he added. Might as well tell her everything, because at some point he was going to have to address the fact that he'd fallen in love with her. He needed her to be well aware of where he came from.

"Not long, though. Right?" Jade asked.

Cash shook his head. "I thought we were it for each other. I mean, we were compatible in bed, so what else did a newly married couple need?"

Jade squeezed his hands. "Considering you're in my bed, let's keep your ex out."

Cash smiled at her playful tone. One tear slipped down her cheek and he reached up, swiping it away with the pad of his thumb.

"I just want you to be clear that I wasn't in love with her." He rejoined their hands and eased her a little closer. "When things started really going all to hell with Dad, she couldn't handle it. I'm not sure if it was me being called at all hours of the night and day to come to his place, or when I had him come live with us so I could keep a better eye on him, or if she was embarrassed the first time we had to take him to rehab. Who knows? I didn't ask, because if she couldn't handle all that, she wasn't for me."

Jade scooted until she couldn't get any closer, then she circled his waist with her legs and looped her arms around his neck.

"I'm sorry you had to go through that alone," she told

him. "I know Jax and Tanner were here, but I'm guessing you were stubborn and tried to do everything yourself."

Oh, how well she knew him.

"Not stubborn," he corrected, resting his hands on her thighs. "I just didn't want to burden them with my problem."

"Like I said. Stubborn."

Maybe he was, but at least she knew what she'd gotten in to. She deserved to know everything if he was going to declare his newfound feelings.

"After the divorce, I swore I wouldn't let myself get caught up with another woman." He rested his forehead against hers. "And then we went to Nashville."

Jade laughed and eased back. "I think that trip took both of us by surprise."

Cash studied her, really tried to see this from her point of view. She hadn't wanted a committed relationship any more than he had. But she was still here, and that wedding had been weeks ago.

For someone who technically pushed through life on her own, Jade was the most remarkable woman he'd ever met. Every day he got to know more and more about her made him want to spend more time with her.

Cash wanted to know all her secrets . . . he didn't want to just *be* the secret.

"I shouldn't have gotten angry with you the day you answered my phone," he said. "I wasn't ready to share that part of my life."

Jade's soft smile never failed to deliver that punch of arousal. "What made you so ready now?"

If only she knew . . .

Cash slid his hands beneath the shirt and found her bare. "I'm done talking."

She wiggled her hips, putting her directly in line with his. "And you conveniently cleared the bed."

In a swift move, he had the shirt up and flung across the room. "You should know something," he said as he dipped his head to trail his lips across her shoulder and down to her breast.

"What's that?" she panted, arching against him.

Cash lifted his gaze and met hers. "I'm staying the night."

Jade fisted his hair and pulled his mouth to hers. "Yes."

Chapter Fifteen

Jade hadn't slept much, but she hadn't asked Cash to leave either. He'd said he was staying the night and, for once, she hadn't wanted to counter.

Sunlight slipped through the slit in the curtains and Jade glanced to the antique clock on her nightstand. Seven. They'd finally fallen asleep so late, nearly two in the morning after Cash had given her a full-body massage that inevitably ended up with another round of lovemaking.

And that was exactly what they'd been doing.

Jade shifted beneath the heavy arm across her chest and attempted to slide out of bed. She'd never had a man sleep over before—not even when she lived in Atlanta. The few boyfriends she'd had always left, and she never invited them to stay.

So, while waking up with someone beside her should feel strange, Jade felt oddly . . . right.

She managed to move slowly enough to ease out of bed and grabbed Cash's T-shirt from the floor. After pulling it on and flipping out her hair, she couldn't help but take in the sight of such a magnificent man sprawled out across her white sheets and duvet. The darkness of his tanned skin, the black ink, the unkempt dark hair, and all of those defined muscles should look out of place.

Jade smiled as she wrapped her arms around herself. Cash belonged here. He belonged in her bed. She'd been moving toward this epiphany for a while now. Ever since he'd brought up the possibility of a relationship, she'd been rolling the idea over in her mind.

No matter how many times she ran every moment through her head, she came to the same conclusion. She'd fallen for Cash Miller, and never in a million years would she have believed someone had they told her this was the man she'd ultimately want in her life.

Cash shifted beneath the sheet, which only covered him to his waist. He settled and let out a slight snore. Jade knew she had it bad when a snoring man made her smile.

Deciding to let him sleep, Jade tiptoed from the room and pulled the door to close behind her. She headed down the back staircase and into the kitchen. The table with three chairs made her laugh as she passed it and went directly to the coffeepot. She needed caffeine and food.

This morning she'd be skipping her fresh greens in the blender. A man like Cash would want something of substance for breakfast, so she pulled out bacon and eggs. Once she had the griddle plugged in and the surface hot, she proceeded to fry the bacon and whip up some scrambled eggs.

She sipped her coffee as she prepared the meal. The creak on the steps had her smiling before she glanced over her shoulder.

Oh my. Cash first thing in the morning wearing nothing but tattoos, messy hair, and black boxer briefs was enough of a reason to have him spending more nights. She could definitely get used to waking up to such a glorious sight in the mornings. Who needed coffee or an alarm clock to jump-start their day with Cash as a motivator?

"I was thinking of making you breakfast in bed."

She turned back to the griddle so the bacon and eggs didn't burn. That man and the promising look in his dark eyes could make her lose focus quicker than anything.

"If you want to have a seat in one of the three chairs we have left, the food will be ready soon."

"You could have woken me up," he told her in a gravelly morning voice that made her want to forget breakfast and see what other furniture they could destroy.

"You seemed so relaxed."

She flipped the bacon and turned down the heat on that side. After pulling off the scrambled eggs, she whisked up a few more and slowly poured them onto the hot griddle.

His bare feet slid over the hardwood floors and her skin prickled as he inched closer. Jade wasn't at all surprised when his arms banded around her midsection and buried his face in the crook of her neck.

"I didn't expect you to make me breakfast," he murmured. His warm breath tickled, and Jade leaned slightly into him. "I would've been happy with those baby shower cakes."

Jade slid the bacon off onto a paper plate lined with paper towels to absorb the grease. "We can have breakfast dessert," she told him as she removed the second batch of eggs.

"I like how you think, Red."

She glanced over her shoulder and smiled. "Why don't you pour the coffee?"

He smacked her lips with his, then swatted her rear end. "Don't you typically run in the morning?" he asked.

When he started searching for mugs, Jade pointed to the cabinet closest to the fridge. "I do, but some things are worth missing a good run."

As she set the two plates on the kitchen table, Cash

laughed behind her. Jade turned and saw him holding up two coffee mugs.

"I know these aren't your style," he said with a smirk.

She laughed at the witty sayings. "No. Those belonged to Livie's dad. He had quite a few of them. We also found T-shirts and hats with equally offhand pilot humor."

When they sat down to eat, Cash kept the mug with an image on the front of a plane that said, "Large Cockpit" and she ended up with the one that said "Pilots: Looking Down on People Since 1903."

"You may not get me to leave if you're going to cook." He scooped up a bite of eggs and followed it with bacon. "But I don't do those green smoothies, so don't try that with me."

"I bet I can convince you of a great many things," she told him, extending her leg and sliding her bare foot up his leg. "You may just fall in love with my green smoothies."

He didn't smile like she thought he would. Instead his eyes darkened as his lids lowered just enough to remind her of that moment just before he let go completely in bed.

"Maybe it's not the smoothies I want to fall in love with."

Jade's heart thudded heavily in her chest, her breath caught in her throat. Cash didn't move, didn't look away. He simply sat there staring at her as if he was waiting on some reply . . . and she didn't have a clue what that would be.

She'd been venturing into these feelings of love, but that had all just been inside her own head. She hadn't known what he was feeling or where he stood really. They'd been so careful not to mention such things.

And now that he'd thrown out that large chunk of his thoughts, Jade didn't know what to do. This was all well and good when it was just sex. Then everything progressed into a little more, then a little more. Now they were sharing breakfast at the kitchen table like it was the most normal thing in the world . . . only it wasn't.

She'd never shared breakfast with anyone. Not even growing up. They didn't do family meals unless there was a party.

There was so much to take in with Cash looking at her like he still wanted her to say something. She had too many words, but none of them seemed right. Maybe because now that she knew how he felt, she wasn't quite ready to admit it. Because everything had changed and Jade was absolutely terrified.

"Cash—"

The doorbell rang, cutting off her thoughts.

"Ignore it," he insisted.

On one hand, she welcomed the interruption because she wasn't quite sure what she'd been about to say. On the other, she wanted to ignore the surprise visitor. Jade didn't want the outside world to interrupt . . . not now, when this was quite possibly the most important conversation they'd ever have.

Not to mention they were still secretive, and she wasn't expecting anyone at noon on a Sunday. Unless it was—

Jade jumped up. "What if that's Livie?" she exclaimed. "She wanted to talk last night. Maybe she's checking on me. I left my phone upstairs. If she texted and I didn't answer . . ."

Cash reached for her hand. "Ignore the doorbell," he repeated. "You don't have to answer it."

The ring pierced through the house again.

Jade pulled her hand from his. "I'll sneak and look out the window. You stay here."

She turned from his disappointed gaze and tiptoed down the hallway. Jade didn't even care how ridiculous she probably looked, sneaking through her own home wearing nothing but Cash's T-shirt.

As she neared the entryway, she squinted to see through the etched sidelight. A woman. A tall woman. Jade inched closer to the front of the house and caught a glimpse through a small square in the glass that wasn't etched. That two-inch section gave Jade all she needed to know.

Her mother stood on Jade's porch.

Muttering a string of curses under her breath, Jade jumped when her mother knocked. There was no ignoring Lana McKenzie. That woman was relentless in everything. Hadn't Nana warned Jade her mother wanted to surprise her? Jade just didn't think her mother would be here this soon, but she sure as hell was surprised.

She threw a look over her shoulder, eyeing the hallway where Cash stood at the other end. With his arms crossed over his bare chest, and standing proudly wearing only his underwear, Jade knew this wasn't going to be a smooth reunion.

Who is it? he mouthed.

My mother.

His eyes widened. *I'll stay out of sight.*

Jade didn't have time to think or to apologize. She turned back to the door and smoothed a hand down the front of Cash's T-shirt.

Nothing she could do about her appearance now.

Jade flicked the dead bolt and instantly received the shocked, judgmental stare of Lana McKenzie. Her eyes traveled over Jade's lack of attire and bedhead.

"Good heavens, Jade, really." Her mother pushed through and entered the foyer. "It's noon. Why are you dressed like that? Are you sick?"

"It's great to see you, too, Mother," Jade said, her tone dripping with sarcasm. "Won't you come in?"

"I thought we could have a girls' day." Lana spun back to face Jade. "I wanted to surprise you, do something nice. I could tell at the wedding you'd been having a difficult time and I realize some of that may be my fault."

Confused, Jade crossed her arms over her chest. "Difficult time?" she repeated. "I've been having an amazing time here, Mom."

A clang came from the back of the house and Jade stilled, refusing to even glance that way. She kept her eyes on her mom, who immediately shifted her attention.

"What was that?"

"What was what?" Jade asked.

Her mom pointed down the hallway. "That noise. Oh, you don't have a cat, do you? Those things can be so filthy."

Jade made a mental note to get a shelter cat tomorrow.

"I don't have any pets." Yet. "What did you have in mind for girls' day?"

Not that she wanted to spend the day with her mom, but she needed to get Lana out of the house.

"I've heard so much about that quaint little spa those troublesome Monroe boys opened." She patted the side of her blond hair, as if something could ever be out of place in that slicked-back bun. "I must say, all my friends have checked it out and I thought we could go get massages and eat at their little café after."

Jade sighed and attempted to smooth her hair away from her face and over her shoulders. "Mom, Bella Vous is booked up months in advance."

Her mother's brows attempted to draw in, but years of Botox prevented too much movement. "Nonsense," her mother claimed, waving a hand in the air. "We can just call. Aren't you friends with them or something?"

"No matter if I know them or not, they have appointments and guests. Just because I call doesn't magically make something open simply because you want it to."

Her mother pursed her glossy pink lips together. "Well, I'm sure we could call and at least check. If not today, then in the next few days."

Wait . . . what?

"Days?" Jade repeated, hoping she'd misunderstood.

"I plan on staying for a couple of days." Her mother smiled and adjusted her clutch beneath her arm. "I didn't drive all this way to just turn around and go home. I think it's time we visit."

Why now? Nana hadn't warned her about an extended visit. Too bad her nana couldn't have come as well. At least things might not seem so awkward. Jade had nothing in common with her mother and to spend an entire day with her would be rather uncomfortable.

"You came by yourself and plan on staying, but you didn't think to call to give me a heads-up?"

"Honey, I'm your mother. I figured I was always welcome here."

Jade sighed and crossed her arms. "You are, Mom."

As much as they rubbed each other the wrong way, as much as Jade just didn't connect with the woman, she was still her mother, and there was a reason she was here extending the olive branch. Jade just couldn't figure out why after all these years.

"Mom—"

The back door opened and closed. Jade stilled. Had Cash left? He wasn't even trying to be quiet.

"Oh my word!"

Livie's high-pitched squeal from the kitchen had Jade cringing and closing her eyes, wishing she could go back to when Cash told her to ignore the doorbell. Why hadn't she listened? They could've snuck back upstairs and kept the rest of the world shut out just like they'd been doing.

But Jade knew all this had to come to an end at some point. She just hadn't planned on this scenario.

"Cash! What are you . . . Where are your clothes?"

Livie's shocked tone carried through to the living room.

"I know you heard all that," her mother scoffed. "If you had company, you should've told me."

Cash came down the hall, with Livie right on his trail. Of course he was still in his underwear, though he didn't seem to be the slightest bit embarrassed. Whereas Jade wished the floor would swallow her whole.

"What is Cash doing hiding in the kitchen in his underwear?" Livie demanded, her eyes on Jade. "And does that have anything to do with the broken-chair pieces I saw by the trash can?"

Livie's gaze darted to Jade's mother. "Oh, Mrs. McKenzie. I didn't see you. Um . . . Jade? What's going on?"

"You've still got the same boyfriend?" Lana asked, completely dismissing Livie. "It's a good thing I came, then. We're going to have to talk, Jade."

"Boy . . . boyfriend?" Livie sputtered.

Jade stared at Cash, and he simply raised his brows as if giving her a silent go ahead to handle this however she wanted.

Turning her attention to her friend, Jade attempted to find the right words. "It's not what it looks like," she started, instantly realizing from Cash's wince that she'd chosen wrong.

"It looks like you're both half naked, there's breakfast for two in the kitchen, though it's lunch time, and a broken chair from my kitchen table is outside in shambles. It looks like you two had a wild night and are just now emerging."

"Exactly why they shouldn't be dating," Lana chimed in, likely happy to have someone on her team for once. "This is not a healthy relationship."

"Mother, not now," Jade growled. "Cash and I are just . . . we're . . ."

"I can see what you're doing," Livie stated as she crossed her arms and pinned Jade with an emotional stare.

The hurt in her friend's eyes had Jade mentally scolding herself. Livie likely didn't care what Jade and Cash had going on; what she did care about were the multiple lies between them.

"I wasn't aware Cash was your boyfriend," Livie added. There was no mistaking the accusation and the pain dripping off each word.

Jade shook her head. "He's not my boyfriend."

"Thank heavens you came to your senses." Lana reached for Jade's arm and patted. "Why don't you go upstairs and get ready and we can go out? We can discuss this unfortunate moment later."

Unfortunate moment? With the angst circling the room and threatening to choke her, Jade knew there was a more apt description for what was going on and it sure as hell was stronger than "unfortunate."

Jade risked a glance at Cash. His jaw was set, his eyes emotionless. He stared at her for only a second, then turned and strode back down the hall. His heavy footsteps echoed up the back steps, and the creaky boards overhead gave away his every movement back into her bedroom.

Jade's heart sank. She'd hurt him. She'd hurt Livie. Two of the most important relationships in her entire life had been bruised, possibly broken, in the span of five minutes . . . and all because Jade had been caught off guard. First by Cash's declaration, then by the shock of her mother.

Not that Jade was putting the blame on anyone else. No, everything that happened had been completely her fault. She'd never been so confused, so scared. She was going to have to answer for so much and she couldn't even begin to think of where to start.

Crazy how her friend and the man she'd been sleeping with had a closer bond with Jade than her mother, but that was the reality. Jade may not know what to say, but she knew who she had to speak to first.

"I'm not going anywhere today," Jade answered her mom, but focused on Livie. "I have a mess to clean up."

He wasn't pissed, he was hurt—which was worse.

Cash shoved one leg and then the other into his jeans and cursed himself. He'd vowed never to let a woman have even the possibility of breaking his heart again.

Yet here he was in Jade's fancy bedroom staring at her fancy bed and hating the way he hadn't spoken up for himself downstairs. He'd just stood there, shocked, stunned . . . broken.

Maybe he'd been waiting for her to come to him, loop her arm through his, confirm that they were something more than two people who looked like they'd just wrapped up a booty call.

But no. Jade had tried to backpedal and act like nothing was going on.

Cash turned from the rumpled bed. He didn't want to

see any reminders of how perfect they'd been together. Apparently, he'd been the only one to think so and he'd let his damn heart override common sense, despite all the promises he'd made to himself.

As he fastened his jeans, he scanned the floor for his shoes, then realized they were still in the kitchen. Fine. He could grab them on his way out the back door and get the hell out of here. No sense in staying where he wasn't wanted.

Cash raked a hand through his hair and figured he should at least be thankful he hadn't blurted out how he'd fallen in love with her while they'd been eating breakfast. He'd been damn close and he'd dropped a pretty heavy hint, but if she brought it up, Cash would blow it off. No way would he ever admit he'd been thinking or feeling anything akin to love.

Whatever they'd had, it was over. Love wasn't something fleeting, but he could try like hell to suppress it and move on with his life.

Cash looked one last time to make sure he left nothing of his behind, then he spotted his cell on the nightstand on the side where he'd slept. He circled the bed and grabbed it just as Jade stepped through the doorway.

"Cash—"

"I need to get going." Major understatement, but he didn't take time to think. He had to get out of there. "Have fun with your mom."

He started around the bed, but she met him at the end and blocked his path. Oh, he could go around her, but he wasn't a complete jerk.

"Stop," she said, holding up her hands.

Cash took a step back so she didn't touch him. "Keep the shirt," he said. "I have more at home."

"That's not why I told you to stop."

He shoved his cell in his pocket and blew out a breath. "What do you want, Jade?"

"Jade? You never call me that."

With a shrug, he said, "Things change."

Her emerald eyes studied him and he pulled up every bit of his willpower not to reach for her. He wanted to shake some sense into her because he'd seen so much in her eyes, felt more than lust in her touch. She could lie to her mother, to her friends, but Jade had feelings for him. Maybe she didn't realize it herself, but he wasn't waiting for her to come to that conclusion. The damage had been done.

Cash wouldn't beg and he wouldn't let her come in here and apologize or try to defend what just happened. She'd chosen her words, chosen her pride over anything they'd had together. Cash saw quite clearly where he ranked in her life.

"So that's it?" she asked, her eyes brimming with unshed tears. "You're just walking out of here?"

"I'm done being the dirty secret you're keeping."

Damn it. He hadn't meant to let that slip out. His statement made it sound like he was bitter and angry. He was neither of those actually. The pain in his heart pretty much erased any other emotion. Maybe later, once he replayed every moment from when she walked into that hangar ready for her Nashville trip until this morning, he'd get bitter and angry.

"You were never my dirty secret," she murmured, swiping at a tear that spilled down her cheek. "What did you want me to say down there? We'd lied to my mother about our being together, then we've lied to our friends about not being together. There was no blanket statement to answer all the questions and I . . . I just . . ."

She bit down on her lower lip as she closed her eyes,

and more tears spilled down her cheeks. The sight gutted him, but his pride wouldn't let him console her or tell her everything was okay when this situation was far from fine.

Cash stared at her for another moment, trying to find the right words, but there was simply too much pain.

He knew exactly what he would've said down there. Had this been Jax or Tanner, and Cash's father had walked in thinking he had a girlfriend, Cash would've gone with the truth. He would've explained the situation and respected Jade in the process.

But Jade's default was to make her mother and her friend happy and to hell with anything she may have shared with him.

"I guess you won't have to worry about what to tell them anymore," he stated. "Seems you covered all that pretty well."

He eased around her and headed for the door. If he could just get to his shoes, he'd be gone.

"Cash."

Stopping just before the hallway, he reached up to grip the doorframe, but he didn't turn around. There was no way he could look at her right now, not when he was on the edge of losing control over his wrecked emotions.

"You were about to tell me you loved me before the doorbell rang."

Cash tightened his grip, yet he still didn't turn and he didn't say a word. There was no way he could admit where he truly stood.

"I know you were," she went on. "You can't lie to me."

Swallowing his emotions, and apparently his pride, Cash glanced over his shoulder. The sight of her standing by the bed wearing only his shirt would've been so inviting only an hour ago. Now, well . . . seeing her in his clothes, her hair tousled by his hands, her body still smelling like him, was simply too painful.

"No. I can't," he agreed, because he wanted her to know the severity of this moment. "Because I'm done lying."

Her eyes widened and she took a step forward, but Cash forced himself out of the bedroom, ignoring her attempts to call him back in. Never in his life had he ever had to use so much restraint. Cash wanted nothing more than to walk back in there, close the door, and remind her how perfect they'd been together. But that wouldn't solve any of their problems. Sex was exactly what had gotten them into this mess.

Wasting no time, Cash grabbed his shoes from the kitchen floor. He didn't look around, didn't wait to see if Lana or Livie were still there. He wasn't in the mood to answer questions or play nice. He needed to get home and figure out the mess he'd made of his life.

From now on, and he meant it this time, his focus would be on his father, on his gym, and on the airport he had a stake in.

There would be no dodging Jade with the project they'd all taken on, and no doubt he'd see her at friend functions like cookouts or when Tanner or Jax just wanted to get together on a whim. But that didn't mean Cash would ever let Jade in again, because this pain cut far deeper than when his wife had cheated and ultimately left.

Having Jade deny their involvement when they stood in her living room barely dressed had been the proverbial slap in the face.

With his head down and concentrating on each step that took him away from Jade's house, Cash headed down the street toward his truck. The ultimate walk of shame— shirtless no less—on this picturesque, tree-lined street with all its old, historical homes. He'd known he didn't belong in Jade's life; he'd told himself that over and over. Now if he could just emotionally remove himself as easily as he had physically, maybe he would recover from this heartache.

Chapter Sixteen

Jade knocked on Livie's front door and then took a step back. Maybe she could at least try to repair this damaged relationship.

After Cash had left her house, Jade had herself a good cry on the sheets that still smelled like him. She'd only allowed herself a few moments, but she hadn't been able to hold the emotions in any longer.

Once she somewhat composed herself, she changed from his shirt and put on a pair of yoga pants and a tank and pulled her hair into a ponytail. When she'd gone back downstairs, Jade discovered Livie was gone and her mother declared she was going to rest and they could do dinner once Jade calmed down.

Calmed down? There would be no calming down. This wasn't some issue over a bad hair day or a burned casserole.

Jade's entire life, her future, had been changed because of her careless words, when she'd let her fear and insecurities consume her. She'd hurt Cash, hurt him so bad he'd completely shut off his emotions . . . at least until his parting words.

He loved her. That stunning declaration should've made her feel so warm, so excited. But knowing he was gone, and she'd virtually pushed him out, only made those precious words hurt her in ways she'd never known.

The click of the lock pulled Jade back to the moment just as the old oak door swung wide. Livie stood in the doorway but didn't say a word.

"Can I come in?" Jade asked.

Still silent, Livie stepped aside and held out her hand in gesture.

As soon as Jade stepped over the threshold, she took in the sight of Piper's blue-and-white-striped teepee in the corner of the living room, a board game laying out on the oversize ottoman, and bed pillows, sheets, and blankets strewn about in what appeared to be a homemade fort.

Things had changed drastically for Livie in the past year. The Livie who'd lived in Atlanta in a posh condo wouldn't have allowed one speck of dust, but this more-relaxed Livie had completely embraced domestic life.

"Looks like you all had a fun movie night," Jade stated, scrambling for words and small talk.

"Last night," Livie stated, her tone almost cold. "Jax took Piper to the store for me because he knew I was going to visit you. We didn't want Piper going with me because we thought you were sick, but that must've just been another convenient lie that rolled off your tongue."

Jade turned and focused her attention on her friend. "We didn't start out lying. Well, we did, but we honestly didn't mean for things to progress into . . ."

What? Where had they progressed?

The beginning had been rash and exhilarating and completely unexpected. Then they'd come home and picked up where they left off. Things seemed to progress faster than she could keep up. She'd been afraid of a relationship, especially when he tossed the idea out there, then she'd started wondering if maybe they could be more.

But in the end, she'd destroyed any chance of having more with Cash other than a few weeks of the most amazing days of her life.

Cash's hint of deeper feelings this morning had scared her, but then, when he flat out declared his love, she'd realized what she'd lost.

"I even asked you what was going on," Livie stated. "More than once."

A sick feeling formed in her stomach as she nodded. "I know, and I wanted to say something. The fling started and we didn't think it would go any further than Nashville, but everything just sort of spiraled out of control and we got caught up in each other. We never meant for anyone to get hurt."

Yet now that the secret was out, everyone was hurting.

Silence settled heavily in the room like an unwanted guest. Jade never recalled a time when there had been any type of a wedge between her and Livie, and she was positive she didn't like this feeling. They'd even gone through the rough, hormonal teenage years together and never had an issue that forced them apart. Jade wouldn't let her careless actions destroy years of friendship.

"You're my best friend and closer than any sister could be," Jade added when she couldn't stand the quiet. "Try to look at all of this from my point of view. Cash and I knew we weren't going to end up in holy matrimony like you and Mel with Jax and Tanner, so we just didn't say anything. We weren't even dating. We figured if you guys knew, you'd think we were more than, well . . . sex."

Livie's brows drew in, then she shook her head and smiled. "You have no clue, do you? Cash is in love with you. I saw it plain as day on his face earlier, and when he turned to go upstairs, you didn't see the pain. That only comes from a man who's broken. I saw it with Jax when he thought I was leaving Haven."

Jade had seen the pain. She'd stared back at the angst filling his eyes as he'd stood in her bedroom. He'd never looked at her with such a cold stare, but she'd seen beyond that to the underlying vulnerability. Cash had put his defense mechanism in place and used it in an attempt to shut down all his emotions.

"I know he loves me," Jade whispered, emotions clogging her throat. "I've messed this all up."

Livie moved across the room and held out her arms. With a sigh of relief, Jade stepped forward and welcomed her friend's embrace. She hated having her heart so exposed, hated even more that she'd screwed up something so amazing and hurt the one man she'd grown closest to . . . the man she'd fallen completely in love with.

But could she trust herself? She'd never known this type of sentiment. Other than Nana and Livie and Mel, Jade hadn't formed very many close relationships. How could she believe that any of this was even real?

"What am I going to do?" Jade sniffed into her friend's shoulder. "He hates me, for good reason, and I'm a hot mess of confusion and fear."

"You're allowed to be afraid. That's perfectly normal, and you two didn't exactly go into this like a normal relationship." Livie eased back and smoothed Jade's hair from her face. "And I'm positive Cash doesn't hate you. Feelings don't just get turned off like that. He's hurting, he's angry, but those reactions wouldn't be so strong if he didn't love you."

Maybe not, but Cash wouldn't give her another chance. He'd been so damaged by his ex and he'd finally just opened up about his father. Taking a step like that, for him, was huge. Cash didn't just reveal his innermost thoughts to anyone. He'd chosen her because he'd wanted more and she'd been too afraid to take what he was so freely giving.

The ache in Jade's heart was unlike anything she'd ever known, but if she went to him and told him she loved him now, he wouldn't believe her.

"I don't know how to fix this." Jade swiped at her damp cheeks and looked to her friend for help. "With you and Melanie, with my mother, with Cash. I've made a complete mess."

Livie smiled. "You have, but you're human."

Processing everything that had happened in the past few hours, trying to regain control over her jumbled emotions had finally drained her energy. Jade turned and stepped over a little blond doll, then took a seat on the sofa. She reached down and picked up the toy, readjusting the twisted purple dress.

"Piper is supposed to clean up the mess when she gets home," Livie stated. "I wasn't feeling great this morning, so I just let it go."

Jade swallowed that damn lump of guilt that kept forming. While her expectant friend had been battling morning sickness, she'd made her way over to check on Jade, thinking she was sick as well.

"I'm really sorry, Liv. How are you feeling?"

"Better," she replied with a smile. "Don't worry about me right now. We need to focus on you and how all this can be fixed."

"I don't deserve such quick forgiveness from you." Jade sat the doll next to the board game on the ottoman. "You know I've never lied to you before and I don't like how all this came out."

Livie nodded in understanding as she came over and took a seat on the edge of the cushion next to Jade. "I know. That's what makes this so difficult. I don't like the position you've put yourself in. What were you thinking, getting involved with Cash?"

Jade laughed and fell back against the cushions. "Honestly, he was so charming at the wedding. But it was before that. When we were flying and bickering like we do, then the plane started causing issues, and I was terrified, I saw a new side of him. He was controlled and almost comforting."

Livie reached across and patted Jade's leg. "Cash is a great guy. I'm more shocked that the two of you . . . well, pretty much everything."

Yeah, Jade had been just as surprised, but then things just clicked. One right after another after another. She'd been unable to prevent the roller coaster and, honestly, she hadn't even bothered trying. Cash had been a good time at first, but then he'd quickly turned into someone she could lean on and still have fun with. She'd never met a man like that before.

"Did you know how he got that black eye a while back?" Jade asked.

"No. He's always got some sort of injury," Livie said as she tipped her head. "Why? Did you give it to him?"

Jade couldn't help but grin. "He got into a fight with Brad, defending me. He wasn't going to tell me, but it slipped out when he was defending me to my mother at the wedding."

Livie's eyes widened. "So the man came to your rescue with your jerk of an ex and your uptight mother?"

Jade nodded. "I told him everything, by the way. The adoption, and why Mom and I have such a strained relationship."

"Are you going to tell him how you feel?" Livie asked. "Because you're so in love with that man. You have been for some time, if I'm guessing correctly."

Nerves curled low in her belly and Jade pulled in a deep breath. How long had she been infatuated with Cash? They'd been so busy irritating each other, maybe that had just been their crazy, emotional foreplay for the past year.

Jade glanced up to the ceiling and struggled with her thoughts and what she should do next. "I don't know. I'm scared."

"Because you messed things up?"

Rolling her head on the soft cushion, Jade shifted her focus to Livie. "Partly, but more because I've never let myself feel this way. I've never wanted to open my heart to someone so completely. I mean, my nana is everything to me, but that was easy, you know? I have no idea what I'm doing, letting my heart get so wrapped up in a man."

Livie smoothed her hair back and down over one shoulder. "Love is scary. There's no safety net, no rules. Every step is a risk, and you only pray you're making the right move."

Jade snorted. "This isn't a very motivational speech."

"Just giving it to you straight," Livie stated with a shrug. "But the best thing about love is that once you fully commit yourself, you'll know why you had to work so hard. You'll understand that there was no other way to the greatest decision of your life."

Jade wished she was that brave. She wished she could just ignore her fears, her worries about being hurt. She wanted to run to Cash and apologize and explain herself and make him listen.

But what if none of that worked? Wouldn't she rather have a little pride and a broken heart than be stripped of her pride and broken?

Livie was right; this wasn't going to be easy. But if

Cash listened to her and could handle her insecurities, maybe, just maybe, they stood a chance.

Music blasted the office as Cash sanded the newly installed drywall. He'd needed an outlet, and when beating the hell out of his punching bag hadn't worked, he figured there was always manual labor to be done on the renovations. Anything they could do themselves saved money.

But he'd been trying to exorcise those demons in his head for the past six hours and nothing. He was still hurt, still angry, still . . . absolutely crushed.

He'd let Jade in, he'd taken a risk no matter how many times red flags waved around in his mind.

Yet even in looking back, he'd do it all again. Call him a masochist, but the time he'd had with Jade was worth the pain rolling through him now. He'd had some of the best moments of his life with her. Never before had anyone matched him and yet been completely the opposite.

Cash dropped the piece of screen he'd been using to sand the rough patches of spackle. He swiped his dusty hands across his old work jeans and took a step back to examine his work.

He'd gone over every single spot, channeling his frustrations into perfection. They should be good to go for laying the new tile in here as soon as tomorrow once the walls were wiped down. Cash didn't plan on doing that. He needed something else to take his mind off Jade and the debacle of this morning.

If his plane were in flying condition, Cash would take to the skies and leave his issues here. Unfortunately, there was still a holdup on the insurance money. They'd finally agreed to pay, once they'd sent their own mechanic out to inspect, but Cash and Tanner had to wait for that check to get their Cessna fixed.

The thumping drumbeat pumping from the radio suddenly stopped. Cash whirled around and discovered he wasn't alone anymore.

"When I first got here I thought there was a concert going on. I never thought this old radio of Livie's dad would play that loud. Then again, I've never tried to drown out my own thoughts," Jax stated as he hooked his thumbs through his belt loops. He scanned his gaze around the room, then landed back on Cash. "Looks good in here."

Cash swiped one arm and then the other, ridding himself of the powdery dust as much as possible. "What are you doing here?"

Jax took a step, then another, and started around the room, examining the walls closer. The silence grated on Cash's last nerve and he wasn't in the mood for whatever game his cousin wanted to play.

"If you're here to lecture me about Jade—"

"Lecture you?" Jax stopped and turned to face Cash. "I'm here because I had to get out of the house with all the women, wine, and tears that had taken over. Well, Jade had the wine. Melanie and Livie were sticking with water."

Confused, Cash raked a hand through his hair, which only produced another round of particle dust floating around him. "What the hell are you talking about?"

"Well, Melanie can't drink yet, Livie can't either with her pregnancy, and Jade is pretty upset over the breakup." Jax crossed his arms over his chest and pinned Cash with a dark stare. "Which is odd, because I didn't even know there was a relationship, let alone a breakup going down."

Cash shook his head and tried to process everything Jax had just said.

Okay, Mel couldn't drink because of breast feeding . . . he assumed.

"Livie's pregnant?" he asked.

Jax smiled. "We'll get to that later, but yes. Piper doesn't know yet, and we haven't made an official announcement."

"Congrats, man."

"Later," Jax warned. "Right now, I want to know why my wife is angry and consoling her best childhood friend."

Gritting his teeth, Cash tried to gather his thoughts. He knew Jax or Tanner wouldn't wait long before coming to him. They'd want answers. Hell, so did he. He'd like to know how he was ever going to recover from this. He'd also like to know how the hell they all could continue to work together when just the thought of Jade felt like a punch to the gut.

"I'd say your wife is angry because Jade and I didn't want anyone to know what was going on."

Cash glanced around and found a handle with a rag on the end. Might as well do something while he was getting raked over the coals. He grabbed the tool and started swiping the dust off the walls.

"Any reason why you guys were sneaking around like a couple of teenagers?"

Cash ran the rag from the ceiling to the floor. "Because it was nobody's damn business and now it's over."

If only the past month was that simple.

"And you're the one who ended things?" Jax accused.

Cash snorted. "You could say that."

He *had* ended things, once she'd made it clear in front of witnesses that he was nothing more than a warm body in her bed.

"You want to give me your version of events?" Jax asked.

Swipe. Swipe.

"Not particularly. What have you heard?"

Jax crossed the room and pulled the bucket of spackle out of the way for Cash. Then he grabbed another rag and went to the adjoining wall to start working.

"I only heard a little actually. I took Piper to a sleepover and then I was trying not to eavesdrop, but I did hear Livie talking about finding you in your underwear in Jade's kitchen. Then Jade told Melanie that she'd made a mistake with you."

Cash didn't think his heart was capable of shattering again, but knowing Jade thought they were a mistake damn near crippled him.

Jade thought everything they'd done had been a mistake. Wasn't that just a smack in the face of reality? He'd been so sure that she was falling for him. He'd clearly read her all wrong when she'd let him stay over, when she wanted to make him breakfast in bed. He'd opened up about his father. Hell, he'd been ready to take her to see him.

Part of Cash had hoped that if his father saw how Cash was moving on with his life, maybe he'd want to do the same.

All of that was shot to hell, and Cash was going to have to pick up the pieces and attempt to regroup.

"I don't want to talk about this," Cash growled.

"Too damn bad." Jax fisted his rag and turned around. "What the hell, man? What were you thinking with Jade?"

Cash slammed his tool to the wood subfloor, the thunk echoing through the near empty room. "What was I thinking? I was thinking that we're adults and we didn't need to ask anyone's permission."

The frustration and agony threatened to overcome him. Cash ran a hand over the back of his neck and glanced down to his dust-covered work boots.

"I was thinking that we wouldn't get caught up in everything," he murmured as he looked back up.

Silence crowded the room, and Cash missed the booming radio. At least he could attempt to drown out the angst . . . not so much when Jax stared at him with sympathy in his eyes.

"You fell for her," Jax accused.

Cash shrugged. "It's irrelevant now."

"Says who?"

"I do." Damn it. "You heard her, Jax. She admitted it was a mistake. I'm not begging. She made her choice this morning, when her mother showed up unannounced and then Livie stopped in."

"What happened?"

As much as he'd like to ignore this entire conversation, Cash knew he wasn't getting out of it so easily. He took a step and sat on the secure lid of the five-gallon bucket. Resting his elbows on his knees, Cash laced his fingers together and started at the beginning. Jax never interrupted, but that didn't make rehashing all of it any easier.

"Surely you're not that blind," Jax finally said once Cash was finished.

"What?"

Jax shook his head and leaned against the wall. "She's scared. Even I can see that. She's never had a real relationship, other than with Livie and Melanie. Her grandmother is close, but she's not in her daily life. Jade didn't know how to handle this morning and freaked out. Hell, I don't blame her. Love is scary."

"Like I don't know that?" Cash shouted. "I've never been so damn scared, but I'm also not naïve. Jade and I are too opposite to make anything work, and I was just a secret to her, nothing more."

"Why do you say that?" Jax countered. "Did Jade ever act like she was better than you?"

"No."

Jax merely raised his brows. "I'd say you overreacted."

Maybe, but pride was a dangerous personality trait, and he had enough of it for five people.

"She's at my house if you want to go talk to her."

Cash shook his head. He wasn't ready to talk to Jade. His emotions were too raw. Besides, as long as her mother was in town, there was no way he could go to Jade's house.

Perhaps this break was best. Maybe they both needed to think about what happened, where they stood with each other. Cash wasn't sorry she knew his feelings. If anything, he was sorry he'd lost all control and allowed himself to be hurt again.

"Can we talk about the fact that you're going to be a dad again?" Cash asked as he came to his feet.

Jax stared for a second and then smiled and nodded his head. "Yeah. I'm done grilling you for now."

Jax may be done, but Tanner hadn't even started. Cash also had a sinking feeling he'd be hearing from Livie and Melanie before all was said and done.

Chapter Seventeen

The tap on her bedroom door had Jade raising one lid to glare across the room. She didn't want to get out of bed. Couldn't a woman just have a pity party?

She'd left Livie's last night and driven home absolutely and utterly exhausted. There had only been two glasses of wine over the course of as many hours. The depletion of her energy had come from sobbing and ugly crying all over her friends.

Thankfully, she'd at least texted her mother before the emotional meltdown to say that going out wasn't a good idea.

"Jade." Her mother's voice carried through the door as she tapped once again. "I called and we're down for brunch at the little café in the resort. You should get up and make yourself presentable."

Jade nearly snorted. There wouldn't be too much she could do to hide her puffy eyes. All she wanted to do was lay in bed and be left alone. Was that seriously too much to ask?

But her mother had driven to Haven for reasons still unbeknownst to Jade. Obviously there was something she wanted to discuss because the woman hadn't set foot back in this town since she left after Jade's graduation.

"I'll be ready in thirty minutes," she grumbled with half her face pressed to her pillow.

"Darling, take an hour."

Yes. It wouldn't do any good for Jade to show up looking sad or depressed. Lana wouldn't tolerate that one bit. Pretenses were positively everything.

Jade rolled to her back and threw her arm over her eyes. Lunch at Bella Vous sounded great. She loved their wraps, and Liam's pastries were absolutely melt-in-your-mouth amazing.

She couldn't stay in bed forever. The open house for the airport was coming up in a few days, she had classes to teach tomorrow, and she seriously needed to get back to her running routine. Maybe training for another marathon would give her something else to concentrate on.

Last night Livie and Mel had convinced Jade to reach out to Cash. At some point she would. Today was not that day.

First, Jade needed to focus on her mother. The heartache would certainly still be there after Lana's intentions were known.

Jade couldn't fathom what her mom could want, and Nana hadn't known either. Nana also didn't know anything about Cash, and until Jade had some sort of handle on the situation, she'd opted not to confide in her grandmother.

Fifteen minutes later, Jade felt somewhat human after a hot shower. Her stomach growled in protest, but that would be fixed soon enough. She dried her hair as much as she could before she grew tired of waving the dryer around. Ultimately, Jade pulled her damp hair to the side and did a fishtail braid to lay over her shoulder.

After throwing on minimal makeup, she found a comfortable green maxi dress she hoped her mother saw as fancy enough. Jade grabbed her favorite silver sandals and slid them on.

One quick side-to-side glance in the mirror and she figured this was remarkable considering how she felt.

Jade grabbed her cell from the nightstand, cursing herself for being disappointed at the lack of messages from Cash.

What did she expect? That he'd message her and suddenly ask to see her? She'd hurt him too deeply for him to be that quick to forgive—if he ever did.

No, Cash wasn't going to come to her. If this relationship was repairable at all, she would have to go to him. She'd have to put her own pride, fear, and worry aside to get him to understand.

And even then, Jade didn't know if he'd let her back in.

She gathered her cross-body purse, slid her phone inside, and headed downstairs.

Her mother sat on the sofa and folded her book in her lap as she met Jade's gaze. "That was fast. Are you sure you're ready?"

Lana McKenzie's cami/cardigan set was just a few shades lighter than her dark pink capris. Of course, her hair had been expertly pulled back and her makeup done with precision.

Jade would rather go for comfort, and the maxi dress would allow for eating room . because she fully intended to not only eat a meal, she would follow it up with a flaky pastry. Carbs would be her best friend today and tomorrow she would go back to her green shakes and protein-filled meals.

"I'm all set," Jade told her. "I can drive."

Surprisingly, her mother didn't say much more. The drive to Bella Vous was actually a little dreary. The gray skies and drizzle of rain seemed to match Jade's mood, but she wasn't going to let it ruin her day. She'd had her pity party and now it was time to woman up and fight for what she wanted.

She wanted Cash, but beyond that, she didn't know. All she really knew was that she had to apologize, and she would likely have to grovel. He needed to understand he was never someone she was ashamed of. Just the idea that he truly believed that had Jade's stomach tightening.

As she turned into the drive leading up the hill toward Bella Vous, Jade tried to compartmentalize her emotions. For the next hour or so, there was nothing she could do about Cash. The only thing she could do was work on her speech, figure out what the hell she'd say to him when she saw him again.

With the mock open house coming up, she had to get with him before that. There was such a fine line, though. If she went too soon, he'd still be hurt and angry and closed off—all justifiable feelings.

On the other hand, if she waited too long, he'd think she didn't care. Jade needed to give Cash his space; they both needed to think. But she wouldn't let too much time pass.

Other than the fact that he needed to hear her side, she just missed him. Since Nashville, she'd seen him nearly every single day, and even when they weren't together, there wasn't this turmoil and tension.

"I've heard their cakes are fabulous."

Lana's comment pulled Jade back to the moment as she turned into a parking spot.

"Everything Liam makes is great," Jade replied. "I recommend the éclairs."

"Then we'll each have one," her mother declared. "There's something I'd like to discuss with you over brunch."

With that declaration thrown in there like Jade wouldn't

notice, Lana got out of the car and quickly made her way to the covered side porch leading into the café.

Jade sat there another second and attempted to take a few calming breaths. With all she had going on, her mother wanted to talk. There wasn't a doubt in her mind that there would be some attempt at getting Jade to move back to Atlanta, or Lana would name-drop and tell her she'd found the perfect man for her.

Part of Lana had been too concerned with Jade's career and husband material, but the other part had simply washed her hands of getting too involved. And by involved, Jade meant her mother didn't want to have to do any actual parenting or doling out solid advice. No, the advice handed down usually had something to do with a move that would benefit Lana or give her leverage within her own little society.

"This will be interesting," Jade muttered as she grabbed her purse and stepped out into the fine mist.

As soon as she stepped onto the porch, Jade took a step and placed her hand over the knob of the entrance door.

"I'd like to have a nice lunch without you setting me up with a friend's cousin's son's best friend," Jade warned. "And I don't want talk of me moving back to Atlanta. Can we do that?"

Lana stared back, then pursed her lips. "You don't even know the offer I have for you."

So it was a career move. Well, Jade supposed that was better than a blind date with a stuffy man who had argyle as a staple in his closet. Jade found she'd much rather have a man who didn't care to get dirty in his job, to be hands-on and work hard.

"I'm happy here," Jade stated.

Without another word, she turned the knob and opened the door. The blessed sugary aroma wafted out and greeted her like an old friend.

Yes. This would do. Sugar and carbs and smiling faces. Jade may not be thrilled with why her mother brought her here, but this would be good for her. Anything positive would help fuel her drive to regain control of her life.

She refused to believe she'd damaged everything beyond repair. That wasn't who Jade was. She never gave up on what she wanted. Apparently, she had learned a few quality traits from her mother.

Jade smiled to a group of ladies seated in the corner. She recognized one woman from her yoga classes. All the tables were full, save for one, which Jade assumed was theirs. She loved this little treasure spot and was thrilled the Monroe boys were so successful at something they'd committed their whole lives to.

The tiny black-and-white-tiled floor in combination with the wrought-iron details around the windows and the brackets for the tables and counter, plus the crisp white chair covers led to a vintage theme. Dark crown moldings and etched mirrors stretching along the side wall added to the ambience, and Jade found herself looking at this place in a whole new light.

She couldn't wait for the airport to get up and running with the new gift shop and restaurant. They wouldn't be in competition with Liam's café. Most people here were guests of the resort, and the airport food would be more Southern-style and home-cooked meals. Something to really welcome their new clientele from all over when they came to Haven, Georgia.

"Hey, Jade."

Liam Monroe stepped from the back and greeted Jade with a wide smile. Once upon a time, the man didn't smile, and that scar running along the side of his face was always turned away. He'd come a long way since settling back in Haven—Jade couldn't help but wonder exactly how this quaint town could heal so many, but it did.

"I haven't seen you in here for a while," he said, resting his arms on top of the pastry display. "Are you having lunch or getting something to go?"

"We're having lunch," she replied, then turned to her mother. "Liam Monroe, this is my mother, Lana McKenzie."

"I remember you," Lana replied, her tone dripping with disapproval.

Jade never knew what would come out of her mother's mouth. Oftentimes she was like a child and honesty, or ill-placed thoughts, just came spilling out. She also wasn't sure if her mother had chosen to come here to judge or to tell her friends she had been to Bella Vous because they'd all raved about the place.

"She called for a table," Jade added quickly, before her mother embarrassed her. "She's heard some great things about the resort, but we couldn't get in for massages, we figured we'd at least take in some of your fine cooking."

"Your table is right over by the window." He moved from behind the counter and led them toward the back. "I thought you might like this view overlooking the pond. Zach and Brock finished that new seating area a few months ago. You should walk out and take a look when you're done here if the rain stops."

Jade glanced out the window and gasped at the semi-circle that framed half of the pond with benches and little tables between each one. There was even a sturdy-looking pergola as a canopy over the space, and Jade spotted wisteria vines already taking shape up the thick posts.

"That's gorgeous. I'm glad he finished so he could dig in at our place."

Liam pulled out Lana's chair for her and then Jade's.

"He's the best. I'll have someone take your order shortly. I need to get my apple pies out of the oven."

Once he was gone, Jade focused her attention across the table to her mother.

"Who's Brock?" Lana asked as she placed her napkin in her lap.

"Zach's adopted son. He's eighteen or nineteen now."

"They adopted a teenager?" Lana exclaimed. "That's not very common."

Jade shook her head. "No, but Brock sort of fell into their lives at the right time. They're good for each other. Brock was a runaway and actually hiding in the basement here. He's a sweet boy."

"That's quite a story," Lana declared. "I guess the Monroe boys have changed."

Jade handed her mother a menu and glanced through the options as an awkward silence settled over them. No doubt once they ordered, Lana would chime in with the true reason for her visit, despite the warning Jade had given her.

A petite blonde named Sara took their orders and left them with a fresh batch of warm yeast rolls with honey butter.

"I forgot about these," Jade said as she reached for one. "They'll literally melt in your mouth."

"You can have mine," her mother said. "I'd better save my calories for the dessert."

Jade shrugged. "Fine by me. I plan on having all the calories today."

"You're not still upset about Cash Miller, are you? Jade, honey, he's not for you."

And here we go.

"Excuse me."

Jade glanced over to the lady she'd smiled to earlier.

"Hi," Jade greeted, thankful for the reprieve. "Stella, right?"

The thirtysomething nodded. "Yes. I don't mean to interrupt, but I was just curious whether you did any yoga classes around here. I've only been able to make it to a few of yours, but since we moved closer to Haven, I was looking for a place here."

Jade tipped her head and rested her hands in her lap. "I'm sorry, I don't. I've been asked to teach locally, but I haven't decided yet."

"I'll keep my eye out," Stella stated. Then she glanced to Lana. "I'll let you get back to your lunch."

Once they were alone, Jade turned her attention back to her mother. Lana had an odd expression on her face, one Jade couldn't quite place.

"What?" Jade asked as she tore apart her warm roll.

"You really like it here."

Her hands stilled over her small plate. "Yes."

"I mean, you really created a life here."

Jade flattened her palms on the table and sighed. "I re-created one. I had a life here before."

"Growing up, you always complained there was nothing to do here," her mother argued. "When we got to Atlanta, you really thrived."

Nodding, Jade picked up her knife and dipped it into the glass bowl of honey butter. "I did love Atlanta when I was there," she agreed. "My lifestyle was quite different from here. I loved my job and my condo. But then I always felt like something was missing."

Something was still missing and he'd left a big, gaping hole in her life since he'd walked out of her bedroom.

Jade had never felt more alive, freer, or more herself than when she was with Cash. He made her laugh, he challenged her, he made everything better. Even through their bickering, she could see what an amazing man he was.

Cash was quite the protector. He protected his father, he'd tried to protect her from Brad and then her mother, and now he was protecting his heart.

"That little scandal you had won't affect you getting your old job back."

Jade clenched the knife in her hand and focused on smoothing the butter. The little scandal and her old job could both go to hell, because she wasn't going back. Her mother thought she'd run from the trouble, but the truth was, Jade had fought, and won, the case. She wasn't running at all. She was starting over and not putting up with anything in her life that didn't make her happy.

Isn't that what she focused on in each of her yoga classes? Exhale everything that doesn't serve a purpose to better your life. She'd taken her own advice and was quite happy.

Well, she was until she'd made a mess of things.

"Mother, I wouldn't take my old job back if they doubled my salary."

Lana scoffed and leaned forward. "Now that's just ridiculous. I spoke to a few people and they'd like to bring you back as an acting partner."

It took every ounce of willpower for Jade to quietly lay her knife on the edge of her plate and not throw it across the room. She dropped her hands to her lap and gripped the cloth napkin.

"You talked to people about my old job?" Jade asked through gritted teeth.

The door to the café opened with the jingle of a soft bell. Customers chatted and laughed. The two waitresses came in and out of the back. Every now and then, Liam's voice filtered through the kitchen door when it opened.

All of this going on around her kept Jade from flat-out exploding.

"I was offered my old job back several months ago," Jade stated. "I didn't want it then and I don't want it now. You wasted your time and likely made a fool of yourself. I don't need a spokesman, Mother. I've got everything taken care of."

The waitress brought their food and silence once again settled heavily between them. Jade wanted her life to be smooth, to be happy. As much as she wanted Cash back in her life, she knew it was also time to have a real talk with her mother.

"We are two different people." Jade took a sip of her sweet tea and slid her thumb over the condensation on her glass. "Our lifestyles are going to be different and that's okay. I don't want the life you're wanting to set up for me. I want the life I create myself."

"There's nothing wrong with wanting my daughter to have the best life possible," Lana argued. "I wish you'd just take what I'm offering."

They weren't going to see eye-to-eye on this. The best Jade could hope for was a truce, but she wasn't even sure that was possible.

"I'm grateful for everything you've given me," Jade started. "You gave me a life I would never have had, but I'm happy here with what I'm doing. Can you respect my decisions? Can we just agree that we're two different people and that we won't always agree?"

Lana's eyes misted. Hopefully, Jade hadn't gone too far, but she couldn't keep dancing around this, and they were both adults who just had to face the reality that they would never have a close mother-daughter bond.

"You're right," her mother whispered. She picked up her napkin and delicately dabbed beneath each eye so as not to mess up her mascara. "We are different. No matter how I tried to make you my little clone."

Jade smiled at her mother's honesty. "You didn't do a bad job raising me. You made me independent."

"Defiant," Lana countered with a soft grin. "But I suppose that's part of parenting. We can only do so much, and then you need to go off on your own."

Never in her life had she thought Lana McKenzie would admit she was taking a step back. There may be hope for their relationship; at least they weren't bickering. Jade sincerely hoped this was a step in the right direction, mending years of animosity.

"I'm staying in Haven," Jade went on. "I've already talked to Livie about buying her house."

"Well, it is a lovely, historical home." Her mother picked up her fork and mixed up her salad. "I would like to know one thing, though."

"What's that?"

Lana's piercing eyes met hers. "Was Cash actually your boyfriend at the wedding?"

Jade shook her head and reached for her turkey wrap. "No. At that point he was little more than a friend, but we drove each other crazy."

"Yet you were parading around in his shirt when I arrived."

"We ended up skipping the whole friend part and going straight to . . . well . . ."

Jade took a bite and just let the sentence dangle. There was no need to spell it all out when her mother had witnessed everything already.

"Do you care for him?" Lana asked.

Swallowing, Jade swiped her napkin over her mouth. "More than I ever thought possible. I hurt him and I'm not sure if I can repair that."

"But you'll try."

There wasn't a question, and there was no judgment. Her mother stared across the table, waiting on a real answer.

"I'll fight for what I want," Jade replied, then quickly added, "just like my mother would."

Lana stared for a moment before she nodded. "Well, I guess I don't always have to approve, but I can respect you enough to step back."

That wasn't quite her blessing, but it was close enough for Lana McKenzie.

A new burst of hope filled Jade, and she had to use this emotion to fight her battle with Cash. Maybe he didn't want to see her, maybe he didn't want to hear what she had to say. But too damn bad. She wasn't done with him, and if he loved her like he said he did, she had all the ammunition she needed.

Chapter Eighteen

Cash circled the empty office and tried to find a spot he'd missed. So far, the pale gray walls seemed to be perfect. Once they were completely dry, he'd be able to see any imperfections.

He rotated his right arm. Lifting weights was one thing, but painting worked a whole other set of muscles, and he hated to admit he was a little sore.

Once he cleaned up his mess, he had a date with his hot tub. He hadn't been home much, other than to sleep. He'd done a pretty good job of staying at the gym or at the airport and keeping himself busy.

Dodging Jade had been necessary for his battered heart. But he wasn't a coward and wouldn't avoid her much longer. They had to talk, no matter how seeing her again would hurt.

She'd texted him twice. Once to apologize, though she admitted that word didn't cover much, and again to tell him she wanted to talk. That last text had come yesterday just before midnight. Cash figured she'd been lying awake thinking of everything that had happened between them, just as he had.

The sleepless nights had been brutal. He'd wanted to feel her body against his, he'd wanted to be able to share his thoughts like he had before. Jade had been the one person he hadn't been able to get a feel for, but then she'd become the one he wanted to confide in. Which was ridiculous. He'd never wanted to get that invested in anyone.

His mother had died, his wife had left him, the only person Cash could fully commit to was his father. And then Jade came along and made him question every vow he'd ever made to himself.

Could he even trust what he felt? Could he trust anything right now? He'd never had his emotions so raw, so exposed. He damn well didn't like it, but he didn't know what to do to fix things.

When he gave the room one last slow perusal, Cash turned in a circle and froze when his eyes landed on Jade in the doorway.

"I saw your truck out front," she said in a small voice so unlike the bold woman he knew. "Then I followed the paint fumes."

He didn't move, didn't speak. For just a moment, he wanted to take in the sight of her. That long, silky red hair tumbled around her shoulders. She had on only a pair of jeans, simple brown sandals, and a fitted green T-shirt. Nothing provocative or fancy, yet his body stirred. Damn, he'd missed her.

Jade remained in the doorway and slid her hands into her pockets as she glanced around the room. Nerves radiated from her and he'd never seen her this way before.

"This looks good," she commented, then finally brought her eyes back to him. "Everything is really coming along."

As much as Cash wanted to cross the space between them and just touch her, kiss her, he remained where he was. Fisting his hands at his sides, he was determined to get through this.

"You didn't come here this late hoping for small talk," he stated.

She chewed her bottom lip for a second before shaking her head. "No. I actually went to your house a couple of hours ago, then I drove to the gym. For the past hour I've been out in my car giving myself a pep talk."

Cash's lips twitched. "And what were you discussing with yourself?"

"If I'd rather turn around and go home or suck up my nerves and come in to face you."

"And here you are."

She blew out a breath and pulled her hands out of her pockets as she took a step into the room. "I won't let this go without a fight."

"A fight," he repeated. "And what exactly do you mean by 'this'?"

Another step brought her closer to him. "You're not going to make this easy on me, are you?"

Cash gave a casual shrug. "I just want to make sure there are no misunderstandings."

Like before.

The unspoken words hovered between them, but he wasn't backing down. She'd come to him for a reason, whether to apologize and move on or try to fight for them, he didn't know.

"No more misunderstandings," she agreed. Tucking her hair behind her ears, she took one more step toward him. "My mother left town this morning."

"So it was safe to come to see me?"

How ridiculous he'd been to have that sliver of hope, thinking she'd come here to actually try to salvage something, or at least admit she'd been wrong. But no, she'd been waiting until her mother was gone.

Cash couldn't help but shake his head as he turned to

the paint tray and roller. He had a mess to clean up—which seemed to be the metaphor for his life as of late.

"My being here has nothing to do with my mother." Jade's words took on a firmer tone than moments ago, but he kept his back to her as he started to pick up. "I was giving you time to think and I was trying to process what all I wanted to say."

He grabbed the tray and wet roller. "So say it," he replied, turning back to face her.

"Are you going to listen or are you going to rush me out of here?"

There she was. That fiery woman he'd gotten used to and fallen in love with. Her cheeks tinged a slight pink and those eyes were wide with anger.

"What do you want, Red?"

She opened her mouth, then closed it. She stared for a moment, and Cash ended up setting everything back down on the plastic drop cloth.

"I thought you were done calling me that," she murmured.

He snorted. "I thought I was done with a great many things."

"Are you done with me?" she asked, her bright eyes holding his. "Because I'm scared, Cash."

Damn it. He knew that cost her. He'd never heard Jade admit defeat or fear. How could someone so strong, so resilient, be this frightened?

"What are you afraid of?" he asked.

She crossed her arms over her chest but never looked away. "Everything. I'm afraid of how much I hurt you. I'm scared you'll never know how sorry I am and how much I regret ever making you feel like you weren't good enough for anything other than a secret."

Tears filled her eyes, and Cash practiced a superhuman

amount of restraint by not taking her in his arms. But she needed to say what she came for, and he still needed to figure out if she was sincere. After all, she had waited until her mother was gone.

"I'm not used to this," she went on, blinking away her tears. "I never had these emotions and I wasn't expecting them with you. I thought we'd mess around, have a good time, and then we'd mutually agree to go back to annoying each other."

Cash smiled. "I never thought it would be that easy."

"Yeah, well, I'm naïve, apparently, because I did."

A tear slid down her cheek and she swiped it away. Her eyes darted around the room and she headed to the step stool in the corner and took a seat. She rested her elbows on her knees and blew out a long sigh as she glanced down to her clasped hands.

The silence seemed to grow more and more deafening as he waited for her to continue.

"You know I was adopted and I never really felt like I fit in my mother's world."

She spoke still looking down, and he knew she didn't need him to reply. Cash waited. He quietly crossed to the overturned bucket that had been used for drywall and he took a seat.

"When I met Livie as a young girl, and then Melanie a few years ago, I felt like maybe I had sisters and a bond that nobody could take from me. But there was still a void."

An ache spread through Cash's chest. He knew voids. He'd learned to live with them; he'd learned to channel his thoughts elsewhere and not dwell on all that was missing from his life.

Or at least he'd been doing a fairly good job of it until Jade.

"I've dated, never feeling a connection," she went on,

then her eyes came up to meet his. "Then I came back to Haven and there you were. Such a pain in my ass, but even then, you managed to captivate me in a way like nobody before."

She let out a soft laugh that had his heart clenching.

"That sounds silly," she admitted with a smile. "But I don't know how else to describe it."

"I know exactly what you mean," Cash replied. "You don't need to explain."

He'd felt that odd connection, too. Yes, they'd irritated the hell out of each other for the past year, but through all that, they'd also challenged each other. As strange as that sounded, their bond had started long ago, and somehow they'd just understood each other all this time.

Another tear slid down her cheek, and Jade swiped it away. Squaring her shoulders, she sat up straight, and Cash watched as she literally gathered her strength right before his eyes. This volley of her emotions from afraid to vulnerable to determined had him admiring her more. Yes, she'd hurt him, but he couldn't help but wonder if she wasn't here now in an attempt to start over.

"I've told you I was sorry for what happened the other morning," she stated. "That's such a blanket statement and apologies are so easily tossed around, but I mean it. Cash, I never wanted you hurt. I never thought we'd get caught before we could figure things out for ourselves, I just . . ."

She shook her head and glanced up to the ceiling.

"You what?" he asked.

Come on, Jade. Don't back down now.

She brought her gaze back to his. "You'd spent the night and I'd started thinking how much I wanted you there, how I've never wanted a man in my bed all night before. I certainly never made a man breakfast."

"The very male part of me is happy to hear that."

She smiled. "I figured I'd throw that in there just for you."

He seriously loved her. How could he ever think that because she'd hurt him by her rash actions, he could just ignore such a strong pull?

Cash stood and closed the distance between them, but he didn't reach for her. Jade looked up at him as her brows dipped in.

"I got scared when my mother showed up," she went on. "You'd just hinted at your feelings and all I could think of was how I felt the same way, but what if we were just two broken people who don't even know what love is? How did either of us know to trust it when we'd clearly started everything based on a lie and sex?"

Unable to resist another second, Cash squatted down and smoothed her hair from her face as he cupped her cheek. She turned into his hand and closed her eyes as her chin quivered.

"Those are all justifiable fears," he told her. "If it makes any difference, I was terrified to tell you how I felt. Hell, I still am. But I couldn't keep it to myself, and you deserved to know. I was done with hiding; I was done with caring what anyone else thought."

"And then I denied everything," she whispered. "If I could go back and change everything, I would. All I can do is tell you that I love you, that I want to try—"

Cash covered her mouth with his. The moment the word "love" slid through her lips, something in him snapped. He'd been waiting for it. He'd known in his heart, but he'd needed to hear the actual words. And now he had them.

Jade's fingers threaded through his hair as she opened to him. He hadn't seen or touched her in days and kissing her still didn't seem to be enough.

Yet he eased back and rested his forehead against hers.

"I didn't want to be another person who let you down," she murmured. "Your father and your ex have, and I just kept thinking I'm no better. I was supposed to comfort you; that's why you opened up to me, because you needed me . . . and I destroyed that hope you had."

"No," he countered, brushing his lips along hers. "You didn't. You're human. I wanted to hate you in that moment; I even tried. But you're part of me, Red. I can't let you go."

She gripped his wrists as he framed her face and eased back to look him in the eye. "I told my mother I'm staying here. She tried to convince me to go back to Atlanta, to take a prestigious position at my old firm. But I said I was buying Livie's house and I may have another job opportunity here in Haven."

Confused, Cash jerked. "You do? Where?"

A wide smile spread across her face. "I got to thinking. Would I rather keep driving thirty minutes to teach my classes, or would I rather drive five to your gym?"

He couldn't help but return her smile. "Is that so?"

Her arms looped around his neck. "Now I have a question for you."

Cash came to his feet and pulled her with him. With his hands resting on the dip in her waist, he tugged her flush with his body.

"What's that?" he asked.

"Would you rather live in your house or would you rather move in with me at Livie's? I do believe her back-yard is large enough for a hot tub."

Cash's fingertips slid beneath the hem of her shirt and grazed her bare skin. "Considering I rent my house, I think I'd be fine moving in with you."

"And the hot tub?"

In a swift move, he had her shirt up and over her head.

"Maybe you should try to convince me just how bad you want it."

Those emerald eyes sparkled as she reached for the button of his jeans. "Oh, I want it pretty bad."

"Then I think we can arrange something."

Cash didn't analyze his feelings anymore. There was no question he was in love with Jade. This was real, being with her, the prospect of building a future, all of it was a thrilling ride he never wanted to end.

Fear and brokenness may be his past, but Jade was his future.

"Do you think people will show?"

Cash pulled his truck into the parking spot near Sophie's office and killed the engine before turning to face Jade.

"Red, you've analyzed and worried about this for days." He reached over and took her hand, bringing it to his lips. "Relax."

How could she relax? This was the mock open house for the airport. Not just any airport, but Livie's father's legacy. Through so many events, all of them had been led to this point, and their futures were riding on this being a success.

But that wasn't all Jade was worried about. This was the night they were going to tell their friends about their relationship. Over the past few days, they'd decided to just be them a little longer. Tonight was the night, though. Jade hoped her friends would be happy. Even though they'd obviously found out about the lying and the sneaking, the crew didn't know just how much Jade loved Cash, and that they planned on living together.

"Are you going to get out or do I need to bring the party to you?" he asked.

Jade stared ahead and spotted Melanie and Tanner crossing the street. Mel had baby Knox in her arms, and the little family brought tears to Jade's eyes.

"Oh, no," Cash demanded. "No crying. You know I can't stand when you do that and I get all awkward and have no idea how to make things better."

"They're happy tears," she assured him. "I'm ready."

"Happy tears," he muttered as he stepped from the truck. He rounded the hood and opened her door, extending his hand to help her down. "You look beautiful tonight."

Jade smiled. "You already told me earlier."

Cash slid an arm around her waist and pulled her against his side. "I plan on telling you every day for the rest of our lives."

Jade's nerves calmed somewhat when Cash urged her forward, keeping her tucked perfectly against his side. They all had agreed to arrive thirty minutes early to make sure everything was set up and good to go. Sophie had made sure the office was ready, and Liam had promised to have everything set up as far as the food and drinks.

The support from friends and other businesses was so overwhelming. This airport was going to be bigger and stronger than ever.

As they reached the stone front of the office building, Cash gave her a gentle squeeze. "You ready?" he asked.

Jade nodded and reached for the handle. "Let's go tell our friends. We've just made this circle even smaller."

He opened the door and ushered her inside. Immediately, Jade took in the grand display she'd hauled back from Atlanta. The 3-D model was just as stunning as she remembered, and everyone was standing around and admiring the details.

"This is absolutely remarkable," Livie stated. "I can't even imagine how perfect the airport will look in real life if this version is so breathtaking."

Cash didn't remove his arm from around her waist as they moved closer to the group. One by one, the crew turned their attention toward them.

"Well, does this mean you two are official?" Melanie asked, patting Knox's back as she swayed.

"We are." Jade smiled. Saying this, showing her friends how much she cared for Cash, felt good . . . it felt right. "Who knew?"

"I knew," Cash stated.

He eased away and dropped down to one knee.

Jade gasped, her hand flying to her mouth as he pulled a box from his pocket. He wasn't doing this. Well, clearly he was, but in front of all these people?

She glanced around and over her shoulder. Nobody seemed surprised, if their soft smiles and nods of encouragement were any indicator.

"You planned this?" she asked, her eyes darting back to the man before her.

"I didn't want to wait," he explained. "I'm the one who wanted everyone here early."

He lifted the box lid and Jade stared down at not one but two rings. Confused, she reached to touch the emerald princess cut on one, and then she admired the simple oval diamond with a ruby on each side.

"Would you rather the ring I saw and instantly thought of you?" Cash asked. "Or would you rather the one that belonged to my mother?"

Tears welled up instantly, and the sight before her completely blurred. "Cash," she whispered.

How could she choose one? Why was he making her? She was so stunned at what this moment meant that she couldn't even think about a ring.

"I'll make this easier on you." Cash pulled the emerald from the box and slid it on her finger. "Would you rather spend your life as my wife or as my business partner?"

Jade laughed as she stared down at the sparkling ring on her hand. "Business partner?"

"You're teaching yoga at my studio."

"I am?"

He shrugged and rose to stand before her. "You are," he said as he slid his finger beneath her chin and forced her gaze to his. "So what will it be?"

Jade didn't hesitate. "I can't choose just one. I'll take both."

Cash pocketed the box. "I had a feeling you'd say that."

She held up the ring and admired it again. "Which ring is this?"

"Doesn't matter," he replied. "They're both yours. Because I couldn't decide."

Jade threw her arms around his neck and sniffed. There was no controlling the tears sliding down her cheeks and she didn't even care that she was an ugly crier. The open house would begin shortly, but all that mattered was that, finally, she belonged. After thirty years of wondering where she should be, what she should be doing with her life, she knew without a doubt that everything had fallen into place.

"I don't mean to interrupt this moment," Jax stated from behind her. "But there are already people outside waiting to get in."

Jade held on a moment longer, wanting to freeze this into her memory bank forever. She'd never expected a proposal this soon.

"Are you sure?" she asked as she eased back. "I mean, this is all so new. Are we making a mistake?"

"New?" Cash raised his brows. "Red, I've known you forever, and over the past year I've gotten to know you even better. I'm pretty sure we can't take this any slower."

She eased up on her toes and slid her lips over his, her fingertips curling into his shoulders.

"We'll celebrate when we get home," she whispered against his mouth.

Cash reached up and swiped her damp cheeks. "You better believe it."

"You know, my nana will probably want the first dance with you at our wedding," Jade joked.

"I hope I don't break her heart when I make her my second dance."

Jade turned around to their friends, and a sense of family warmed her heart. Bonds weren't always made by blood relatives. The closest people in her entire life were right here, and they were all moving forward into a new chapter in all their lives.

Glancing to Livie, Jade smiled through a fresh crop of tears. She crossed to her friend and went into her open arms.

"I'm so happy for you," Livie said, her voice thick with her own emotions. "I'm so happy for all of us."

Another set of arms wrapped around them. "We're pretty lucky," Melanie stated.

Jade shifted so they were all in one circle of arms. "Are we ready to show this town what's about to take over?"

A tear slipped down Livie's cheek. "My dad would be so overwhelmed with this."

"He'd be proud," Jade countered. "He's looking down on you and smiling. I just know it."

"If you all want to go in the back and take a minute to compose yourselves, use my office," Sophie stated as she moved toward the front door. "I'll get this party started. Liam has all the food set up in various rooms. I've put pamphlets and fliers and information on the restaurant and gift shop throughout the office. I'll get people mingling."

Jade glanced to her friends. "I think we need to touch up our makeup."

As they started toward the back office, Cash gripped her elbow and turned Jade to face him.

"I love you."

Jade's heart flipped. "I love you, Flex."

He moved from her elbow to her hand and slid his thumb over the stone. His eyes focused down, he pulled in a deep breath. "Maybe, if you don't care, we could go see my dad this weekend?"

Those dark eyes were raised to hers. "I'd like to tell him about this in person, but if you're not ready to—"

"I am. I want to meet your dad and tell him about us." Jade briefly touched her lips to his. "From here on out, we're doing everything together. I don't care how difficult things get. You're stuck with me now."

A corner of Cash's mouth kicked up into a grin. "You didn't even give me a choice."

"No, but I'm giving you my heart."

Cash laced their fingers together and started down the hall. "There's nothing more I could ever want."

Books by Bestselling Author
Fern Michaels

Available Wherever Books Are Sold!
Check out our website at **www.kensingtonbooks.com**

31901065209258